First Published 2020 by Kristin

This Edition Published 2020 by Kristine Ceirane

ISBN: 9798558098099

Text Copyrights © Kristine Ceirane 2020

Image Copyrights © Kristine Ceirane 2020

Moral rights asserted.

All rights reserved. No part of this publication may be reproduced, stored in or introduced into a retrieval system, or transmitted in any form, or by any means (electronic, mechanical, photocopying, recording or otherwise) without prior written permission of the publisher.

Any person who does any unauthorised act in relation to this publication may be liable to criminal prosecution and civil claims for damages.

Written in Norwich, Norfolk, England.

Contents

Tiredness - Page 5

Stillness - Page 60

Puzzlement - Page 112

Lucretia - Page 142

The Encounter - Page 197

The Flash - Page 267

Voice of Blood - Page 321

The Return - Page 377

Revelry - Page 443

Conciliation - Page 507

Disappointment - Page 533

Sparks - Page 576

Tiredness

Sadness, loneliness, depression and hopelessness. My constant companions. Over the years, they have taken me over completely. No matter how colourful the world is I see it grey. For me, the sun is always shining through the clouds. The air is always damp. This is my world. And this is what it would remain, forever.

I've met so many people who I have loved and lost them all, there was nothing I could do about it.

My story started many years ago, in 1820, when I was 18 years old. Despite my age, I had already seen a lot in my life.

London of those days was completely different from the present one. I was born and raised up there. Smog covered the city. Black smoke was rolling from factory chimneys. One look at them was enough to cause a lump to form in your throat and feel shivers running down your spine. Working there was a pure inquisition although factories could not be compared to workhouses. No-one wanted to get there. No matter how hard living on your own was, it was a thousand times better than living in a workhouse. The reason for that was very simple. People who lived on their own usually had longer lives than residents of a workhouse.

My home was one of London's countless shacks. A labyrinth of numberless dirty and narrow streets led to it. Our dwelling consisted of two small and faded rooms, I shared them with my parents, my brothers and my sisters. There were five children in the family and all of us had a job.

I started working at the age of five. My first job was sweeping up the streets. They were so dirty that I was never without work.

Over the years my memories have faded away and there are things I remember quite vaguely, like the death of one of my sisters. She caught a cold and died after a short illness. How old was I then? Maybe ten years old. How old was she? I don't remember.

I felt some sort of relief in the family after her death. Now we had one less mouth to feed. No-one seemed to be sad about the loss, but maybe that was just the way it seemed...

My remaining sister got married and left us. Her husband was as poor as we were and they led a humble life.

When I was about 14 years old my mother died, leaving my father, my two elder brothers and myself. One evening she said she felt a bit sick and went to bed. She never woke up. She had lived a long and hard life and at least she didn't suffer. Despite this great loss, we had no time for sorrow: industrialised London didn't care about people like us. On the next morning I, as usual, went to work. At that time, I worked in one of London's many factories.

Twelve-hour workday seemed easy to me. It was because I worked sixteen, sometimes even eighteen hours. Work was monotone and unhealthy; the pay was miserable. My health gradually worsened.

When I was about 16 years old, death visited my family again. My father died. No-one told us the cause of death, I think some accident happened at the factory where he worked.

So, there I was. My family was destroyed in only a few years. It was like a candle's flame had been blown out, but the smoke was still in the air.

My brothers and I had become orphans. We couldn't afford the two roomed place anymore and moved to a small and miserable room with a low ceiling and walls that had been blackened by smoke.

The following weeks or maybe months were all the same, until one day.

When I woke up in the morning, my brothers had already left. I went to work and, as usual, came back late. To my big surprise, they were not at home. It felt as if something bad had happened. I looked around. All their belongings were missing, they had left me. In my life, I've cried only a few times. That night was one of them.

Once I had overcome the initial shock, I started to think about what to do. I couldn't afford to rent this room alone, so I had to run away. Besides, maybe my brothers had fallen behind with the rent.

I wrapped up my belongings in a parcel, I didn't have many. I decided to spend one last night there and leave in the morning.

I became homeless for a while and spent nights in different places – gateways, abandoned buildings. Sometimes I stayed in cheap night shelters.

Another two years passed. Luckily, I didn't have many opportunities to see my reflection. I was skinny, lumpish and always starving. Rags covered my body. I was exhausted and unwanted. Nevertheless, I desperately wanted to live. Deep in my heart I felt that life could be something more. I had seen rich Londoners: they had beautiful clothes, posh carriages and faces that showed no signs of need and hunger.

Of course, I couldn't change anything in my life then. However, I held onto life desperately.

XXX

The night that turned my life upside down started just like many others. The weather was dank, another workday in the factory had ended and I was on my way home. It was either late November or early December.

Suddenly someone grabbed me. I couldn't believe it. I hadn't heard anyone approaching me. Up until this moment I had thought I was the only person on that street.

Crime was quite common in London but, still, it was so unexpected that I couldn't do anything. The stranger was holding me and suddenly I felt a sharp pain. He had bitten me in the neck. It felt like he was trying to suck blood out of me. I had never been afraid to walk through London because I was too poor to attract any interest. That's why he took me unaware.

I was already puny, but now I felt even weaker. The stranger's hold loosened. He realised that he had made a mistake by attacking me. Considering my way of life, my blood must have tasted awful.

The stranger released my neck and tried to pull away from me, but I caught hold of his arm and didn't let go. The balance of power was not on my side. I didn't realise what I was doing, but my mind was telling me not to let go of him. He tried to break free, but I was holding onto him with every ounce of strength.

Suddenly the stranger calmed down. He looked into my eyes and understood. Although the street was illuminated with a pale light, I could see his eyes. They were lifeless.

"All right. If you want to live, release at least one of my arms," he said.

I obeyed. That moment changed everything.

The stranger bit into his arm. Blood started to trickle from it. He pressed his arm to my lips and said:

"Drink it."

That's how I became what I am now. And this is where my story really begins.

I reached a building and clung to its wall. I felt so weird that it's still difficult to describe it. I don't remember how long I stood there, but it was still dark when I returned to my dwelling.

I woke up upon hearing a noise. I opened my eyes and looked around. Someone was pounding on the door. I got up and opened it. It was Grames, my landlord.

"Hard night, ha? Took a day off?"

"Umm… What?"

I could barely put my thoughts together. Grames told me that it was late in the afternoon and that I had done the right thing by leaving my job in the factory. He said that I could find something better instead. I had been living there for a while and we were somewhat acquainted. Grames told me a few other things before he let me know the purpose of his visit which was that I was due to pay the rent. He sneered when he was looking at me. He probably thought that I had started to drink. I stood up slowly and, in the twilight of the room, started to look for my purse. It was just as frayed as the rest of my property. I gave Grames the requested money, he took it and walked away.

Afterwards, when I was alone, I could think about what had happened. According to Grames, I'd slept for many hours. That was quite unusual as normally I slept no more than five hours a day. Then I remembered about my job. I'd never missed a single day before.

Now I had done it and felt nothing. There were no regrets, nor eagerness to go there immediately. I was still me, but something had changed. I didn't know what exactly had happened to me, but something in my mind or, to be precise, in the pieces of mind I had then, told me that my life would never be the same again. I didn't know what to expect and this thought scared me.

Prior to this I hadn't had the time or need to think. I lived day by day, hoping that it wouldn't be the last one for me. I vegetated. My life was predictable. It consisted of poverty, hunger and hard work. Now I understood that things would be different from then on and had no idea about my future.

The only window in my room was boarded up. Rays of light were shining through it. I looked at the window and then went over to it. I wasn't interested in what was happening outside, I was looking at the sun. It was slightly covered by clouds, but I don't know why, I felt some unspeakable loathing. Weather had never interested me much, but now, taking a look at the sun, I understood that I wanted to see it no more. I wanted darkness. I wanted to merge with it, as well as with the dark streets of London where I would keep walking endlessly.

Everything was so strange. I was still "me" but I felt that some other "me" had developed. A part of me I hadn't even known about.

Of course, now when you're reading this, everything seems to be so simple and sometimes unbelievable. But don't forget, dear reader – these strokes are written by the current me, the one who knows how to express his thoughts and talk in proper sentences.

moved on and had walked a few steps when an idea came into my mind. I returned to the stranger and checked his pockets. His wallet was heavier than I thought. I had never seen so much money in my life. It took my breath away. I put the wallet into my pocket, hoping that it would hold its weight, and returned to my dwelling.

Weeks, maybe months, followed each other. I don't remember. All days were the same – during the day I was sleeping, at night I was meandering, exploring London, going to the parts of the city I had never been to. I saw London in a different way. The need for blood, pint by pint, decreased, which made my existence a bit easier, for my mind wasn't so occupied with that one obsessive thought.

I changed my resting places regularly, mostly staying in derelict houses. I was reluctant to rent a room. I was still wearing my ragged clothes, I slept all day, woke up at night, had no job yet always had money. That was more than enough to cause suspicion.

I soon got used to my new lifestyle. But as time passed by the question – what was I? - started to prey on me. I felt very lonely and wanted to find someone like me.

xxx

I had found my usual meal and was going back to my sleeping place. It was a typical London night. The weather was wet and raw. I turned onto a street and froze in shock. I saw him – the stranger who had made me like this. I understood that he could give me the answers to my questions and decided to follow him. It seemed that he, too, had got his catch and was on the way to his dwelling. I kept my distance hoping that he would not notice me.

The stranger walked over to one of London's most refined districts. The streets had become cleaner. He walked to a massive house with a high wrought iron gate and a big yard. The place didn't look welcoming at all, maybe because it was so dark. There was hardly any light in the windows. I dove into darkness. The stranger opened the gate, crossed the yard and went into the house. I didn't see him using a key, it looked like he had just opened the front door.

It took some time for me to gain courage and open the gate. Nervously, I approached the house. I stared at the door knocker for a while. It was a lion's face and it, too, didn't create a welcoming atmosphere. The fangs were so sharp and looked so real that I thought it could actually bite me should I knock.

My intuition told me not to use the door knocker. It would be so easy for the stranger or whoever would open the door to tell me to leave and shut it right in front of me. No, I had to make sure I got inside the house. It would be more difficult to kick me out then.

Instinctively, I pulled the door handle down and the door opened. I was right, the door wasn't locked when the stranger had arrived. What a strange place. I had never thought that rich Londoners could be so careless.

I stepped into a poorly lit hallway. Everything - the walls, the floor, the ceiling - looked almost black. There were massive stairs with beautiful banisters some twenty feet from me, leading to the first floor. I noticed a few pictures on the walls but it was so dark that I couldn't see the faces of the people in the portraits. I thought I saw a round shaped table with a big vase full of flowers on the left side of the stairs but I wasn't entirely sure because of the darkness.

I had always wondered what a rich person's house could look like and now I was in one of them. However, my intuition told me that it was not a typical house.

On my right, there was a big door and I could hear voices coming from the other side. It took me a moment until I dared to walk in. Inside was a big room with dark grey walls and many windows. Unlike the hallway, this room was brightly lit. There was a huge table in the middle of the room. About ten figures were sitting around it. Everything looked ordinary except for one thing. The table had absolutely nothing on it. One of the individuals drew my attention. He was sitting at the end of the table and looked as if he was their leader.

As I walked in, all conversations stopped and everyone started staring at me. The stranger whom I had followed was there, too. He looked puzzled when he saw me. The possible leader was looking at me in a frosty way, at the same time studying me from head to toe.

"Who are you and what are you doing here?" he asked.

I was overcome with confusion and didn't know where to start. My rhetoric was miserable during that time. I briefly explained what had happened.

"Walther, is it true?"

I was fidgeting. The stranger I had spoken with was thinking about what I had told him, drawing a finger over his lips.

After a short moment of silence Walther said a quiet "yes". He had a very nervous look on his face. I was right, the person who sat at the end of the table really was their leader.

"Walther, aren't there enough people in London? *Why* on earth did you attack someone like *him*?"

Walther didn't say anything.

"It's not enough that you grabbed that rabble," he gave me a look full of contempt," you made him one of us! And let him go! Do you have any excuse for that?"

The others looked shocked. No one stood up for Walther.

"I guess you want to join us, don't you?" he asked me.

I looked at them. They all had new, expensive clothes and massive jewels on their rings. It was obvious that none of them knew what neediness was.

"Yes," I replied.

Despite their hostility, I decided to gather all my bravery and stay there no matter what. The leader looked straight into my eyes and said:

"It seems that we have no choice. We can't let you go because you can get yourself into trouble and that may affect us, which would not be good. However, there will be a few rules. Firstly, you will follow everything we say. Secondly, we'll turn you into a human looking being. You will come to know what it's like to have a bath regularly and wear clean clothes. Thirdly, you'll have to become educated. We will teach you how to talk, read and even how to speak French. If you fulfil these conditions, you'll be allowed to stay here as long as you want. We'll give you two years of time. If you fail, we'll find a way to get rid of you. Do you understand?"

Everything I had just heard was unbelievable to me. I said the only possible answer:

"Yes."

I was sitting on my bed; no candles were alight and the only source of light was the dim moonlight cascading through the window in front of me. The room that was given to me was simply decorated: dark walls, a bed, a desk, a chair and a wardrobe, yet it was the most exquisite of all the rooms I had ever lived in. I didn't know how much time had passed since my arrival there - maybe a few days, maybe a week.

I was thinking about my life. Shaky thoughts were running through my head. I felt at ease and troubled at the same time.

Time was moving slowly. No one took interest in me. I heard a commotion on the ground floor, but I didn't make a move to leave the room and go downstairs. I understood that they were hardly tolerating my presence and I didn't want to cause anyone's annoyance.

Another hour passed until I heard someone coming towards my room. The door opened and a girl stepped in. I remembered her. She, too, had been in the room on the night that I arrived.

Despite twilight, I could see how dissatisfied she looked. It was quite clear that she didn't want to be there.

"My name is Beatrice and I'll be some kind of a nanny for you. Come with me, I've prepared a bath and I have new clothes for you. If you want to be one of us, you must look accordingly."

Despite the poorly hidden dislike towards me, her voice was very pleasant. It was low-toned and silky. I followed her into the hall. She took me to a room with a bathtub, steam rising up from it. I found a towel, clothes and a brush prepared for me in the corner.

I couldn't remember the last time I had taken a bath and I hadn't changed my clothes for years. I looked at Beatrice's luxurious, stitch craft covered dress, her blonde, curly hair and rosy skin. Her appearance made me feel more miserable.

"I'll be back in one hour." Then she looked at me again. "No, better in two hours."

I had forgotten how pleasant it was to wash and brush up. Given my previous way of life, it was no surprise that the water was terribly black after I had finished.

I dried myself with the towel and focused on my hair. I hadn't cut it for years. My hair was halfway down my back.

I had black hair, just like my mother, also I had the same coloured eyes, blue-green.

I hadn't brushed my hair for a long time. I had to work hard at it until I managed to untangle my knotted hair.

Then I focused on my clothes. My new costume consisted of long, black trousers, a black waistcoat with golden buttons, a white lace shirt and long black boots.

Curiosity filled my mind. I wanted to see how I looked. There was a mirror in the room. The glass was steamed over, so I wiped my hand over it and froze in surprise.

Every time I had looked in the mirror before, I had seen a threadbare and thin factory worker with a sad look. Now I saw a very handsome young man in nice attire. My eyes no longer had hunger and despair in them, they were powerful and piercing instead. My new clothes made me look almost noble.

I don't remember how long I stood there looking at myself, not being able to take my eyes off of my reflection. I was still in front of the mirror when Beatrice came in. As our eyes met, her face changed immediately from scornful to surprised.

"Who would have thought..." she said.

I smiled. Since that day, Beatrice always treated me nice.

My second "nanny" was Arifay. He had the difficult and unenviable task of educating me. I had never attended school and couldn't read or write. Luckily, Arifay was friendly and took things easy. He explained everything to me: who I had become and how it would affect my life in the future. He confirmed what I had already suspected. I couldn't eat human food anymore because it would be damaging to me.

"Of course, you can risk, but believe me – you'll feel very bad for a long time. Even vomiting won't really help," he said.

Also, I came to know that I would never age. Years could go by but my face and body would remain as they were then. And, the most important thing, I came to know that I had become immortal.

"Immortality may be frightening sometimes. Try not to think about it too much."

I asked how long Arifay had been like this.

"For a while, it doesn't really matter," he smiled, but never answered my question. It was the only time when I noticed sadness in Arifay's smile.

I had difficulties with perception and concentration, but I wanted to learn. Arifay tried to explain everything as simply as possible. To my surprise, I noticed that slowly I was starting to remember some things.

A few weeks passed by. I hadn't been introduced to the others and spent my time with Beatrice or Arifay. When I needed to hunt, one of them always came with me. The leader didn't trust me much, or to be more precise he didn't trust me at all.

One evening, when I was in my room with Arifay, I asked him what kind of house this was. He explained that the house belonged to them all and they owned it legally. They had bought it a few years previously.

"Where do you get money from?" I asked.

"Oh, it depends. Some of us were already rich when we joined, some got their money from the stock market – it brings in big returns."

Suddenly I remembered about my money. I had taken wallets from some of my victims and hidden them in my previous dwelling. Since I had attacked only wealthy men, I had a nice sum there. The last time I had counted I had about fifty pounds.

"I... I have money, too," I said slowly.

Arifay gave me a surprised look. Of course, he wanted to know how I had acquired the money. When I told him Arifay started to laugh. His sincere laugh was probably audible throughout the whole first floor.

"Fifty pounds? It's pretty much for a poor man but small change for who you are now. However, we can collect the money if you want. Do you remember where you hid it?"

I nodded. We decided to retrieve the money immediately. We put on our cloaks and left.

I hadn't been out much since I had arrived there, mostly only when hunting. The house where I had hidden the money was on the other side of the city and it took us about one hour until we reached it.

I could feel that Arifay was feeling uncomfortable when he followed me inside the house. It was obvious that he wasn't used to being in places like that.

"Did you really live here?" Arifay asked. I felt disbelief in his voice.

"Yes. Here and in many similar places."

The money was hidden under a floorboard. I couldn't remember how many wallets there should have been, so far, I had found five of them. I checked my "safe" carefully but didn't find any more.

I went to Arifay.

"Here they are."

He looked at me approvingly and smiled. I opened one of the wallets and looked at the coins.

"Did you attack moneylenders and manufacturers?" he asked.

"I hope so," I replied.

Then we left.

xxx

I was studying every day, putting my whole heart into it and enjoying my progress. I still remember the happiness I felt when I read a word for the first time.

I spent hours writing different kinds of texts and noticed that slowly I was starting to develop good hand-writing. I wasn't allowed to read books, so I read newspapers instead.

That's how I spent about half a year. I was still kept away from the others and spent most of the time in my room. Sometimes I went out to the garden. It was very beautiful: there were fountains, flowerbeds, paths and benches. Of course, it would look more beautiful in the daylight, but I didn't feel any desire to see it.

Sometimes Arifay joined me. He gladly showed me different constellations and explained things about astronomy. I admired him and wanted to become as smart as he was.

One night I was sitting in my room, looking out of the window, when suddenly the door opened and Arifay came in.

"They want to see you. You must come downstairs."

Although I knew that sooner or later this moment would come, I felt scared and insecure. Arifay went to the table and started to study some of the newspapers and sheets of papers with my exercises on.

"Keep calm. They just want to see what you have learnt so far. Remember: they gave you two years."

He took a few sheets of paper and newspapers from the table and told me to follow him. It was easy for him to say "keep calm". I remembered my previous meeting with the others and how hostile they were. I had a feeling that they would have gladly torn me into pieces but since it wasn't possible, they just tried to burn me with their eyes.

I followed Arifay into the big room. Everything looked the same as it had been - they were sitting around the table, with the leader sitting at the bottom end of it. His chair was the largest and most luxurious I had ever seen.

My presence drew everyone's attention. Of course, during the past six months some of them had seen me in the garden or in the hallways, but now they saw me in the light. No one had expected that the changes would be so drastic. The leader looked impressed.

"Oh, who would have thought," he said. "Well, then it's not that bad of you as I had thought, Walther."

Walther looked baffled. It was obvious that the leader had punished him somehow. Then the leader focused on me again. This time I accepted his gaze without feeling so uncomfortable.

"But as you know, appearances can be deceptive. That's why we want to see your current progress. After all, you've already been here for six months. However, whatever your success will be, I'll keep my promise and you'll have one and a half years left to prove yourself."

I was asked to read some articles from the newspapers. Long words presented difficulties to me, but in general I was reading quickly. When I had finished, I looked around. I couldn't say that the faces surrounding me were friendly, but at least they weren't aggressive anymore. Arifay showed them examples of my hand-writing.

"He really couldn't write before he arrived here? I would say he is very diligent," one of them said. She nodded to heighten what she had said. Everyone agreed with her.

Only the leader remained silent. He was looking off to one side, drawing a finger over his lips. Then he started speaking:

"Given who you are and how you've lived until now, your results are very good. I think it's time to explain some things to you. Let's walk out to the garden."

Everyone livened up. It was obvious that they would like to know what he was going to say. That's when I started to worry again. Arifay put his hand on my shoulder and whispered in my ear:

"Keep calm. If the worst comes to the worst, remember that he can't kill you with a spade and bury you somewhere in the garden!"

I chuckled. Arifay knew how to calm me down.

There was a glass door that led to the garden. The leader opened it and stepped outside. I followed him.

"I presume you've noticed the kind of district this house is situated in, how well it's maintained and that it is worth a lot of money."

"Yes, I've noticed that."

"So," he continued, "you've probably noticed that despite our lifestyle – the hustle at night and our specific food – no-one is bothering us."

I said that I had noticed that too.

"Why do you think it is that no-one finds us strange?"

I looked down. I didn't know the answer - I had only a suspicion.

"Money… Reputation…"

He gave a laugh:

"You're smarter than I thought! Exactly - we've got money, tons of it, and it's a guarantee for good reputation. In society's eyes we're just a bunch of eccentric rich people. We don't hide from others, on the contrary - the door of our house is wide open for guests. There's just one small nuance – not everyone who steps in goes out."

I grinned.

"If we want to continue this lifestyle and do what we want, we can't afford any mistakes. That's why I was so furious when I came to know what Walther had done. You could endanger us all. I felt that you probably didn't know much and that your manners were... if honest, you didn't have any manners... That's why I gave you two years to learn. Your stay here depends on your own will. If you have to leave then at least you'll be educated enough to live on your own and won't be a threat to us anymore."

Silence fell. I was thinking over what I'd just heard.

"Let's go back," he said.

I could feel the curiosity that was filling the room. Everyone wanted to know what we had talked about. The leader sat in his place and turned towards the others:

"So, as you all have seen, our guest has achieved certain results. I think we should partly tear away from this mysteriousness and at least get introduced," he said and looked at the girl who sat the furthest from him.

She gave me a look:

"I'm Marisa."

"You already know me," said Arifay who had sat next to her.

Everyone introduced themselves, except for Walther who rather mumbled his name. Only the leader hadn't said his name yet.

"And now since everyone's introduced, we would like to know your name," he said.

"My name is Vince."

"Vincent... Well, considering that you'll live here and probably meet some of our countless guests, we'll need to introduce you." He fell silent and sank into his thoughts. "From this moment your name will be Vincent Andrew Styles. What do you think about that?"

What could I say? It sounded much better than my real name.

"All right."

He smiled:

"Good. And now I'm sure you would like to know my name, wouldn't you? My name is Yuri."

xxx

Seasons changed one after another. A new period in my life had started. Every day, for me that meant evenings and nights, I spent many hours improving my reading and writing skills. My handwriting became neater and neater. I was reading not only newspapers, but also books. The others had lent me some money and invested it in the stock market. I came into contact with everyone more and more, especially Yuri. He taught me many things about history, music, art and literature. Little by little, I started to take part in receptions. They were organised at least three times a month. Most of London's well off attended them. I was introduced as an orphan from a noble family who had no surviving relatives. Yuri had felt pity towards me and took me under his wing. Except for the part about rich parents, everything else was true. I still wonder how none of our guests noticed quaintness in our behaviour. It was true that sometimes in the morning our house was occupied by fewer guests than had arrived the night before. We hated all these arrogant manufacturers, moneylenders, businessmen and other people whose snobbishness had no boundaries. Thus, if the desire to drink their blood arose, we just couldn't resist it.

I started to pay more attention to my looks. I already looked very good, but I wanted to look even better. I wore black waistcoats with golden, silver or bronze buttons, black trousers and white laced shirts. My boots caused envy in many of our guests. My long, straight hair was always down. The jewels from my massive rings shone on my fingers.

I looked so excellent that none of our female guests could resist me. Some of them were really tiresome and followed me everywhere. It was a rare occurrence when I could go outside to the garden without any of them in my wake. However, I was courteous to them all. Recently I had started to learn French and that charmed them even more. I kissed their hands, did small talk and took them on walks in the garden telling them things that I had learnt from Arifay, Yuri and the others. Many of my admirers had husbands who couldn't hide their jealousy. As for the young and unmarried, they cherished a hope that they would become Mrs. Vincent Styles. Some of them even pulled me into a corner and kissed me passionately. After that, tears, excuses and pitiful sighs followed. "Oh, I couldn't do anything about it! You are so charming!"

I relished their attention although I felt nothing towards any of them for they were all empty and boring.

Life seemed like a fairytale back then. When two years since my arrival had passed the question about my stay wasn't even discussed. My friendship with Yuri had become stronger. I was fascinated by his life experience, his personality. He had become like this many years previously, by his own choice. He was born into a rich, titled family. He relished life and wealth, but was depressed by the thought that he was mortal. When he had the chance to obtain eternal life, he took it without any doubt. The price that he had to pay for that didn't scare him.

With time, Yuri had surrounded himself with others just like him and they lived together, moving from place to place. Apart from England, Yuri had lived in Scotland, Ireland, France and Germany.

"It's been five years that we have been living here in London. We can stay for a few more years, then we must leave. As you see, eternal youth has some disadvantages," he said and gave a loud laugh.

I wanted to be like Yuri. He was intelligent, charming, sophisticated, wealthy and led a lifestyle I had dreamed about for years. I watched his moves and tried to imitate them. It was he who taught me how to fence.

"I would gladly teach you my knowledge about wines and cognacs, but you won't have any use for it," he said and sighed. It was the only time I saw him sad.

xxx

Three more years passed by. I had turned 23 years old. Life still seemed like a fairytale to me. I had changed from a factory worker to an aristocrat, I had friends and had forgotten what need was. I enjoyed life and never stopped learning. I read almost everything that was available: fiction, books about astronomy, chemistry, physics, biology... My French was perfect. Thanks to successful investments in the stock market and a few clever schemes, I had earned a lot of money and could return the money that was once lent to me.

I had started to think about living on my own. There was no specific reason for it. I had spent five years under one roof with my friends and we hadn't had any disagreements. I had enough opportunity to be alone when I so wanted. However, I wanted to have my own house.

When I made my decision known to the others they were dismayed, but didn't try to stop me. I started to look for a suitable house and found an estate close to London. It was a much smaller house than my friends' place as it was not supposed to be a shared house. Walls were covered with dark brown wooden panels and the windows were quite small so that there wasn't much light coming in yet it was much brighter there than in my friends' house. My house had a nice garden which needed some maintenance so I hired a landscape architect.

I moved in there quite fast and continued with my previous way of life. I attended countless receptions and also hosted them myself.

I employed servants. Remembering my past, I treated them well and paid good wages. I knew how hard life was for poor Londoners and employed more servants than I needed. I donated money to charities and had started to think about founding my own charity.

That's how a few months passed by. My servants had an attachment to me. They admitted that they found me a bit strange, but my friendliness compensated for it. I told my cook that I had a serious stomach disease and many dishes were bad for me. The cook prepared a clear soup and sometimes served me some fruit. Of course, I never actually ate them.

I had a chambermaid named Elisa. She liked everything that was related to me and often stayed in my rooms, cleaning up non-existing dust. She leafed through pages of my books quietly, touched my belongings with deepest admiration and cautiously studied me. When I noticed her looking at me and looked at her, Elisa blushed and turned away. She was so sweet and touchingly beautiful. It was obvious she had fallen in love with me.

Elisa changed something in me. I liked her presence and I soon realised that I used every opportunity to spend time with her. To me, she was the most charming girl in the world: tall, with rosy skin, light brown hair and blue eyes. Her look was naïve and enthusiastic at the same time. She had never gone to school, but had that kind of wisdom that comes from the heart. I realised that I, too, had fallen in love.

I should have rescued her by sending her far away from me. Instead, I did the opposite thing and married her. I sent invitations to my friends at the last minute. Soon I received a letter from Yuri. He said that I was making a huge mistake. "For your own but even more – for Elisa's sake – cancel the wedding."

Now, when I look back, I understand that the cancellation wouldn't have helped. I would have hurt Elisa so badly that she would never have recovered from it. It was too late to put everything right.

Our wedding was one of the rare occasions on which I left the house during the day. My friends were deeply dissatisfied with what I had done, but didn't say anything. They knew it wouldn't help.

The first few weeks after our wedding were wonderful. I had adapted myself to Elisa and started to stay up most of the day. We took long walks, rode horses, attended plays and operas.

After a few months Elisa became pregnant. My initial joy was replaced by doubt. Arifay had once said that I would never have children. I didn't take interest in it then, so I didn't question him in detail. Now thoughts were gnawing at my mind. However, I waved them away, telling myself that every rule has an exception.

Being so in love with Elisa, I started to contact the others less and less and stopped organising receptions. I didn't want to waste the time I could dedicate to Elisa and the child we were expecting on people I had no interest in.

That's how nine months passed. Soon our child had to come into this world.

I had to go out for my night hunting. Elisa had fallen asleep and I thought she wouldn't notice my absence. When I returned, I saw lights in almost all the windows. An unimaginable bustle was going on in the house. I wanted to go upstairs but one of our maids saw me. She grabbed a hold of me. She was shaking.

"Sir, the labour has started!"

I ran upstairs. I wasn't allowed to see Elisa so I went to one of the other rooms and paced up and down. Time was lingering for what seemed like an eternity to me until finally one of the maids came into the room.

I hurried up to Elisa. When I came into the room, the first thing I noticed was Elisa's face. It was pallid and grim. Elisa looked at me. I saw tears in her eyes.

"Our child…was stillborn," she said.

Our relationship gradually changed. The child's death was a huge shock. I shrank into myself. I felt so guilty. Elisa was suffering not only because of our child, but also because of me. She had started to understand that something was wrong with me, although she never found out the truth. I understood how everything would end but couldn't prevent it.

A few months later she passed away. The doctor said that she had a tumour. A tumour? Elisa was absolutely healthy until she had met me. It was the suffering that broke her down. She died because of me.

After her death, I swore never to let anyone become so close to me again. It was a promise I, unfortunately, was unable to keep.

I sold my estate, moved elsewhere and began to organise receptions again. It was a chance to forget myself, but as time went by it became boring to me. I felt lonely and unhappy. For the first time I sensed my immortality as a burden. I remembered *them*. I had seen tiredness, sadness and depression in their faces. Gradually the world started to lose its colours.

During these years, I've thought about that fateful evening over and over again. Sometimes I think about what my life would have been like if nothing had happened and I would have stayed a simple worker. Maybe with time I would have found a better job and got somewhere in life and saved some money. Maybe I would have stayed where I was and died in poverty or because of some accident at work. Maybe... The only thing that matters is that I would have lived the life I was supposed to live.

I've tried, but I can't remember when exactly the tiredness took a hold of me.

Stillness

December 31, 1999

It was ten o'clock in the evening. I was sitting in a massive leather chair near the cold fireplace. From outside my house looked empty and depressing. From inside, it wasn't any better.

There used to be a time when I would have a glass of cognac in my hand whilst sitting near a kindled fireplace in my big, splendid house, enjoying another wonderful day of my life. Now there was no need for any of that.

I remembered New Year's Eve many years ago. It was completely different from all of the previous ones. I had gained what I wanted the most. Immortality.

It was 1769 and I was in my family home. The glow from the fireplace was the only source of light in the huge library.

There were a few hours left until midnight and I was standing near the fireplace, feeling very odd.

Everything seemed so surreal. I looked out of the window and saw a typical winter landscape. It was snowing. The huge yard was covered with snow, the bare trees looked a bit ghostly. I looked around the library. It also looked as it usually did: one of the walls was completely covered by a bookshelf, the table was still in front of the window, the chair, decorated with wood-engravings, was almost as massive as the walnut table.

Everything in this room symbolised power and authority. It had a depressing effect on some people. After entering this room, they felt like there might be something wrapping and squeezing them. This feeling enchained them and took away their self-confidence. I knew it very well, so I received everyone I didn't like in this room. The furnishing hadn't been done by me, but by one of my ancestors many years before. Apparently, he had done it with the intent.

My feelings were intensifying because the world and things around me had remained the same while I had changed.

Many things didn't affect me anymore. I thought about all the people I knew – they all had the same fate: aging, writing of a last will, bitterness seeing their old bodies in the mirror, pondering about how short life is, fear of death and, in the end, death. I visualised all of them in my mind for a moment and realised that I didn't feel any compassion towards them. There hadn't been many people who had ever meant anything to me and none of them was with me anymore.

I had gained immortality and felt very elated. The depression, which had followed me for years, had disappeared. Of course, there were things I had to leave behind, but they seemed insignificant in comparison to what I had obtained. Immortality was worth more than everything I had sacrificed.

I had found what I was looking for after having spent only four years searching. I was 32 years old and it was one of the last chances I had to become forever young. Of course, many years of debauchery had left traces in my features, but still, I was very handsome. I imagined how it would be to become immortal at the age of 50: an old man with more bald spots than hair on my head, bad teeth and a body that barely keeps together. I was dreading it. Thoughts about aging and death, which had always caused dislike, had become terrifying in the last years. I was glad I had escaped such fate.

People called me a dissolute aristocrat. I never objected because that was exactly who I was. Unlike many others I didn't hide it, so I had at least one virtue – honesty.

I lived alone in my family house. My parents had died when I was very little and I didn't have any other close relatives.

My days were filled with entertainment, nothing doing and waste of money. I considered practising shooting, fencing and archery to be entertainment, too. I was well-read and considered myself to be one of the most educated people in the country. I liked to show my eminence over other people and see confusion in the faces of people who had once tried to drive me into a corner but failed.

xxx

1765

One morning, when I hadn't fully woken up yet, Reginald visited me. He was my best friend and also the only one who was allowed to visit me at any time. My butlers knew that, so I wasn't surprised when I saw Reginald standing in the middle of my room, leafing through one of my books. When he saw me rising up from the pillows, his face brightened.

"Good morning, Yuri! It looks like you had a good time yesterday."

"That's possible. To be honest, I don't remember much. What's the time now?"

Reginald looked at his watch.

"One o'clock."

I had already put on my usual – cold blooded – facial expression and said in a worriless voice:

"Excellent. It means I'll have enough time to prepare myself for the duel at four."

After I had said it, I looked at my hands, trying to look careless. Hopefully, from aside it looked as if I wanted to check whether my nails were still manicured enough when actually I wanted to see that my hands weren't shaking. Luckily, they didn't, otherwise I'd be in trouble.

Reginald gave me a surprised look.

"A duel? Again? May I know the reason?"

Still having a careless expression, I said:

"Oh, nothing too exciting. Some lord was a bit dissatisfied with the fact that I had an affair with his wife." I sighed. "It was so easy. Just nineteen, newly-wedded…"

"Mmm… I'm interested. What's her name?"

"Is it important? In truth, I don't know. I didn't ask."

Reginald's sincere laugh filled the room.

"Oh, Yuri, this is so characteristic of you – to get into trouble because of a woman whose name you don't know."

"So what? It's just a trophy. Sometimes I feel really bored. I can get any woman I want. If at least one would reject me…"

Reginald stayed for a while and then left. I started to prepare for the duel. I didn't feel any fear. I was one of the best shooters in the country, my reaction was perfect and I was absolutely sure that I'd return. Before I left, I looked at the mirror. I liked what I saw. Regular debauchery hadn't affected me much. I had beautiful lineament, ice-blue eyes and looked younger than I was – I was 28 years old then. My arrogant facial expression put off anyone who'd attempt to exploit me. Just one look and they had already run away.

I deliberately alienated myself from others and my appearance was part of it. I had long, black hair and always wore black clothes, apart from my white laced shirts.

I put on my cloak and gloves, then had a last look at my reflection and headed to the field where the duel was about to take place.

I hadn't really overstated when I said I don't remember that woman's name. I had forgotten her first name, but, of course, I knew the surname.

My carriage was almost near the duel place, but I was still calm.

My antagonist was already waiting for me. Not hiding my boredom, I went to him, wanting this to end as soon as possible. There was a reception in the evening and in my thoughts, I was already there.

Everything was as usual: we took the guns, made ten steps and shot after the command, but this time something unbelievable happened – a bullet flew very close to my ear, slightly scraping it. My skills hadn't deceived me and it was me who returned from the duel, but nothing was the same anymore. At the moment when the bullet flew past me, I hesitated. My hands started to shake and my breath quickened. I felt a weird flutter. Later I realised it was fear.

I immediately left the duel place and went home. I didn't want to see anyone. I locked myself in the library and emptied one bottle of cognac after another.

This wasn't the first duel in my life, not at all, but it was the first one where my antagonist had made such a precise shot. I had never been so close to death. I was shattered.

I thought about my parents. I had no memories of them because they died when I was two years old, so I couldn't judge what kind of people they had been. Everything I knew about them had been told to me by other people.

They were a harmonious couple. According to pictures, both were good-looking and self-confident. They were conscious of their money and power. My father was an excellent fencer and shooter. He spent at least two hours every morning practicing.

My parents were killed during a robbery. Their carriage was attacked while they were on their way to somewhere. One of my father's friends who was with them that day said that everything had happened surprisingly quickly. He had his own horse and was riding behind the carriage. Suddenly shots rang out and the carriage was attacked. He was injured, my parents were shot dead. The robbers took jewellery and money and vanished.

I had never thought about this before, now I did. My parents were rich and powerful, but it didn't protect them. They were shot like dogs. Their money, their position in society – none of that had mattered. My father had spent countless hours learning how to use the foil, the sword and guns, but when he really needed to use these skills, he didn't even have a chance.

After my parents' death, I became dependent on my relatives. They hired governesses who changed quite often. I didn't have a friendly relationship with any of them.

My relatives didn't show much interest towards me. They preferred their interest to go towards my money. I don't know how much of my parents' money they took for themselves, but at least they didn't try to kill me to get the whole fortune.

Two more luckless duels took place. After thinking them over again and again I realised I hadn't made any mistakes, I only had strong antagonists. But they were missing something and that was the reason why I was the one who returned.

In the first one a bullet scraped my arm, in the second one it scraped my shoulder. Usually my antagonist hadn't even managed to make a shot because he was already shot dead by me. There was a time when I was partaking in duels a lot, but when people noticed that I returned from all of them without any injuries and rumours about my shooting skills started to circulate, I was defied less and less, only in those cases when ignorance would mean a public outrage. In all other cases people just pretended that nothing had happened. Of course, my insolence grew with every day. I could afford a lot and I knew that no-one would dare to say anything. Being a reject of the society didn't scare me, I was too rich and titled.

Those duels made me think about death. Awareness of my mortality depressed me. My money and power had made me an overman, but a single thought about mortality made them worthless to me. Nothing I owned could protect me from death.

Soon a period of unrest started. My mind rejected the undeniable truth, saying that there must be a way to avoid death or at least to prolong life. I was determined to find it.

Dejection, suspense and the search for something unknown – this is how I spent the next few years. At first, I just read all the books from my library, hoping to find something there. I found sagas and tales about different mythical creatures, but none of them interested me.

Almost one year passed until I finally found what I was looking for. Vampires. Eternal youth, eternal life. Perfect. There wasn't much about them in the book, so I had to continue my search. A few months later, when I had finished, I concluded that information, available in my library, was not sufficient.

I visited almost every bookstore in London, although I didn't expect to find much there. When the shopkeepers noticed my interest in such a specific literature, they told me the addresses of other, secret shops I should visit. Most of them were in the worst districts of London and my first impression about them was negative, but this is where I got books and manuscripts that weren't available anywhere else.

My knowledge about vampires increased significantly, there was only one thing I didn't know – how to find them? I had to continue the search. Time went by.

xxx

It was an evening and I was going to a reception. I was about to step into my carriage when I heard a voice behind me:

"This is such a nice evening, isn't it?"

I turned around and saw a man, maybe 60 years old. He had a friendly look and warm smile, which made a strange contrast with people I usually met and with myself.

"Yes, it's nice," I said and looked at the sky. It was a bit bleak and only some stars were shining through the clouds, but the weather was pleasantly warm.

The man was unloading his carriage. I looked over at him and saw books and notes.

"I haven't seen you here before," I remarked.

"I bought this estate one and a half years ago, but I haven't really lived here yet. I have spent the last eight months away from home," he replied.

Given my unconcern about the world around me, it wasn't surprising that I didn't know my neighbours.

"I'm a scientist," he continued. "I explore nature and various creatures and I spend a lot of time outdoors. When I'm at home, I don't go out much. After I've spent months living on my own with no other people around me, feeling absolutely free, returning to so-called civilised society is a bit traumatic."

I smiled. I didn't know why but I liked this man.

"However, I can't do my work alone, so I have several assistants. While I'm away, they keep my house in order, when I come back, they help me to cope with my notes and other things."

"Sounds exciting," I said in order to show I was listening.

"If you're interested in an old man's adventures, tales and discoveries in biology, you're very welcome to visit me. Whenever you see light in the windows, you can come."

"Thank you for your invitation. I accept it with pleasure."

"Oh," he said and smiled even wider. "I didn't introduce myself. Professor Terence Clanwell."

"Count Yuri Rokosovski."

"Nice to meet you. Have a pleasant evening."

"The same to you," I said and stepped into my carriage. This was one of the rare occasions when I was polite to someone.

A few days later I decided to make a visit. I knocked on the door of the Professor's house. It was opened a minute later. I expected to see a butler, but instead I saw a young woman. There was no doubt that she was a chambermaid, although chambermaids didn't usually wear expensive embroidered dresses with such a deep cleavage that for a moment I was unable to look at anything else.

"We're glad to see you, Count Rokosovski. Come in, I'll take you to Professor Clanwell."

While following her, I thought – how could I not notice someone so beautiful and charming living in the neighbouring house? My visit had already become much more interesting.

I was taken into a room. The Professor was sitting at the table, reading. When he saw me, he gave me a wide smile and stood up immediately.

"Count Rokosovski! How wonderful to see you here! Please, sit down," he pointed at a chair opposite his. "Thank you, Angela, you may leave now."

She slipped out of the room, closing the door behind her. The Professor noticed my look and smiled.

"I didn't warn you. All my assistants are women. Life has proved to me that they are better employees than men."

I smiled too.

"Do they all look like that? This could be a separate reason for my visits."

"Be careful – they're not ordinary women. At least, not the kind of women you've met before."

"Well, that's even better. I'm tired of the women I've met before."

Instead of a reply, the Professor made a helpless gesture, as if he'd be saying "do as you like". Then he went to the drink's cabinet and offered me cognac.

"With pleasure. I never say "no" to a glass of good cognac."

My first visit to the Professor's house wasn't long and the conversation wasn't specific. However, I liked that place and I decided to visit it again soon.

xxx

"You know, people have started to wonder if you're not ill."

"Do they? I wonder why."

"You haven't attended any reception for a while. I started to think that something was wrong with you and decided to make a visit," Reginald said and snickered.

I smiled. I forgave Reginald for everything that for anyone else would end with a challenge to a duel or a touch of my fist to his jaw. It was impossible to be mad at Reginald.

"No, I'm absolutely fine and, as you see, quite alive. I've just found a new way to while away my time. However, I'm pleased to hear that people are worrying about me just because they haven't seen me for two weeks."

It was Sunday morning and we were sitting on my outdoor terrace. I was in a good mood because I had spent the previous evenings at the Professor's house. That place had a very good aura. I tried, but I couldn't remember the last time when I had been in a place where I felt so well.

And, of course, Professor's assistants were another reason that made this place more inviting to me. I had seen them all, but none had left such an impression on me as Angela. She always opened the door and took me to the Professor and pretended she didn't notice my interest, which made me like her even more.

"Where do you go and what do you do?"

"You will not believe me – I'm visiting a professor who lives in my neighbourhood."

Reginald whistled.

"Unbelievable! Yuri has noticed he's got neighbours! And he even speaks to them!"

"Everything is simple: I was used to having ignorant people around me, but then I met someone who is not like that. Besides, and it is also an important reason, he has a lot of beautiful chambermaids. Especially one of them."

Reginald sighed.

"I should have expected that. I suppose I'll hear the details now, right?"

"No. She doesn't pay attention to me. For the present."

"Oh. That is something! Where is she? I must see the woman who has rejected Yuri Rokosovski!"

He stood up and pretended he's going to the Professor's house. I smirked.

"You know, I even like that. Life has become more interesting."

In reality, my disappearance from society was an overstatement. I was still attending receptions, but less than before. I felt bored. I didn't really want to admit it, but I preferred the Professor's company over all those receptions.

I still perceived life with mixed emotions. On the one hand, a depression that had followed me for years had started to disappear and I started to feel a strange easiness. On the other hand, I was still searching and hadn't got any closer to my aim. I supposed I knew everything about vampires, but I didn't know how and where to find them.

To my own surprise, I realised I hadn't got into any trouble for a while. No duels, no scandals, not even arguments. I was 31 years old. There was nothing in my life I could be very proud of. I simply lived by following my desires and I wanted my life to remain like that.

xxx

I woke up when someone ran into my room. The door slammed and one of Reginald's butlers was standing in front of me. He was pale and out of breath and looked very nervous.

"What has happened?"

"Count Rokosovski... Lord Kensington was killed in a duel."

I immediately went to Reginald's house. My friend was lying in his bed. His face was very calm and it looked as if he'd just fallen asleep. In some way, he had, only it was eternal sleep. I don't remember how long I stood there. A single tear fell down my cheek. For a person who never cries it was equal to a flood of tears.

My friend had died in a duel for nothing. Being young and fearless, he had accepted the challenge.

Right after Reginald's funeral I went to search for the person responsible for his death and challenged him to a duel for some ridiculous reason. As I heard later, being afraid of me he had planned to run away from London. Of course, he could decline my challenge and gain a coward's reputation, but I would keep challenging him again and again. He, too, understood that.

When we met each other at the duel place he was nervous and prepared for death. I don't know what his usual shooter skills were like, but nervousness took its toll and he didn't have a chance. After I had won, I went home. I had avenged my friend's death, but I didn't feel any better. My depression came back with full force.

Once again, I was forced to think about life and death. For this reason, I didn't like to be alone. I attended receptions and parties, but it didn't help much. Although I was surrounded by people, I felt lonely. I slept until late afternoon, but pressing thoughts sometimes didn't leave me even in my dreams. Only visiting Professor Clanwell could make me feel better. Soon I was spending every evening there.

XXX

"If you've devoted so many years to your explorations, you must have seen many unusual creatures."

"Yes, of course, but it happens very rarely. You see, the laws of nature are very tough – usually only the strongest and those who don't differ much survive. But I've seen many unusual animals, for example, a fox with two heads and a deer with five legs. But usually such animals don't live long..." He sipped some cognac before he continued. "If honest, I'm not interested in such things anymore. I'm interested in creatures that are considered magical, dangerous or mythical. The ones, people would be scared of if they'd see them. For instance, unicorns. Or dragons."

Although I had seen none of them in my life, after what I had found out in the past few years, I had no reason not to believe in the existence of such creatures. Suddenly a thought came into my mind.

"And werewolves?"

The Professor nodded.

"I've seen them too."

This unexpected turning of our conversation was perfect for me.

"Vampires?"

He nodded again.

"Yes. I've seen and explored many mythical creatures. You can't even imagine how many there are. Unfortunately, human life is short and one has to decide whether to explore a little bit of everything or to explore something thoroughly. This is why I've chosen only a few of all the thousands."

"And how about all these explorations you told me about before? You don't explore flowers and animals?"

"Not really. I still explore plants, but only magical ones. If you mean such animals as deer or wolves, then I dare to say I know everything about them. I explored traditional plants and animals when I was young. The last thirty years have been dedicated to something completely different."

"Are you saying that all the adventures you have told me weren't true?"

I felt a little bit strange. On the one hand, I had found out something unexpected and useful. On the other hand, Terence had fooled me from the first day we met.

He shook his head.

"No, not at all, all the stories were true. I just didn't tell you how old they are."

"Tell me about them."

"What do you want to hear? Which creature interests you?"

I tried to look incurious.

"I don't know. Werewolves."

Terence looked at me and, after a short pause, said:

"I think you know. You only hesitate to ask."

I smirked. Indeed, why talk around it?

"You're right. I'm interested in vampires. I've spent the previous three years searching for all possible information about them."

"Three years? Then tell me what you already know so I'd know what to tell you."

After listening to my narration, Terence said:

"You already know the essential information. I don't see anything I could tell you."

"There's one important thing I don't know. How to find them?"

"That's an unusual question for a young nobleman, isn't it?"

He gave me a serious look.

"If you had asked me about something else or spoke about books in your library, I'd think that you simply are interested in such things. But you asked me only about vampires and, besides, asked me how to find them. Why?"

He looked at me again.

"Your parents died many years ago and you don't have other relatives. You aren't married and you don't have a lover. Your only friend died in a duel six months ago. There's no-one who would be incurably ill and for whom eternal life would be the last resort. And that means... You want eternal life, don't you, Yuri?"

There was no reason to say anything but the truth.

"Yes."

Without realising it, I had made a huge step closer to my aim.

Since that evening our conversations became much more interesting. Terence told me how he had studied unicorns, chased werewolves and collected different magical plants. It was exciting, however, I always tried to make him mention vampires. Terence didn't mind, but he never gave me a clue how to find them.

"Once again, Yuri, why do you want it?"

"Rather – why do I need it?"

"No, Yuri, no... Eternal life can't be a need. You can want it, but you can't call it a need."

"Whatever... I'm frustrated by the thought that I'm mortal. I like life, I like to enjoy it and I hate to think that my body will age and I'll die. So, if there's a possibility to obtain eternal life, I'll use it."

"When did you decide that?"

"I started to think about it when I was in my mid-twenties, but this thought became obsessive three years ago."

"There must be events that have influenced you deeply."

"Yes, several. At first, the death of my parents." I paused. "They were among the richest people in the country, but died in a forest during a robbery. They had money, but it turned out to be worthless. Money didn't protect them. Then there were several duels where I almost lost my life.

I've never been afraid of duels, I consider myself to be one of the best shooters in this country, but three times I literally escaped from death. It was frightening. The awareness that I've been so close to death, stayed alive and that a day will come when I won't be able to escape anymore... And... The last one... Reginald's death. He was the only person I've ever called a friend."

Something like that repeated during the next few evenings. Mine and Terence's conversations had turned into some kind of a duel – I insisted I want to become a vampire while he explained why I didn't need that. With every evening, while listening to my arguments, his face expressed more and more hopelessness.

"You'll have to give up many things. For example, you'll never have children."

"Children? I think I already have a few. Somewhere…" I said and smirked.

Terence sighed.

"You're hopeless."

Finally, a few weeks later, Terence shrugged and said:

"As I see, you won't change your mind."

I nodded.

Terence's eyes brightened and he gave me a wide smile. He stood up from the table corner he had sat on and started to walk around the room.

"All these weeks I was testing how strong your determination is. You stood like a rock and sometimes it looked like you were ready to attack me to find out what you need."

"True, I really had considered such an option."

"You see, we're talking about very serious things here, about the decision that will change your life completely. Forever. I can't discuss it with a person for whom it's just a whim or who doesn't know what he wants. I've got to know you well enough to see that you really understand what you want to do. And this is why," he paused, "I'll tell you what you want to know the most."

Finally! After four years of effort I was only a few steps from my aim.

"Where?"

"I'll give you a clue. You're a wise man, you'll understand."

Then he made a gesture without pointing at anything in particular. Terence wanted me to play by his rules. Why not? So, he pointed around. Books? No, it couldn't be there, that would be too simple. His notes? Maybe, but I knew he had meant something else. I glanced over. The answer had to be somewhere in the house. A person could turn into a vampire with the help from another vampire. And, besides Terence, the only inhabitants of this house were…

"Your chambermaids! Angela…"

He gave me an appreciative glance.

"You're right."

What I was looking for had been so close the whole time!

"How come that you have worked with them for many years, but are still alive and haven't been bitten by werewolves or bewitched by a wizard?" I asked Terence later that night.

"Precaution, extreme precaution. I knew I must be very careful, I can't lose my alertness even for a moment. So far,

I've been fortunate." Then he hung down his head and said: "I'm old and I should start to think about how to end this. I've had an amazing life but soon I won't be able to work outside my house."

"Have you ever thought about becoming immortal?"

"Yes, when I was young and also in the first years of these explorations. However, it is a very serious decision and I hesitated to make it. Now I'm happy I didn't. I've realised that death is not an evil. People should be happy that they're mortal, but they don't appreciate it."

It sounded like the greatest nonsense I had ever heard, but I didn't say anything. Terence noticed that.

"It's hard for you to understand it, right? Don't worry, our agreement still stands. I knew from the beginning you're the kind of person who will be able to accept immortality. It will never become a burden to you, although it's possible that you will not always like the time you're living in, but you'll be able to alien yourself from it. However, there's an opposite type. Usually they turn into vampires by a hasty decision or against their own will. The first years are fine, but then... An event or a chain of events make them realise how serious immortality is and they become hapless. They get estranged from everyone, their life loses colour and they wander around lonely and depressed. They're around us, but you can't see them, only feel them."

I asked Terence how he could be sure that my determination was unchangeable if he only knew me for less than a year.

"You're right, I have known you personally for less than twelve months, but actually I started to follow your life shortly after I had moved in here. I was told that you're showing interest about specific literature, especially the one that is dedicated to vampires. While I was away, my assistants kept an eye on you. When I returned, all I had to do was to choose an appropriate moment when to address you."

It wouldn't be a lie if I'd say that I felt the biggest surprise in my life. All this time I had thought that I'm the one who runs this game, but it turned out that it was him. Although the result was good to me anyway, I felt like I'd been deceived. For the first time in my life I was outsmarted.

My transformation was supposed to take place in December. I'm not sentimental, but I thought it would be the best time. Right before the New Year's Eve, when people usually want to start a new life or hope that something good will happen in their lives. In reality they all will be one step closer to the grave, while I… Isn't it a perfect joke?

Terence didn't ask for anything for his help.

"I don't need money," he said.

We agreed that he would be allowed to describe my transformation in his notes, without mentioning my name, of course.

"You can choose any of my assistants."

"Angela."

"I already thought you'll choose her. She has made a strong impression on you."

"Why did you plan all this to help me?"

"For a very simple reason: if someone has an aim, it is very likely that he'll reach it. And there are only two options: everything will work out well or... What if you suddenly realise that you have made a mistake? What if you don't have enough knowledge? What if you won't be able to adapt yourself to the new lifestyle? What will you do then?"

A few days before New Year's Eve I went to Terence's house. That evening the door was opened by another chambermaid. Angela and Terence were already waiting for me in the room. Terence nodded to her, she stood up and came to me. That was the only time when she touched me. On that evening, at the age of 32, the time stopped for me.

Next spring Terence and his household packed their belongings and left London. This time – forever. He wanted to conduct one more research somewhere in Scotland before he retired.

"I think it's been long enough for me to run across forests and deal with various dangers. I'm old and my strength and dexterity are not the same anymore. I want to put my notes in order and decide how to leave them for the next generations."

We said our farewells and I watched his carriage disappearing out of my sight. It was the last time we met.

I knew that in a few years I would become a nomad too. For a while no-one would notice that I was not aging, but with time I wouldn't be able to hide it and would have to leave London for decades.

Many years later I had a strange encounter that reminded me of my past. I was sitting in a dodgy bar with a glass of indefinable alcohol in my hand pretending that I was drinking it. In reality I was waiting for an appropriate moment to go hunting.

Suddenly the door opened and a woman entered the bar. I looked at her and couldn't believe it. May! She saw me and was as surprised as I was. She had become older since we last met and looked about 40 years old. It wouldn't be anything abnormal, if only May wasn't eight years younger than me. She couldn't decide for a moment, then came over to my table.

"Yuri... Of all people you're the last one I ever thought I'd meet again..."

"I can say the same about you."

May glanced over and said:

"I think we don't need to explain to each other how this is possible, do we?"

"No."

"How old are you?"

"Thirty-two. And you?"

"It's not polite to ask such a question to a woman. I'm in my early forties."

"Tell me how you have been living all these years."

I had an affair with May when I was 26, but she – 18 years old. May became pregnant. I knew it, but didn't do anything.

"Well, after you lost any interest in me, I had to get rid of the child. Rumours started to spread about me in the village, but I managed to stop them when I got the mayor on my side."

"How did you do that?"

"Let's say that he personally ascertained my innocence and virginity," she said in a sarcastic voice. "Later I got married and gave birth to two children. My husband died when I was thirty-five and I realised that life could be something more.

My children had grown up, left the house and I stayed alone. I started to go out more and seek a new life, but it wasn't enough."

"And then?"

"Let's say that an unexpected opportunity appeared and I took it. If you want to know if I regret it, then – no. As for you, I don't even need to ask."

Both of us felt strange. Many years had passed since our last meeting. We said farewells and I left the bar hastily.

xxx

With time, I met other vampires and we started to live under one roof, owning a shared house. This is how I have lived in different cities in England, Germany, France, Ireland. The time I enjoyed the most was from the beginning of the 19th century until the 1840s. Later others preferred to live on their own and our company dispersed.

We presented ourselves as young aristocrats who were travelling around the world and using kind offers of foreign acquaintances to stay with them. There was always someone considered to be the owner of the house. Usually it was me. At first people found it a bit strange but later they got used to it. Our money and titles were also a reason for that. All of us were wealthy: the ones who hadn't been born rich made their fortune by closing different legal and not so legal deals. As rich people usually do, we often organised receptions, but ours were slightly different from other receptions because sometimes not everyone who entered our house in the evening left it in the morning. That is how we skimmed the cream of society from some of its sourest members.

For many people, the 20th century is the time of surprising progress and development. For me it meant the end of the world I belonged to. Men in suits and women in dresses and hats are rare now. Good manners aren't fashionable anymore. Rush has taken over people's lives. Any smear may be called art. Such sports as fencing, archery and horse riding have become old-fashioned. Aristocracy is almost a swear word, there are no borders between social classes anymore.

The world I belonged to is gone and I'm learning how to live in the new world. I need to constantly purchase a new fake passport and look after my fortune, part of which is deposited in many banks. Once I already lost some of it – I didn't do anything with it for decades and later found out that the money didn't belong to me anymore.

After living in different countries, I came back to England. On several occasions I moved into some of my old estates in the countryside. They're weather-worn now, but it doesn't bother me. This is how I felt connected to my time.

Most recently I had been living in one of my old houses. The place was quite distant, so no-one could notice my presence and disturb me. Considering the last 230 years of my life, I realised that I had never regretted my decision. Eternal life hadn't lost its affinity. I just missed my world and, sometimes, although I had spent most of my life in solitude and felt fine about being alone, I wanted a companion or just someone to talk to. I remembered the ones that used to be around me. Reginald... His joy of life, his ironic approach to life and eternal smile contrasted with my cynicism and my rising myself above others. As a result, our friendship became so close that it surprised everyone including ourselves. Professor Clanwell... I wondered how his life ended. Where were his notes now? Arifay... He was a vampire too. I met him at the beginning of the 19th century. He reminded me of Reginald. Arifay could get out of any situation with a smile on his lips and he had his own opinion about everything. I haven't met him for a very long time. Beatrice... She was a big self-made woman in a time when such a thing did not exist, and also a very outspoken one. Unfortunately, we lost touch many years ago. Vincent... I had never met anyone with such a story of life. An ordinary London factory worker, rather dead than alive, became a vampire in absolutely unbelievable circumstances and joined us in the same – absolutely incredible – way. At first, I wasn't happy about his appearance, but I couldn't send him away. That's why I gave him two years to master some manners and gain the right for further stay in our house. The result surprised everyone. An illiterate became an intelligent young man and a pleasant conversationalist. The last time we met was around 1829, although I think I saw him on the street somewhere in America in the 1930s... Vincent alienated himself after the death of his child and wife. Marriage to a mortal was his fatal mistake.

Soon the Millennium would begin and I didn't have any idea what changes it would bring. Stillness had taken over my life and I wanted to get rid of it. I looked at the clock. It was five to twelve.

Puzzlement

I was at a crossroads, not figuratively, but literally, trying to choose which direction to go. After a rather short consideration, I decided to choose the road that led to London. So, tossing my bag over my shoulder I started my long journey. I had decided to go on foot because I didn't want to meet other travellers. I preferred to travel after sunset as sunlight always slowed me down and wanted to do as many miles as possible before the morning.

It was sad to leave the town, I had spent many years there, but there was no other option.

To understand why everything had ended, I had to remember how everything had started. The memories were coming back one after another.

Everything began in 1757 when I was 25 years old. There was nothing remarkable about my life then. I was born in a wealthy family and had enjoyed a careless life since the day I was born. I received a good education and had never worked a single day in my life. When I was younger, I was thinking about joining the army and later considered seafaring as my family lived in one of Britain's port cities, but never actually did anything about it. I was a thinker, not a doer. Sometimes I was surprised that I was in a relationship because I was also quite shy. I could have a thousand thoughts running through my mind but not a single word would come out of my mouth. It must have been Elizabeth who showed initiative, not me.

Elizabeth and I had known each other since childhood. We were neighbours and often played together. She was the only child, while I had two brothers and a sister. Elizabeth did play with my sister, but for some reason she always preferred my company.

As we grew up, new feelings started to develop. At first, we didn't understand them, later we realised it was love. Our families knew about it and didn't object. We had never talked about the wedding, not even to each other, considering it obvious that one day we would get married. How naïve we were!

I remember that evening clearly. It was summer, the weather was lovely and I was out in the garden when I heard Elizabeth calling my name and running towards me. She fell into my arms and embraced me so strong as if she was afraid someone was going to take her away from me. I saw tears in her eyes.

"Elizabeth, what's happened?"

She didn't reply. I was caressing her hair, trying to help her to calm down. Silence fell. Elizabeth embraced me even stronger.

"My parents... They want me to get married... To another man..."

I froze.

"I said that you're the one I want to marry but they said it's not possible. They've already chosen a husband for me." Elizabeth's voice sounded strange. "The date has not been chosen yet but from now on I'm a bride. A bride against her will."

Then she started to cry hysterically.

We stood there for a long time, discussing what to do. We decided to talk to our parents. I was sure that my family wouldn't object against my intention to marry Elizabeth. Her family... Their decision had surprised me.

It was a sleepless night. I felt shocked and confused.

I went to see Elizabeth's parents the next morning.

"Children, I understand that you grew up together and are attached to each other but we can't accept your proposal, Arifay. We have other plans for Elizabeth's future. She is going to marry Lord Valence. We deeply respect you and your family but we and The Valence's are old friends. We want to cement our friendship. Elizabeth is our only child and Lancelot is their only son."

"But... Why him and not me? Old friendship joins our families too. Besides, I love Elizabeth."

"This is more than just a friendship. It's about wealth and improvement of social status."

"My family is rich too."

"The Valence's have more money and a title."

Elizabeth's mother had never spoken to me like that before. Her words surprised me. What did she want to say? That I wasn't good enough for Elizabeth? This conversation felt like a dead-end right from the beginning.

"Yes, I don't have a title and my family is not as rich as The Valence's are but there's something I can offer. Love. I love Elizabeth and Elizabeth loves me."

Up until that moment Elizabeth's mother had been patient and polite. Now she looked at me as if she was talking to a misbehaving child.

"The fact that you love her doesn't change anything. Elizabeth is going to marry Lancelot and this decision will not be changed. Now I will ask you to leave," she said and, before I had time to say anything, walked out of the room. Elizabeth's father followed her, silently.

As I returned home, I went to my father.

"Elizabeth? Well, I would have nothing against your marriage although our family wouldn't gain anything from this union."

"Does it mean you'll help me?"

"No."

Once again, I couldn't believe what I was hearing.

"Father...." My voice was pleading. "You must help me. I love Elizabeth..."

"Arifay..." My father's voice sounded tired. "There are more important things in life than love. Obligation is one of them. Obligation to your country, your family, other people. This also applies to marriage. Marriages are not based on love but on a mutual benefit, the need to intermarry or an obligation. Love doesn't matter. This is why I'm not going to help you. Interests stand over feelings."

The conversation with father only made everything worse. I had thought he would support me.

xxx

The next few weeks passed in a haze. Elizabeth and I were determined not to give up.

"Interest, obligation... This is disgusting! Who are we to our parents then? Human beings, their children? No! We are commodities that can be sold in a market!"

"Commodities... Indeed! We are commodities. When I think that you could belong to another man..."

"Do not mention it!" Elizabeth shouted.

Here I must add that Lord Valence wasn't an old or disgusting man. No, he was my peer, a handsome aristocrat with refined manners, popular in high society. Many girls would be happy to call him their husband.

"Calm down, Elizabeth, calm down. We will interrupt their plans. You will never marry Lancelot."

"I won't. I will marry no-one but you."

As we looked into each other's eyes, we realised what to do. We would run away, marry secretly and then come back. Our families couldn't separate us anymore.

Unfortunately, they anticipated that we were planning something. My father called me to come to him and, in a very strict voice, said that I should forget about a secret marriage otherwise I would be excluded from his last will and would have to leave the family house immediately.

"A man must be able to accept his fate. I hope this is the last time we talk about this," he added.

Elizabeth's parents reacted the same way. They said that if Elizabeth would dare to marry me, she would not be their daughter anymore.

"I hope you won't shame our family by marrying Arifay," Elizabeth's mother had told her.

So, we didn't run. Life without each other was unimaginable but so was life in poverty. It was scaring us. What could I offer to Elizabeth being penniless? How would she live penniless? We were absolutely unprepared for life on our own.

"I guess there is no other solution." Elizabeth's voice was dry and blank. "If we can't be together in life, we can be together in death."

"I hoped that we wouldn't need to say these words but... Our parents don't leave us any other choice," I said. "How shall we do it?"

I was surprised how easily we were talking about our own death.

"Revolvers?" Elizabeth suggested.

"No, it shouldn't be anything where we would need to kill each other. I couldn't do that. I'm a good shooter but you...You could only injure yourself and then... No, I couldn't kill you."

"Poison?"

"Yes, that could work... But which one? Definitely not arsenic. It's a terrible and painful death. I don't want you to suffer. And it's difficult to get other poisons."

"Maybe we could jump from a high place?"

Since our city was located near the sea, it had plenty of cliffs and places with dangerous currents and underwater rocks. Jumping from one of them was almost a sure death. I thought that would be the most appropriate solution. We would join our hands and step over the cliff together...

The wedding day was coming and so was our suicide. Emotions were crushed. I did everything by inertia. I felt like a dead man before I had become dead physically.

One evening, Elizabeth visited me. She wasn't allowed to visit me anymore so she had to sneak out of the house. Her face looked radiant and... happy.

"Arifay," she said, falling into my embrace. "I think I've found another solution. A friend of mine visited me recently. She told me an old legend. Of course, I don't know how truthful it is but... She told me about immortal creatures – vampires. Eternal life. Eternal youth. Do you understand? We won't need to die; we could be together in life... forever."

I looked into Elizabeth's eyes. I didn't have any idea what she was talking about but I saw that life and hope had returned to her. I didn't have any idea if vampires existed or not. I didn't even know who they were, but I was so desperate that I was ready to believe anything. We discussed both the pros and cons of turning into vampires, many times.

"We would need to leave our homes forever..."

"Yes, but we will always be together."

"They drink human blood..."

"We could try to drink animal blood instead. After all, blood is blood. Does it matter where it comes from?" Elizabeth was fading away my doubts with every word she said.

"Eternal life.... Forever young, always together... Eternal life sounds better than eternal death, doesn't it?"

"Yes, indeed. Eternal life sounds better than death."

This time we ran. We had a small amount of money, enough for a few weeks, and one small suitcase each.

Our destination was London.

"Everything can be found in London," Elizabeth had once said. I couldn't disagree.

We had no idea how to find vampires and how much time it could take. Elizabeth had an idea: since vampires are the undead, we could try to find them in cemeteries. Our plan was simple – at night we'd go to a cemetery and Elizabeth would walk around there, hoping to attract the attention of a vampire. She thought that a young girl would be better bait than a young man. It's amazing how Elizabeth, not knowing much about vampires, instinctively did everything correct.

During the first week, nothing happened. We had no idea if vampires even existed because there was no proof.

Later, one evening we put our cloaks on and went to a cemetery. It was cold outside and it had been snowing. When we reached the cemetery, I hid behind a tree. Elizabeth began slowly walking around tombstones, stopping from time to time to read the inscriptions on them.

Suddenly I noticed a silhouette. His face was covered by a hood. I hadn't noticed him coming. Instinctively I made a step forward but then stopped.

It happened almost in an instant. The silhouette was already near Elizabeth, bending her head back and biting into her neck. Oddly, but she didn't look neither surprised, nor scared.

I saw that she was staggering and becoming paler. I ran to her.

"Elizabeth!"

The silhouette startled. When I had come very close to him, I heard Elizabeth whispering:

"Transform us."

He looked at us.

"Why should I do that?"

However, he loosened his grip although he didn't release Elizabeth. She told him everything. The vampire's head was still covered by the hood. We couldn't see his emotions.

After Elizabeth had told him our story, he didn't say a word for a moment. I could foresee that now we're absolutely in his power. He could help us or... kill us. Oddly, but in our case both options were acceptable.

Then, the vampire took off his hood. Finally, we could see his face. It was a young man with chiselled cheekbones and black hair. His beauty contrasted with his icy stare.

"So, you want to become vampires to be together in eternal life? I suppose I could help you."

Then, as it would be the most ordinary thing in the world, he bit himself in the arm and outstretched it towards Elizabeth. She pressed it to her lips so tightly that the vampire gave her a surprised look.

"Enough," he said. "My blood is like venom. A few drops are enough."

Then he came to me. There were small blood drops in the snow. I was looking at them, feeling fascination and fear at the same time. His fangs cut into my neck.

After the transformation was done, there was no need to linger.

"Good luck in your new life," the vampire said to us before leaving.

We also wanted to leave but felt too weak for that. Elizabeth tried to make a few steps but collapsed. I wanted to rush to her but I couldn't. I felt dizzy and collapsed, too. We both slipped into unconsciousness.

I remember clearly the period just after the transformation. I felt weird all the time. Feelings, unknown to me before, developed and even the ones I knew before weren't the same. My skin became icy and pale, I didn't feel the cold, I became more handsome and my physical strength increased. I even changed mentally. Character traits that had been considered good and honourable lessened while the ones that were considered bad grew. I no longer liked sunlight. I slept in the daytime and woke up in the late evening, feeling thirsty for blood.

Elizabeth, too, had become more beautiful, I couldn't take my eyes off of her.

Initially we had decided we wouldn't attack people but soon we realised that we didn't care. When we went to hunt for the first time, our thirst was so strong that we just grabbed the first person we met along our way. We didn't feel any guilt or regret, only thirst. Hunting, an issue discussed so often during the first days, became ordinary and neither of us mentioned it anymore.

During the evenings while we were lying in bed, embracing, we were still unable to believe that we had succeeded.

"We accomplished it," I whispered, caressing Elizabeth's face.

"Yes, we really did it."

There was another issue discussed a lot in the past but not mentioned anymore – the wedding. We wanted to get married because that was how we were raised. We had spent a lot of time considering if we could get married being vampires. If the legend was true, we'd become creatures whose existence is against the laws of nature. Could we go near a church? After the transformation this issue had died, too. If we were outside the law it didn't matter if we were married or not. Mentally we felt like a married couple and nothing else mattered.

The first years, spent together, were wonderful. Our love became stronger and we were discovering something new in each other all the time.

"Mmm, you've got a birthmark here. I hadn't noticed it before. Let me kiss it."

Elizabeth giggled when my cold lips touched her spine.

I was watching her moves, discovering new gestures and mimics. Now we could spend all of our time together and barely separated. I remembered how often I had been told that love doesn't matter. Those people didn't realise what they were missing. Sometimes I remembered my family and my heart filled with sorrow. I would never see them again. I hadn't even said goodbye to them. Unfortunately, there was nothing I could do about it.

Being a vampire made things easier. We could live without worrying about money most of the time. We didn't need food, heat, new clothes. Of course, we didn't live on the street but our household was very simple. When our own money ran dry, Elizabeth sold her jewellery. We weren't against dark deals. Elizabeth could break into a house without blinking an eye in the absence of the owners and steal a lot of valuable goods: manuscripts, silverware... Then we fenced them.

After a few years in London we moved to a town near the sea. Of course, it was far away from our hometown. It was big enough for us to hunt and small enough to remind us of the countryside. We still loved water and nature very much. London with its drabness and bustle had started to annoy us.

Previously, when we still lived with our families, we really liked going on walks. We often strode in my garden or in the nearest wood. During warm spring evenings we could spend hours walking around and watching everything: plants, animals... And we still loved to do that. The only difference was that now we were having walks only at night and winter had become our favourite season.

One-night Elizabeth was walking ahead of me. We were about to cross a small bridge. Suddenly she started to walk faster and after a brief moment had already climbed onto the railing. I could only admire her dexterity – from my point of view it looked so easy as if she wasn't wearing a heavy velvet dress and a cloak. She outstretched her hands to the side and smoothly walked forward.

"Elizabeth, what are you doing?"

She turned her head and looked at me:

"What are you waiting for? Join me!"

I went to the bridge but, instead of climbing onto the railing, clasped my arms around Elizabeth and lifted her off of it. Then I pressed her body to mine and our lips merged in a fiery kiss.

Unfortunately, our happiness didn't last long. After less than three decades we realised that there was something missing in our relationship. We knew each other inside out. There was nothing to discover, no excitement left. Emptiness appeared in our relationship and there was nothing we could fill it with. Time passed by but we remained the same: young, beautiful and... boring to each other.

Our feelings became weaker and weaker. We started to avoid each other and spent more time separated. We tried to save our relationship but we realised that we didn't know how.

In my thoughts I often returned to the past, to the moment when we had made the decision to enter into eternal life. We were young, in love and didn't know what it would mean. Then it had only meant an opportunity to be together. We knew many couples who had spent their lives together and, looking at them, we thought how beautiful it would be to age together. We didn't know anyone who would have been in a similar situation and our understanding of love was limited with what we had read in books. Eternal life had seemed to be a dream come true, it was an opportunity to be together forever and enjoy love that would never end. It turned out that in reality everything was different. I realised what an awful mistake we had made. I wished we had chosen death.

Elizabeth felt the same only in her case things were much worse. At first, I didn't realise exactly how much worse.

Children were the most painful issue for us. Once we had wanted to start a family, now it wasn't possible anymore.

Elizabeth had started to walk around town in the afternoon, watching children playing. She looked at them with eyes full of love and insatiable tenderness started to tear her.

She started mentioning it more and more often. She was telling me about children she had seen on the streets and it was one of the rare times when I saw life in her eyes. I couldn't reprove anything to her. After all, she was only 20 when she was transformed.

I noticed that her behaviour was becoming stranger and stranger. She started to talk to herself. Once, when I opened the door, I noticed that she was singing a lullaby as if she was standing near a cradle. I felt true compassion. Poor Elizabeth! Suddenly I realised that there were so many things we hadn't considered...

Then the third, the most unpleasant, phase of our relationship started. The love, so strong that we were ready to die for it, had faded away completely. Emptiness and disappointment turned against each other. Elizabeth and I looked at each other and thought of ourselves as unholy. Our faces were becoming less beautiful to each other because of the growing disgust. We tried to avoid each other as much as possible. The fact that our favourite places were the same made everything worse. Quite often I had gone, for example, to the beach and ran straight into Elizabeth.

Our rare conversations turned into rows. Usually they ended with yelling terrible things to each other and running away. An argument could start any moment.

"Arifay, can you imagine how beautiful it would be if we'd have a child?"

"Elizabeth, you know it's not possible."

"But what if we... could obtain ourselves a child?" A strange note sounded in her voice.

"Elizabeth, do you want to steal a child from someone?"

"Yes, that is exactly what I mean!"

"We can't do that! We can't steal a child from anyone!"

"Why not? I want a child!"

"We can't have children! And we can't steal them from anyone! Two vampires raising a child! That's absurd!" I exclaimed.

Elizabeth sprang up indignantly and ran to me, striking me in the chest with her forefinger.

"That is your fault! Yours, yours, yours! It was your idea – to turn into vampires and be together forever! And now your plan has failed and we can't alter anything! You've turned me into a blood sucking monster!"

I was listening to her with undisguised surprise. My fault? The idea about eternal life belonged to her!

"My idea? Who ran to me saying that she had found a way to stay together, remaining alive?"

My answer only maddened Elizabeth. She let out a screech and started to scratch my face with her sharp nails.

Before I realised what I was doing, I had pulled her away from me and thrown her across the room. She landed heavily on the floor and looked right into my eyes. Terrible swearing words started to flow from her lips - she could make a sailor blush.

I didn't care about it until she said:

"I hate you! I curse the day I fell in love with you!"

That was The End. There was no reason to continue torturing each other. I took my belongings and left.

We had wanted to be together forever but this eternity had lasted for only fifty years.

I had sunk into my thoughts so much that I hadn't noticed it was morning already. I went off of the road and slipped into the forest where the treetops gave rise to a pleasant shadow.

I was going to find a place for myself until the sunset. Then I would continue on my way.

Lucretia

Autumn of 1864

I looked outside the window to see if he really had gone. The dark silhouette slowly withdrew and reached the gates. He stayed there for a moment as if he was taking a final glance at the house. Seeing him leaving, I went away from the window. Standing in the middle of my drawing room, holding my head in my hands, I was thinking about what to do. I wanted to pack my bags and leave immediately, but was worried that it would cause suspicion. I needed to plan everything through and leave properly. I was about to go to Edinburgh where I had recently purchased an estate. I suppose I had already anticipated that it would be useful someday.

The brightly lit room and crackling fire were making a strange contrast with the coldness inside me and the outdoor terrace where, just a few moments ago, I had been with him.

I had to distract myself with something, so I decided to start packing the most necessary belongings. I literally ran into my bedroom and threw my travel bag on the bed. Unfortunately, this task was distracting only my hands. My mind, repeatedly, was attacked by the same thought – why did I allow this to happen?

Nigel and I met at a reception. I never knew who was behind it but they definitely hadn't put their heart into it. I felt bored and decided to take a look around. Because of the lighting, the house was sinking in semi-darkness and shadows were slipping from one room to another. Nigel had been leaning against the door frame. His pose was suggesting he'd like to leave this place. I was going to pass him by when suddenly he addressed me:

"Are you looking for something to distract you, as well?

"Yes. I'm trying to find a place here where something is going on."

"This isn't a very exciting reception, is it?"

For a moment, silence fell.

"Are you waiting for someone?"

"Yes, for my aunt." He sighed. "She is in London for a few days and wants to use the opportunity to attend some receptions. My parents assigned me to accompany her."

He sighed again and it sounded as if he'd have a heavy burden on his shoulders.

"And you agreed?"

"I'm trying to be a good son." He smiled.

"Let me guess: at first she lugged you around, presenting you as a charming young man who, by the way, is single and then she'd said that the girl who you'll marry one day will be very happy, but later she found an old acquaintance and forgot about you completely? And now she's probably brisking around with a glass of champagne in her hand. "

"How did you guess?" He laughed and filled the whole hall with wonderful, warm laughter.

"Sometimes human behaviour can be predicted so easily…"

"Have you arrived here alone?"

"Yes, I always arrive alone."

"Oh, excuse me… I didn't introduce myself to you. Nigel Greneville."

"Lucretia Lockwood."

Suddenly a loud shout was heard in the hall. It was accompanied by quick steps.

"Lucretia! I hoped to see you here!"

It was Derek, one of my countless London acquaintances. He hugged me and kissed me on both cheeks.

"I've attended several funerals that were more exciting than this so-called reception. Lucretia, will you join us? If we can't find entertainment here, we'll have to create it."

"Of course."

Then I turned towards Nigel.

"I must go now. It was a pleasure talking to you."

"Mutually. I hope we'll meet again."

"So do I."

xxx

Two days later I was fidgeting in front of the mirror making sure I was looking absolutely gorgeous for this evening's reception. As usual, I did. My green eyes could stop anyone who looked into them for a long time – my look was so piercing that it seemed to be able to break into one's soul and see all their thoughts and darkest secrets. My Roman nose only added to my appearance. I guess it was an heirloom from a distant ancestor. My dark, brown hair was tied in a tight knot. I put the top hat on and gave my clothes a final look: a white blouse, black trousers, a black jacket and long, black boots. I hadn't worn a dress for more than a year. Of course, in the Victorian era dressing like this was a huge challenge for a young woman. At first my look caused condemnation, but later people got used to it. It wasn't the first time I'd ever looked different from others – I was 5 feet 9 inches tall, which was quite rare at that time.

I had barely arrived at the reception when I spotted a familiar face in the crowd. Nigel, too, saw me and came to me.

"Accompanying your aunt again?" My voice sounded a bit sympathetic.

"Yes. Luckily, she's going home soon."

He took a look around.

"Oh, there she is, waving at me desperately… I must go now. I hope to see you later."

As soon as he had left, I was approached and invited to join a discussion. As usual – when a lively discussion was necessary, I was addressed. It was enough for me to enter the door when people were ready to fight for my attention and company.

"Unfortunately, we didn't meet again that evening." I heard a pleasant baritone right next to me.

Once again Nigel and I had encountered each other. I was sitting in a chair near the fireplace enjoying a quiet moment after a passionate exchange of opinions.

"Yes, and it was a pity. However, I must say the reception was excellent and I enjoyed it."

Nigel moved closer to the fireplace, which was the only source of lighting in this room, and looked at the flames.

"I usually try to avoid receptions, but…" He cast down his eyes. "Relatives are relatives."

"That's why we all have a family – we do something for them and expect that they will later do something in return, for us."

"Would you like to go to the garden? I'd like to have some rest from being introduced to all the unmarried women here..."

We went outside. The autumn was soon going to be replaced with winter but the air was still warm. The evergreen trees and plants stood out against the grey sky and gravel on the long, seemingly never ending, footpaths.

Although Nigel and I barely knew each other, we felt like two old friends who had met again after a long separation. I didn't know how much time we had spent out there when suddenly someone yelled:

"Nigel, Nigel! Are you here?"

He sighed.

"That's my aunt. I suppose she wants to go home now."

"Well, there's nothing we can do about it. Thank you for the pleasant evening."

Nigel took my hand and kissed it.

"I can say the same. I hope to meet you again sometime soon."

"So do I."

I enjoyed Nigel's company. It felt like I had found a true friend, so it wasn't surprising that I started to invite him to my house. When Nigel's aunt had gone back home and he stopped going out it was almost the only way to meet him.

My garden was slightly overgrown and had a mixture of trees, evergreens, flowers and wild plants, and a frog pond with a few resident toads. I liked it that way. It felt real, with a character. I liked spending time outdoors, either sitting in the shade under a tree with a good book, going for a walk or practicing archery.

The house itself was a combination of chaos and order. Despite having been here for eight months I still didn't know how many bedrooms it had. I only ever used three rooms: my bedroom, drawing room and library. I wasn't fond of the Victorian fashion of lots of vases, porcelain figurines and other bric-a-brac everywhere and only tried to have things that were useful. I loved books and maps and had a large globe on my desk in the library, which was also my office. My desk was always covered in letters, invitations, newspapers and documents. I enjoyed spinning the globe and picking places I'd like to travel to one day.

Nigel loved my place straight away. We both shared the childhood horror of accidentally breaking something useless but precious simply by trying to move across a room. It was nice to be in a place where one could feel free.

"Nigel, I want to ask you something... Usually I don't do it because men always say "no"."

I looked at him and let out a laugh. Nigel looked bewildered and curious.

"Will you fence with me? I really like doing it, but other women become shocked upon hearing about it and men reject my proposal because they want to avoid injuring me."

"Well... I don't know... And what if I really injure you?"

"Don't worry. I've been training since childhood, with my brothers. Nothing has happened to me so far."

"With your brothers? Then why don't you ask them?"

Here I had to use my usual lies.

"They are all abroad. My elder brother is a doctor in France, the middle one joined the navy and is currently in India, and my younger brother is an anthropologist. The last time I heard from him he was in Romania."

Nigel was doubting.

"Please… I promise nothing will happen to me. It would make me very happy."

I looked at him sweetly. I knew he wouldn't be able to resist.

"All right. Let it be."

Of course, nothing happened to me. At first Nigel took caution and fenced worse than he actually could but soon he realised that I'm a strong antagonist and the battle heated up. I didn't let him lose deliberately and I wasn't going to lose deliberately either, so the result was a draw.

"Thank you for accepting my proposal. I haven't had so much fun in a long time," I said and touched my forehead, pretending that I'm wiping away sweat. I didn't want Nigel to notice that my skin is just as cold and dry as it was an hour ago.

"I didn't expect anything like that from you. Which one of your brothers taught you to fence like this?"

"My middle brother. We could train for hours."

"That's very impressive though I hope you'll confine yourself to fencing and won't propose, for example, duelling."

"Don't worry, I won't. Although... I'm a very good shooter. Living together with men has taught me a lot of things."

Growing up with three brothers and their friends, I was well adjusted to the presence of men and felt completely relaxed in their company. I could talk to them, play together with them, ride a horse with them or be a judge for their 100-yard sprints. They saw me as one of them, so I didn't know that sometimes a friendship could transform into different, deeper feelings.

Of course, I had received a lot of attention from men in my life, but it had never come from men who were my friends. That's why I didn't notice that Nigel's feelings towards me were starting to change. This revelation came unexpectedly. We were sitting on the terrace, talking about something. He looked at me and our eyes met. I saw a familiar expression in them – desire.

That night, just after Nigel left, I realised that we had to part ways. There was no other choice. But then a thought ran through my mind – I didn't want it to happen.

To explain why Nigel and I couldn't have a future together, I had to go back to the summer of 1862.

I was 21 years old then and was living in a coastal town in the South of England with my father and three elder brothers. My hometown was notable for the amount of myths and legends about different magical creatures that were passed down from generation to generation in the form of bedtime stories. There were rumours that some of the creatures had lived in our town and the locals had fought them. I was the youngest child and the only daughter in the family. My mother died when I was little and I had spent most of my life in the company of men. I followed the stock market news with my father, played hide-and-seek with my brothers and their friends and lived in a more relaxed atmosphere than many of my female peers. However, I wasn't boyish – my father, worrying that I'd become a tomboy one day, ensured I did needle-work and piano lessons. I liked pottering in the garden. We had an orchard, a garden and a gardener but one corner was given to me and only I took care of it. I mainly grew flowers there: roses, sweet peas, peonies, hyacinths, tulips, lilies, freesias, as well as lavender. Surrounded by love and care, I couldn't imagine any other life.

I had another reason to feel happy. His name was Jack. His family had moved here three years ago. Willing to make an acquaintance with neighbours, they organised a party and that's where we met. Already then, I realised that I look at him differently than to other men. Our families became friends and we invited them to our house from time to time and they did the same. We fell in love with each other and had been a couple for about a year. We had talked about getting married a few times but those weren't serious talks.

My father didn't rush with giving me away in marriage and neither did Jack's family – none of his brothers were married and 22-year old Jack was the youngest child in the family.

On that fateful day I was coming back from visiting a friend. She liked my flowers so I made a bouquet for her and we spent a few careless hours drinking tea and eating cake. I was on my way back when I heard a voice behind me.

"Good day, Lucretia!"

It was Nancy, one of my neighbours.

"Good day, Nancy!" I said, turning to face her.

"I just wanted to ask if your family is going to the party at the Abysses' house? After all, you're one of their closest friends."

I looked at her, becoming very surprised. I didn't have any idea that Jack's family is organising something.

"I never knew anything about it. When is the party?"

"Really? Strange… The party will be this Friday. It's nothing big, they just want to celebrate their son's engagement."

"The eldest one's?"

"No, the youngest one's."

Suddenly it became hard to breathe.

"Jack is getting married?"

"Yes, to a girl from a neighbouring county. Their families are old friends."

Cold sweat appeared on my forehead and my knees began to wobble. We were outside my house now and I had to lean against the flint wall. I felt like someone had thrown a rock at my chest. What I had just heard sounded unreal.

After a moment I recovered for a bit and, forgetting about Nancy's presence, ran to Jack's house. Thoughts were running wild inside my head. I hoped that Nancy had been mistaken and it's not Jack who's getting married. Jack couldn't do that; he was with me!

When I ran into the yard, I saw someone coming over the path. It was Jack. He stopped and gave me a surprised look.

"Lucretia, what's happened?"

"Jack, is it true? Are you getting married?" while saying this, I had subconsciously grabbed his hands.

"Yes."

"But... how?"

"I'm sorry, Lucretia… You're a wonderful girl, but it's the will of both families. Everything is over between us."

He was looking straight into my eyes but I couldn't sense any regret.

I tried to calm down before I came home but I couldn't fool my father. He immediately asked me about what happened. I had to tell him everything.

"I didn't know that everything was so serious between you both."

"What did you think then?"

"That you simply like each other…"

"It was serious… We met often… In secret.. He's the love of my life, father…"

It was then that it dawned on me how little trace there was of this relationship. Jack and I did not display our feelings in public, that would have been considered bad manners at best and scandalous behaviour at worst. In private we enjoyed a certain degree of freedom, in public we were bound by strict rules.

What my father had just heard was preoccupying him. Being a man of action, he waited until I had recovered a bit and offered to go to Jack's house and talk to his parents.

1862 was a year of many firsts for me. Up until that day I had never thought about how one's perception of a place can change. I had so many fond memories of the Abyss family house, I always looked forward to visiting Jack's family, his mother had always been very nice to me. However, things can change. That day the place suddenly seemed so cold, the reception room was uninviting and

Jacks' mother seemed very keen to get us out of the door as soon as possible.

"Lucretia, we're really sorry for this. I understand that you had romantic feelings towards Jack and we probably should have mentioned the arrangement, but…"

"The *arrangement*?" I exclaimed.

"Yes, he and Cornelia were promised to each other five years ago, when they were seventeen."

I felt like something had stabbed me right in the heart. It became hard to breathe. I fell into semi-consciousness. My vision clouded and the voices around me fused.

An arrangement. No-one had considered it necessary to inform me! Never, not even with a single word, had Jack mentioned Cornelia or her family. I remembered countless times when Jack and I had ridden a horse, walked in the gardens, remembered visits to his house. I sat in the front room while Jack was reciting poetry in his charming voice. I remembered what a great dancer he was and how easily we had glided over the dance hall. I remembered our first kiss in the meadows. I remembered how he confessed his love for me. We were in a field, lying in the grass; my head was on his chest and he was sliding his fingers through my hair.

"Lucretia, you're an extraordinary girl. And this is why I like you. I love you."

xxx

"I've never said I'm in love with you, what are you talking about?"

A memory came back. Jack gave me such an innocent look that I started to think I'm going insane.

"I've never been in that field with you."

That was our last conversation. It turned out that mine and Jack's relationship was a creation of my girly fantasy and he had kissed me just once, on the forehead.

"Lucretia, you were like a sister to me. I'm very sorry if you thought it was something else."

He looked at me again, with the same innocent look, then turned around and walked away.

Unbelievable. At first he said it was his parents' will and he couldn't do anything about it. Later it turned out that the agreement about his and Cornelia's marriage had been finalised five years ago. And now Jack was swearing to me that he had loved me only like a sister and had never thought I could feel anything more towards him.

Memories were stabbing me like sharp pieces of glass. I felt like I'm bleeding. I was standing in front of the mirror but, of course, there were no traces of blood. All I saw was my pale, jaded face.

Betrayal was slowly eroding me. At first, I simply became grey and silent, then I stopped noticing the world around me and shrank into myself. I could stand near the window for hours, looking outside but not seeing what's there. I stopped eating.

Soon I started to spend more and more time in bed. After a while I didn't leave it at all. I lost sense of time. Once I was looking outside the window and saw that trees are leafless. When I had looked outside the last time, the leaves of the trees had just started to change colours.

Liar! He was such a liar! He had been with me for three years, one of them – as my beloved, and I had thought I knew him. Now I realised that I didn't know him at all.

Apathy was replaced by fever. I thought I'm burning. The last thing I remember – I woke up in my bed. I didn't have enough air to breathe, it was unbearably hot and I heard voices around me. I saw chambermaids, the doctor, my brothers, father... And then I sank into unconsciousness.

When I woke up, it was dark and silent. I didn't know where I was. I wasn't in my room or even in the house. The air was strangely chilly and wet. The next moment I was standing in the garden. Still not understanding anything, I went to the house. My head was full of questions I had no answers for. Why was I outside the house? How did I get here? Suddenly I shuddered. I remembered something else we had on the estate. A family crypt. What was I doing here? I didn't have keys in my hands. How did I get in here? How did I get out?

The house door wasn't locked. I found it strange too – during such a late hour all doors were always locked. Maybe I had left them open when I went out? But... Why would I do it?

There was light in the front room. I went there and warily opened the door. My father was sitting by the fireplace. He was so immersed in thoughts that didn't notice my presence.

Suddenly he felt that he's not alone anymore. Father turned his head towards me and our eyes met. He didn't look surprised when he saw me. A foreboding overtook me.

"I have been waiting for you," he said with eyes full of sadness.

The conversation was painful. To prepare me, my father told me an old legend I had already heard when I was a child. More than a century ago a young man had died in our town. His bride ran away with another man and he died from sadness. Shortly after his death weird things started to happen in the neighbourhood: at first people noticed some strange creature walking around at night and then later people started to disappear. The locals thought it was some kind of wild beast and went to hunt it but it turned out to be much worse: the beast was the young man. He had woken up from the dead and turned into a vampire – a creature who feasts on blood. He was caught whilst drinking a kidnapped person's blood. Thunder-struck locals attacked the vampire and killed it.

I had never believed this story but now I knew that the legend was true. My father loved me too much to allow the recurrence of the second part of it. He always stood on my side, no matter what. He had decided to let me go.

"Lucretia, you must leave immediately. During your illness people were talking that if you die, it may happen again. We tried to hide the real reason for your illness and said that you died of pneumonia."

Father had prepared a horse and new clothes for me. I think they belonged to one of my brothers.

"You'll look less conspicuous in this," he said.

Father also gave me a considerable amount of money and jewelry.

"Go as far away from this place as you can and never return. It will be too dangerous."

We embraced. Then I jumped on the horse and vanished into the November night.

For the first time I thought over my destiny. Becoming a vampire had gradually changed me. There was almost nothing left from the old Lucretia. Instead of her a cynical and cold being was born who decided to accept the life she had now and to enjoy it as much as possible.

After one year of solitude I realised that I need a change. I invented a new name and identity and slowly started to look for a company. And then I met Nigel.

The thought that Nigel would soon leave my life depressed me. He had brought me the ease and joy I had been missing. However, our farewell was inevitable. Humans and vampires couldn't be together.

Nigel continued to visit me and I continued to remind myself that it can't continue this way. I had given him the cold shoulder recently and hinted that it would be better if we wouldn't meet anymore. I told him that it was because of me, not him.

"Lucretia, do you think I haven't noticed the strange things that surround you? You mention your family quite often but none of them is in England; you live in a large house but have no servants; you can barely be seen in daylight. It looks like you're hiding from something. You live as if you have a dark secret and I don't understand what it is. But I shall say this to you – whatever it is, you can tell me."

That was unexpected. Nigel turned out to be far more attentive than I thought.

"And.. that's not all. You never feel tired, barely eat and drink at receptions, your skin stays cold even sitting in front of a fireplace. Your eyes are like an abyss and have strange expressions I can't understand. Sometimes I think that you're not human."

Nigel had noticed surprisingly much. If his knowledge would have been broader, he would have guessed my secret. Now it was absolutely clear that he loves me. Only a person who's in love is so observant, noticing things other people miss even when seeing each other every day.

In other circumstances I probably would have lied, but now... I told him about my love for Jack, his betrayal, my illness, the rumours that accompanied it and death.

While talking, I had been standing with my back to him, looking away. Now I turned and looked into his eyes. I was waiting for his reaction. After everything I had told him, I'd understand any kind of reaction: fear, horror, the willingness to destroy me. I wouldn't have been angry at Nigel if he'd run away to tell everybody that there's a vampire amongst them and would return with a crowd of people to kill me. It didn't scare me. I'd manage to run away.

I just hoped that Nigel's feelings towards me would be gone. But there was no fear or hate in his eyes. Quite the reverse – his look was full of sympathy and compassion. He saw in me not a vampire but the Lucretia who was able to love so deeply, that she died of pain when she was deceived.

I realised that with my confession I had made everything worse. Instead of turning his back upon me, Nigel had fallen in love with me even more.

I should have taken action then. However, instead of making a step back I made a step forward. It was obvious that we can't be together but in my mind it didn't mean we needed to separate now.

I relented. I even started to wear gloves, so Nigel wouldn't feel the icy touch of my hands.

It was evening and we were walking in my garden.

"Aren't you afraid that I could bite you?"

"No."

"That's good because I'm not going to do it."

I didn't like the look I saw in his eyes.

"If you've ever been thinking about it, then put this thought out of your mind! I'm not going to turn you! You don't have any idea what it actually means to be a vampire!"

I was so furious that I felt like I could spit fire. How could he even consider giving up human life!

Nigel had to run to catch me. I had forgotten how fast I can move now. Of course, he said that I've misunderstood him and apologised for this misapprehension. I wanted to believe he was honest.

Being in people's company I knew that they could feel cold, but being at home I had already forgotten it. I remembered it only when Nigel politely asked if we could go inside the house.

"Oh, sorry…" I got bewildered.

I still liked to spend time outdoors and together with Nigel we spent a lot of time riding horses or walking around my garden. The fact that it was December didn't bother me. Even on the coldest days I could be outdoors wearing just a shirt. I wore a cloak only because I was supposed to.

"You must be freezing. Let's go inside."

A moment later we were sitting in my drawing room. Nigel was warming himself near the fireplace. I handed him a glass of cognac. He gave me a surprised look before he took the glass.

"I thought you can't consume food or drink. Why do you have cognac in the house?"

"It is for guests. By the way, there's a difference between "I can't" and "I shouldn't". I eat and drink a bit in public. It would be too suspicious if no-one had ever seen me doing that. Human food simply causes me a stomach ache. Alcohol – even in small amounts – causes something similar to a hangover."

I sat in the chair opposite him, only moved myself further away from the fireplace. I didn't feel cold, but I felt heat.

"You said you don't feel cold, but you always have a fire burning…"

"I can't leave the house unheated. The rooms will become damp and my books will get ruined." I smiled. "What else do you want to know about me?"

"Why do you always wear men's clothing?"

"Correction: these are clothes men usually wear, but they all are made especially for me. I like my costume and... it's more comfortable. Unlike many others, I'm not willing to suffer in the name of beauty.'

xxx

I had accepted an invitation to join a small party. I was sitting by the fireplace, discussing the latest gossip and having a few drinks with a group of people. The darker it got, the more the hosts wanted to talk about all things mythical, mystical or simply unexplainable. I felt a bit bored until...

"Have you ever heard about bloodsuckers?"

"What kind of? The ones in the Government? Or did you mean someone else?" someone said and laughed. Others joined him.

"No, I was being serious. Have you heard anything about the so-called... *vampires*?" he held his breath and gave everyone a scared look.

I could tell them a lot, I thought and smirked. Of course, I wasn't going to do it.

"I have," a man said. He must have joined us recently because I had no idea who he was.

Everyone turned towards him. He enjoyed this attention for a minute and then continued.

"I heard a story recently: in a town in Sussex, locals had broken into a crypt. There were rumours that the dead person might have turned into a vampire after death."

Women gasped.

"Tell us more!" an old lady demanded.

These people didn't care what they listened to as long as it was entertaining.

"And, what happened next?"

The teller smiled. "I'll better tell you the whole story. A girl had died in that place a few years ago. She had fallen in love with some boy but he left her because of another girl. The girl endured a lot of heartache and died from suffering. Although her illness was hidden, rumours started to spread in the village that the poor girl may turn into a vampire after her death – it sometimes happens to those who have died a premature death. Something like that had already happened there. This is why it was necessary to make sure that didn't happen again, by driving a wooden stake into the girl's heart, putting garlic into the coffin and so on. The family was firmly against it. She was buried in the family crypt which was locked and guarded."

"What was the girl's name?"

"Lucy Westmoreland."

I froze. My hands clutched the arms of the chair. I almost turned them into sawdust. Lucy Westmoreland was no-one else but me – my full name was Lucy Lucretia Westmoreland. Friends and relatives called me "Lucretia"; "Lucy" was used only in documents.

"And?"

My heart continued to beat wildly. If someone had opened the coffin, the family secret would be revealed!

"I'll have to disappoint you. What once used to be Miss Westmoreland was in the coffin."

Everyone gave a sigh, full of disappointment, but I lost peace completely. The coffin wasn't empty! How was that possible? Those couldn't be my bones – I wasn't a spirit, but a physical being. Who was lying in my coffin? Would my family have killed someone to hide the secret? No, it couldn't be, I said to myself, they would never do that.

A voice brought me back to reality.

"Miss Lockwood, what do you think about this? Is it possible to grieve about a betrayal so much that it leads to death?"

I had to pull myself together to pretend careless.

"If you're asking me that, you don't know how a woman's mind works. We're sensitive beings and there are things we perceive intensely."

"Can you imagine such a situation in your life?"

"Why are you asking me that? Oh, right, I'm the only unmarried woman here... No, I can't. I'm quite selfish and can't love strong enough to grieve like that poor girl did."

"Good for you. Poor Miss Lucy..."

The others nodded:

"Yes, poor Lucy..."

After what I had heard I had to see my father. I realised how dangerous it is, but I didn't see any other option.

I only had to travel 50 miles but the journey was exhausting – not physically but mentally. The closer I came to my father's house, the more I felt my memories weighing me down. It was late, but the light was on in the front room. The back door wasn't locked and I sneaked in quietly. I looked through the keyhole and gave a sigh of relief. My father was alone. I opened the door carefully. He looked towards it and, seeing me, sprang to his feet.

"Lucretia!"

We ran to each other and embraced. I felt tears flowing down his cheeks. He regained self-composure after a moment and pushed me back.

"But... What are you doing here? I told you to never return. It is too dangerous... Especially now..."

"I heard about my coffin being opened and couldn't not come. Tell me – who is lying in my grave?"

His face clouded.

"A chambermaid."

As if he had guessed my thoughts, he quickly continued:

"I didn't kill her. A few months after your death I gave employment to a new chambermaid. Unfortunately, she fell ill and died. She had no relatives, so I offered to pay for the funeral. I was about to bury her in the local cemetery but then a thought came into my mind… Your grave was empty and she looked a bit like you… I put one of your dresses on her and buried her in the Westmoreland crypt and put a coffin, filled with a bag of sand, in the cemetery. It was the only way to stop the local obsession with vampires."

I shuddered. My father had to go through so much because of me…

"When we said farewell, I told you – people were obsessed with the thought that you'll become a vampire after death. Two days hadn't passed after your funeral when they were already here, asking for permission to go into the crypt and…" he said these words with disgust "to assure themselves from your waking-up. I said that I won't let them abuse my poor daughter's body, but I knew they wouldn't give up so easily. This is why your brothers, servants and I started to guard the crypt. We caught someone who wanted to break in there almost every week. When the locals finally managed to break in, they found a coffin filled with someone's remains. Since that day, the rumours have stopped. Your name now is as clean as it was during your lifetime."

I looked at my father. He had aged a lot in the past two years. The corners of his lips had weighed down, his hair was grey and his face was filled with worries.

"Oh father, how can I pay you for all you've done for me?"

"Just live. Be happy in this life if it wasn't meant for you in the previous one."

I realised that I should leave now otherwise my presence will slowly start to become even more painful for both of us. But there was one thing I wanted to do before I go.

"Are my brothers sleeping?"

"Yes."

"May I take a look at them? This is the last time I will ever see them."

He nodded.

I went upstairs and looked into the rooms of my brothers through a small open bit of the door. I said good-bye to them in my thoughts. I felt immense gratitude. They continued to take care of me even after my death.

I felt that I can't stay here any longer. I bid farewell to my father – this time forever – and rode away in the dark night.

I felt depressed. The recent events had been too much for me to bear. I was falling to pieces. My doomed relationship with Nigel was tearing me apart and keeping me sane at the same time.

On the one hand, I liked to be with Nigel. I always felt good in his company, I liked his kisses and caresses, and enjoyed his visits. On the other hand, two years of solitude, one absolute and one relative, had changed me. During my human life, I thought I couldn't spend my life alone, I wanted a husband and children.

Now I had realised that I felt fine being alone. I didn't have to consider others and I was free to do whatever I wanted when I wanted. I disappeared when I wanted to be alone and found someone when I needed company.

Because of Nigel I had to think about different things I hadn't considered before.

If we'd separate, the future would be simple: I'd disappear and we'd never meet again. If we'd try to stay together...Nigel would need to adapt to my lifestyle and move from place to place every few years. A wedding would cause additional problems. A few years would pass and Nigel would have to hide me from his family. They would notice that my face hasn't changed even a bit. Or... Nigel would have to abandon his family and disappear. Lies would become part of his life. He'd age and see how wrinkles start to cover his face and his hair turns grey. Every time when he would look at me, he would see my forever young face.

Children's laughter would never be heard in our house. The longer we'd be together, the more painful it would be for us both. Did I want it? And could I let Nigel spend his life like this because of me?

XXX

"Which marriage do you think is better: an arranged one or a marriage for love?"

What a pity that I couldn't see my face at that moment. I hadn't expected such a question.

I don't know how I did it but I usually found the most interesting and open people in London's high society. I was accepted despite the fact I didn't behave in a manner a young Victorian woman should.

Many doors were open to me and people were keen to hear my opinion on various, often controversial, topics. I came to a conclusion that every society – even the most conservative - needed outsiders and rebels. It produced them to keep things in balance.

"Both are acceptable to me. I can't even say which would be better. Feelings may be unstable. What does one do if the love ends? An arranged marriage at least has a specific aim, usually – to strengthen two families. It's hard to say which would be better… People may be happy in both kinds of marriages. I think it's important for people to know why they are getting married, so there would be no situations when one is getting married because of love, but the other – because of convenience."

"Yes, it's very important. For example, my wife and I were wedded to combine the fortunes of our families but later we fell in love with each other and have been happy together for forty years," an elderly man said.

"I, too, had my marriage arranged. I respect my wife and she knows she can count on me. I wouldn't call it love but I'm happy," another man supported his opinion.

"And what do the others think?" Derek, who had started our discussion, said. He was widely known for his interesting and often provocative topics. He liked to see people having lively discussions and defending their beliefs.

The rest of the opinions didn't differ from mine. Soon I decided to see what is going on in other rooms and left. I wasn't in the mood to discuss relationships. I had gone out to have a break from the subject.

The more I thought about Nigel and me the clearer it was that we need to separate. Our relationship would come to an end anyway and this end would be possible only on a sad note. All we could do was to choose how deep this sadness would be. I knew that Nigel wouldn't leave me so I was the one who had to take action.

"Lucretia, why don't you let me love you?"

This is how the hardest of our conversations started. It was supposed to be the last one.

"Because this love won't lead to anything good. I can't turn you into a vampire. I don't believe in eternal love. I believe in a love that lasts a lifetime. A human lifetime. I can't allow you to stay with me as a human. I'll always look exactly the same as on the day we met while you'll age. You'll waste your life staying with me. You'll spend your days in seclusion, separated from the world that is full of exciting things. And then a day will come when you die in my arms. You'll pass away happy but I'll stay alone. Forever. So please go and let me go too."

"Lucretia…" he said and stretched a hand towards me.

I took a step back.

"Nigel… If only we had met earlier… I'd still be alive then…"

He came closer to kiss me but I took another step back. "No. If you'd kiss me now, this kiss would be full of sadness and unfulfilled expectations. I don't want your last memories of me to be like this. I want you to remember the good times we had. Now go."

I turned around and, not letting him object, went into the house closing the door behind me.

A day later I got into a carriage and went to Edinburgh. I issued a short statement informing everyone that I have accepted an invitation from friends in Scotland to visit them. The London bustle continued without me and soon I became a fading memory.

I didn't come back to London for nearly half a century. I never tried to find out anything about Nigel. I hope that he followed my advice and forgot me. I also hope that he died happy.

The Encounter

London, summer of 2002

The street was full of people and the crowd was literally pushing me forward. The noise, diesel fumes and heat only worsened my mood. This was one of the rare occasions when I left my flat during daytime. I didn't like to do that because daylight was physically uncomfortable to me – my head seemed to be leaden, my skin was prickled by many tiny needles and it was difficult to concentrate, but today I had a meeting at the bank and unfortunately even private banks weren't open at night. I hadn't felt this bad for a long time. Luckily, I was nearly home. I got out of the crowd and slipped into the staircase.

My life had changed a lot during the last two years. I decided if I can't accept this world, I would at least try to get on with it. The world around me had changed and I adapted myself to it. I left behind even more things I had used to and started a brand-new life. Right after the Millennium I moved out of the neglected house that had been my residence for years and bought a flat in Central London. Although I liked space, I realised that a house would be too large for me alone. Previously it hadn't bothered me because I was deliberately living in an empty house with no living being around me and furniture covered by a thick layer of spider-webs because it reflected how I felt inside. However, I was tired of such life. I made a few drastic changes and stepped into the 21st century. I gave up part of my snobbery and reminded myself that from now on I would need to do everything myself. No more butlers and chambermaids. And so I, without blinking an eye, paid my bills, washed and ironed clothes, did household chores and many other previously unimaginable things.

I spent a lot of time at home. The interior of my flat was a successful combination of two centuries. 19th century furniture mixed with brand new pieces. I had a good taste and had furnished everything by myself.

Also, I had changed my look. I wore suits when I was going out or had business meetings and kept the clothes I actually wanted to wear – replicas of 19th century clothing – for wearing at home.

Recently I had bought a new false passport with a false name. I hadn't used my real name for decades. Yuri Rokosovski was a rare name and asked too many questions. Besides, I was afraid of meeting a descendant of the Rokosovski family. During my human life, there hadn't been too many people who belonged to it. Later, of course, I didn't care whether or not the family still exists. I had never had children – or at least I thought so – but, still, I decided to take a precaution and used only ordinary-sounding British names. Another thing I left behind was my earldom.

It was an evening when I had gone out – I wanted to buy new books. Usually I visited book stores, but today I wanted to find something old. I was standing at a shelf in one of my favourite antique stores, browsing manuscripts, when suddenly I found something very familiar. Professor Terence Clanwell. The person, who helped me to become a vampire and... also a friend of mine. I started to read the manuscript, which was more like a diary, full of his adventures and explorations. Werewolves, vampires, warlocks... I was turning over the pages when I saw something very interesting. Terence had described someone's voluntary transformation into a vampire. A young aristocrat who wanted to enjoy life forever and who valued nothing but himself. It was me, of course. He wrote he had met this wish because he knew that this person wouldn't have rested. "I couldn't say "no". Eternal life was what he was craving for and my refusal wouldn't have changed his mind. He would have continued his searching and wouldn't rest until he would obtain what he wanted. I knew that he's that kind of a person who can be turned into a vampire. There would be no disappointment, no regret. He would accept his fate and be happy in his new life. That's why I did what I did. However, I felt pity for him. He had money and power and he enjoyed life, but if you looked beneath the surface you saw a lonely and unhappy man. He lost parents when he was just two years old and was fostered by relatives. They paid little attention to the young boy and Y. became a secluded and cold person. He liked company, but he never knew such feelings as love, care and selflessness. To him, people were just toys. However, I hoped that the transformation would change him, his frozen heart would thaw and he would be able to experience true happiness. Y. was a natural born leader and I knew that it was in his powers to help others, in particular to those who felt depressed and lost. I hope I was right. Otherwise he would have failed me. And not just me, but also many others."

Terence never showed me the notes he made about me. To be honest, I didn't care about their content because my mind was occupied with different things back then. Thus, what I had just read was a true surprise to me. He had done it again! At first Terence simply tried to dissuade me, but then transformed me saying that it would never do an ill turn to me and that eternal life would never disappoint me. Now I had read his thoughts. Indeed, I had acted exactly how he intended. Terence had known me better than I thought and foreseen my fate. Our friendship lasted only a few months, but I had a feeling that Terence managed to see my soul. I mean, when I still had it. He had foreseen not only the fact that I would change, he had also foreseen *how* I would change.

"Addictive read, isn't it?" the shop keeper said.

"Yes, it is. The topic is interesting and it's very well written."

"You know, many people read the manuscript, but no-one wants to buy it. Probably it's because it is more about the inner world of magic creatures and not about them in general. I suppose it scares people."

"Well, I'm not among them. I'll take it."

"Great. I was trying to sell it for ages."

"By the way, do you know anything about the author?"

"Yes, but the information is contradictious... Some say he died in his bed in his late seventies, others say he died during one of his expeditions."

xxx

Once again, I was forced to leave my flat during daytime. This time I had a meeting with one of my wealth managers. Looking after my money demanded a significant effort and it was one of the few things I couldn't do alone.

I thought that it was going to be an ordinary day but it wasn't. I was returning from the meeting and, again, the weather seemed to be against me - the sun was shining and the air was stuffy. I put on the pace and hurried back home when I collided with someone. I was about to shout "Watch your step!" when I realised who's in front of me.

"Vincent!"

"Yuri!"

I overcame the surprise first. Vincent was hurrying somewhere, so I gave him my address and invited him to visit me someday.

A few days later, much sooner than I expected, Vincent knocked on my door. Already then, on the street, by giving him a quick look, I understood that he hadn't become any better since we last met. When Vincent was still living with us, he had a piercing look. He wasn't too self-confident, but knew his worth. Now his eyes were sad and full of pain. Despite his height - more than 6 feet - he seemed small and fragile. Vincent was dressed all in black, he was wearing boots with a thick rubber sole and iron buckles and his face was covered by a thick layer of make-up. It was obvious that Vincent is trying to dissociate himself from everyone and hide his feelings. Depression, which had started after the death of his child and wife, still hadn't left him.

Despite all that Vincent seemed happy to see me.

"Welcome to my plain-looking house!"

"Given that it's yours, it really *is* plain-looking," he smirked. "Where are the servants?"

"Times have changed… I'm trying to be modern and do everything by myself."

"Are you telling me you furnished this?"

"Yes."

"However, some things never change," he said and pointed at my laced shirt.

"This is what I wear at home. When going out, I always wear something plain. But you have changed. Have you become a goth?"

"Yes and no. I like the look."

While talking to Vincent, I soon noticed that he could talk for hours about various neutral topics. As soon as questions touched himself, his answers became very short.

"I hadn't met you since... Can't really remember... Since eighteen..."

"...twenty nine. Then you disappeared."

"Yes, I left London without telling anyone."

"You could have returned to us. Of course, we were dissatisfied with your decision to marry a human, but no-one would have reproached you."

"I know. However, I couldn't return. In your house life would have been exactly the same as when I left it, while I had changed. I couldn't fit in there anymore."

"What did you do after you left London?"

"I was travelling from a country to a country. I've lived in many places throughout Europe. In the 1920s I moved to the States and lived there until 1990."

"Hmm... Once when I was in America, I thought that I saw you on the street, but I didn't have a chance to make sure if it was really you."

"When was it?"

"In Chicago in 1934."

"It could have been me. I was living there then."

"What have you been occupied with all these years?"

"I felt guilty about what happened to Elisa and our child and devoted my life to medicine. During the First World War I was working in a field hospital, then, in America, I was a hospital porter. Later I went to university and became a doctor."

"You are a *doctor*?"

"Yes. I save people during daytime and kill them at night." Vincent laughed. His laugh was dark and sarcastic. "How about you? Has anything changed in your life?"

"The past sixty years have been difficult for me. The 1940s was the last decade I enjoyed. The following decades... Life and habits changed so fast and there were a lot of things I just couldn't accept. I spent almost twenty years in solitude, unable to decide what to do with my life. I saw the Millennium in an abandoned house that once used to belong to me. Then I realised I can't continue like that anymore."

"I have nothing against the twentieth century. On New Year's Eve in 1899, I had no idea that the new century would bring such changes. It seems that everything has changed."

"I prefer the nineteenth century. On the one hand, it was the time when unprecedented development started – electricity, railways… On the other hand, many things that make life more complicated didn't exist. Technology hadn't disappointed people yet and what was intended to make life easier really made life easier. I could have a luxury lifestyle and employ servants without fearing to get into newspapers. Now I live alone because people have become too shameless. I can never be sure that someone won't find out my secret and won't sell a story about me to TV or tabloids."

"Of course, the twentieth century has its drawbacks, however, in my opinion it is one of the best periods of history ever. Yes, people saw how destructive wars can be and how evil humans can be, yes, technology really has turned against them, but, still, so many things have changed for the better. For instance, working conditions in factories today and one hundred and fifty or two hundred years ago can't be compared."

I knew he would mention this at some point. Vincent still remembered his humble beginnings very well.

"Medicine... Since the beginning of the twentieth century the progress has been breathtaking. Diseases that used to kill millions of people in the past can now be cured," he continued. "The environment... People often complain that London is a dirty city. I remember the London of my childhood – the city has become much cleaner since then!

People have opportunities they didn't have before. It doesn't matter who you are and where you come from – if you have a dream, you can fulfil it."

Vincent continued to stay with me from time to time. His first visit lasted almost nine hours, which wasn't anything extraordinary - long conversations were characteristic to us. Little by little Vincent no longer hesitated to talk about himself.

"You know, those five years in your house were the best in my life. I had everything and life was like a fairytale. For the first time in my life I had friends and even tutors… You were like a role model to me. I wanted to be like you."

"I know. Although I wasn't the best person for that. Though, over the years, I became more tender-hearted and sympathetic than when I was mortal… But you were so young then. Now, many years later, you're grown-up enough and you don't need me anymore. By the way, how old are you now?"

That made Vincent think.

"I was born in 1802, which means... This year I became two hundred years old!"

He looked amazed. Apparently, he hadn't thought about his age for a long time.

"Do you know exactly when you were born?"

"No. My family was too busy to pay attention to such things, so I chose the date by myself – February 19. And what's your age?"

"I'm two hundred and sixty-four years old. I was born in 1737. As you see, I'm not much older than you, our age difference is only sixty-five years."

"Do you know the date?"

"Of course. My family had a special book where they registered all births and deaths in our family. My birthday is on October 22."

One evening Vincent began to speak about what bothered him the most.

"Love is my problem. From time to time I fall in love and then I don't know what to do. All relationships I've ever had have fallen apart. Now I no longer want to be with someone. I'm scared by the thought that I might find someone I'd want to spend my entire life with. I'd have to reveal who I am. Years would pass and she would age. And again, I'd experience the death of a woman I love."

For a moment, neither of us said anything.

"Never be afraid of love. Love can be painful, but it's much more painful when you prohibit yourself to love. In the worst case, love from a distance. If it's too painful for you to see your beloved one aging, do not stay with her for so long." I looked at Vincent and smiled. "You didn't expect to hear something like that from me, did you?"

"No, I didn't."

"Yes, I've spent my life alone. Yes, I've never loved. But it doesn't mean I know nothing about such things. Vincent, you and I are very different. You can't live without love, so don't prohibit yourself from loving. And remember – there's a little chance that you'd actually find someone to be with until the end of her days, especially in this century when people have become shallow and barely have true feelings. And.. another thing.. Do not dream about something that doesn't exist. I'm talking about eternal love. Do you remember Arifay?"

"Of course, I do."

"Have you heard his story?"

"No."

"He became a vampire because of love. Arifay fell in love with a girl who had to marry someone else. They decided if they couldn't be together in life, they would be together in death. But then someone told them about another option – to be together in eternal life. Being young and naive, they chose it. Over the years emptiness which they couldn't fill appeared in their relationship. Usually, when it happens, a couple decides to have a child or finds lovers. For them, the first option was impossible and they had no interest in the second one. They split up after only fifty years together. Arifay lost his reason for eternal life."

"He never told me this."

"I was the only one who knew it. When Arifay met me, he realised that finally he had someone who would understand him and told me everything. He had carried this burden for too long. He never spoke about it again. What can I say... poor children. They were born in an era when marriages were arranged and love existed only in the books they read. They didn't know anyone who had been in a similar situation and had no idea that reality is different from fiction. "And they lived happily ever after..." Arifay once said to me he wished they had chosen death. That's how disappointed he was."

xxx

"Apparently we've lost our skills," I sighed and lowered the foil.

"It's not surprising. We haven't practiced for years"

Since both of us liked fencing, I took out of the closet my rusty foils – Vincent didn't have his anymore – and we arranged an improvised duel.

The duel took place at Vincent's house, because my flat was too small and had no garden. Vincent lived in an abandoned factory.

"I really like this place," Vincent said. "Distant and quiet. No police, no squatters. No other unexpected visitors."

"I prefer to live in a place with running water, electricity and a door that can be locked."

"I can live in such places as well, but right now I want to live in a place like this."

At that time Vincent and I saw each other more and more often. Sometimes I visited him, but the collapsing factory building repelled me. Vincent found it amusing – after all, he knew that I had spent nearly twenty years in an abandoned house. I said that the past is past. Vincent had no option but to visit me. Soon he got tired of walking back and forth and moved in, although he disappeared on a regular basis without giving any explanation.

xxx

I entered the staircase and was going upstairs when I suddenly collided with someone. I hadn't heard anyone approaching, which was odd. Surprised, I saw a young woman in front of me. Our eyes met. There was something so familiar in her mesmerising look. She was a vampire too! For a moment we both froze but then she pushed me aside and ran out onto the street. There was no point to chase after her in the Covent Garden crowd. Who was she and what was she doing here? Did she live here? I had never seen her before. I hadn't met other vampires for a long time. Now Vincent was here, but still, I would like to meet someone new. Will she return? I looked at the empty staircase for a moment, then went to my flat.

A few hours later the doorbell rang. It didn't surprise me although I wasn't expecting anyone. Vincent had his own key now, so it couldn't be him. From time to time one of my neighbours bothered me – usually either wanting to borrow something or asking to sign a petition. I opened the door and, to my surprise, I saw Her.

"May I come in?"

I made an inviting gesture and she stepped into the living room, slowly glancing over and examining everything, while I was examining her. She had changed her clothes and was currently wearing a navy skirt suit with a red belt, a white blouse with ruffle and black high-heeled ankle boots. Everything was expensive and, probably, made to order. The way she carried herself suggested she was born at least a hundred years ago. She had chestnut brown hair, freckles, green eyes and chiselled cheekbones. Her Roman nose only added beauty to her face. She is so charming, I thought.

"It's a pity you didn't wear this earlier today."

"Skirt and boots wouldn't have stopped me from running away, believe me."

"How did you find me?"

"I worked it out. I know everyone who lives on my floor, so I thought that you probably live one or two floors down. A bit of surveillance work in the staircase and I figured out that this should be your apartment."

"Why did you run away?"

"I don't know. After I had run three blocks, I realised that my behaviour was silly."

"I haven't seen you here before."

"I moved in this week."

"Are you here for a long time?"

"I have absolutely no idea. Maybe for a couple of years. Maybe for a couple of months. Depends on my mood."

She looked around again.

"Do you live here alone?"

"No, I share this place with a friend."

She raised an eyebrow.

"He's a vampire too."

"Interesting, isn't it... You don't meet anyone for ages and then bump into several at once."

"Indeed. That's how Vincent got here. We have known each other for many years, but hadn't met for a long time."

"I think of myself as a lone wolf but every now and then I appreciate company."

"Would you like to come later when Vincent is at home? He told me he might be back around eleven pm."

"Yes, that would be nice."

She went to the door, then stopped and gave me a smile.

"Oh, I didn't introduce myself. Lucretia Lockwood."

"Yuri Rokosovski."

***

Vincent

I came back home, which at the moment was Yuri's apartment, and closed the door behind me. As I entered the living room, I noticed a female guest. I didn't think much of it until she turned towards me and looked into my eyes. This look literally burnt me. It didn't belong to a human. She was one of *us*.

"And here's Vincent," Yuri said. "We have been waiting for you."

She gave me a smile and introduced herself.

"Lucretia Lockwood."

I nodded.

"Lucretia is our neighbour," Yuri explained.

"Three vampires in one building, what's the chance of that happening? One has to seize an opportunity," she said.

My arrival had changed the atmosphere from relaxed to stiff. I had nothing against guests, but I knew that Lucretia would definitely want to know more about me. However, she was a stranger and I wasn't going to open up to someone I've just met.

"You come from the nineteenth century too, don't you?"

"Vincent became two hundred years old this year," Yuri replied instead of me.

"How about letting him speak for himself?"

"Sure. But I need to warn you – it may take some time. Vincent is not very talkative."

"It depends on the situation," I said and sat on the sofa opposite them.

"Only I come from the nineteenth century. Yuri was born in the eighteenth century."

"Oh, so I'm the youngest of us all. I was born in 1841."

"You're quite well preserved," Yuri smirked as he took a quick look at her.

"It is one of the advantages of living in a twenty-one-year old's body." She smiled. "I hope I won't insult you, but – what is your background? You," she pointed at Yuri "are an aristocrat, there's no doubt about it. But you – you have good manners, but I don't think that you come from a wealthy family."

"You're correct. I was born in a working class family and spent my human life in poverty."

Her curiosity levels increased straightaway.

"I'm sorry, but I won't tell you more tonight. I barely know you."

"That's all right. I understand."

"And you? Lockwood isn't your real name, is it?" Yuri asked.

"No. I'll tell you my story. When the time is right."

"Oh, how mysterious everyone is..." Yuri said sarcastically.

After that we started to talk about various neutral topics. Lucretia soon farewelled and left.

Who would have known that that evening would be the start of a very close friendship... Less than three weeks later Lucretia had become one of us and both Yuri and I had the feeling that she's always been around. Every time when I came back to the apartment, she was there.

"How about breaking the ice and starting to talk about what *really* interests us all?" Yuri suggested.

I made no reply. Lucretia was biting her lips and didn't say a word. Yuri sighed.

"Fine. I'll start with myself then. I guess I'm the only one here to whom the transformation wasn't a serious mental trauma."

More or less, I knew Yuri's story, however, when he told it again, I found out many things that were previously unknown to me. As I had listened to the whole story, I thought – he was wrong when he spoke about the trauma. Yuri had grown up in an environment where almost no-one cared about him. He grew up alone and got used to following only his own wishes and desires. Later, when he started to socialise, Yuri examined whether or not he could continue to live that way. And it only worsened everything. Yuri realised that almost anything was allowed to him and didn't hesitate to use it. I had to make a choice between life and death, while Yuri made his decision hoping that something would change in his world – so rich from outside, so poor from inside. Meeting him now I realised that he had almost succeeded.

***

Lucretia

Many vampires I had known had transformed deliberately, but I had never heard a story like this. Yuri decided he wanted to live forever and reached his goal. It sounded so simple and... stupid.

Vincent's story was completely opposite. Now I understood why his look was so sad and why he felt so miserable. Vincent's whole life was grief and pain with short spells of happiness. If he wouldn't be so sensitive it wouldn't have affected him in such a destructive way.

My feelings towards them changed. I started to dislike Yuri, although we had got on quite well. I just couldn't understand how someone could wish to become a vampire deliberately. For me it sometimes still was an unpleasant reality which I had to accept. It was the other way around with Vincent, I became very attached to him. I knew that at first he didn't like my presence but now he viewed me as a friend.

The ice really had been broken and now it was my turn to speak. Memories that had lied untouched for many years suddenly came back to life.

"You wanted to know my real name… I was born as Lucy Lucretia Westmoreland."

"Westmoreland.." Yuri said. "The widower Westmoreland and his three sons?"

"Yes."

"He had a daughter who died of an illness, but it wasn't true, was it?"

"No."

"Maybe I shouldn't have asked that... We have probably had enough for one evening..."

"No, it's just... I haven't told this to anyone for a long time. But, since you shared your stories with me, it would be fair if I tell you mine..."

***

Yuri

I knew that it was possible to transform after death, usually premature or violent, but I had never met anyone who had become a vampire this way. And now there was Lucretia, sitting in front of me. Her story was so sad and seemingly incompatible with who she was now. Lucretia as a human and Lucretia as a vampire had nothing in common. If, while talking about her childhood and family, her face wouldn't have lit up and her voice softened, I wouldn't believe that this tough and cynical woman was once loving and warm-hearted .

I always thought that Vincent's story is the most unimaginable. Now I couldn't understand which of them was unluckier.

***

Lucretia

As I had thought, my story had affected them greatly. Vincent told me that, while listening to it, extreme grief had overcome him. Yuri, too, was thinking of it a lot. Four evenings later he still returned to the topic.

"Lucretia, excuse me, but don't you think you overacted?"

Yuri was trying to understand how a betrayal could hurt so much. So far, he hadn't succeeded. It didn't surprise me – it is difficult to imagine things you've never experienced yourself.

"Well… There's one thing I didn't mention."

I looked at them. Yuri understood immediately and started to grin. Vincent gave me a puzzled look. How typical.

"I slept with Jack."

Now Vincent looked shocked, but Yuri was shaking his head in a fake condemnation.

"Who would have thought…" Yuri said.

"I was twenty years old, in love and my body craved him. It just happened.. Besides, I considered him to be my fiancé and thought that we would marry one day."

"Lucretia, didn't anyone teach you that you shouldn't do such things unless you know how to manipulate the other person?"

"No. Oh, I'm sorry, I forgot that I'm talking with the planet's main sexpert with three hundred years' experience!"

"Two hundred and fifty," he corrected. "I'll become only two hundred and sixty-five years old this year. By the way, if we started to speak about it... Vincent, and how about you?"

Vincent wasn't thrilled about the turn this conversation had taken. In fact, he looked well pissed off. Vincent had a long list of things he didn't like to talk about.

"Twenty-three," he muttered. Vincent knew that Yuri wouldn't have let him alone.

"Twenty-three? How is that possible?" The surprise in Yuri's voice was real. "Lucretia I could understand, she was brainwashed by the Victorians, but you?"

Vincent sighed.

"Have you ever been hungry for a long time?"

"No. I always had plenty of food on my table and in case I thought it's not enough, I had a nice basement full of goods."

"Then you won't understand me. I spent the first eighteen years of my life in deep poverty. When you've been starving for years, you forget that *that* part of your body can be used not only for peeing."

After he said that, he looked straight into Yuri's eyes and grinned. Yuri started to laugh. Who would have expected such words from Vincent?

"All right, the first eighteen years. But later... You spent five years in my house. Are you telling me that despite the crowd of women who visited it you never..."?

"No. I wasn't interested in any of them."

"What kind of excuse is that? And how about Beatrice? She fancied you."

"Yes, but she didn't interest me either."

"Please do not tell me that it happened on your wedding night."

"It did."

"Unbelievable! Did anyone really do that?"

I sighed. Apparently, Yuri was going to keep pestering Vincent.

"Yes. Many people, by the way," I said.

"That is something beyond my comprehension."

"Does anyone doubt it? I can bet that you were a polite host and entertained your female guests in all possible ways."

"I only gave them a short tour of the house: the library, the picture gallery, the garden, my bedroom... If I had known that Vincent is such a prude, I would have sent at least half of them straight to his room."

I ran my hand over my hair and turned to Vincent.

"There's a statuette on your left. Use it."

Vincent smiled, but didn't do anything. He was way too sweet and put up with Yuri's teasing. Me, I would have taken the statuette and thrown it at Yuri.

"Sometimes Yuri can be such a bastard!" I said to Vincent. We had climbed onto the roof and were enjoying London at night. We could hear the hustle and bustle from surrounding streets and feel part of it: music coming from local pubs and bars, people laughing, talking, shouting, arguing, cabs moving up and down the narrow streets hooting the horn.

"He's only showing off. Yuri is delighted to have us in his life and that's how he's expressing it. "

"I know. Otherwise it would be difficult to tolerate him."

"He's not that bad. If he's your friend you may consider yourself very lucky. As an enemy he shows no mercy, as a friend he will always be there for you."

***

Yuri

Our company made Vincent feel better. I noticed it when he started to use less make-up. Part of former strength reappeared in his eyes and his laugh sometimes sounded quite careless. Partly it was because of Lucretia. Vincent was smitten by her, so was I. Lucretia pretended she hadn't noticed it.

***

Lucretia

I soon realised that both Yuri and Vincent fancy me. I wasn't naive and knew that it might happen, however, I didn't like the situation. I really valued our friendship and knew that if I replied to their feelings it would ruin everything. I had already experienced it and it was also the reason why I didn't live with other vampires anymore. Three times I had helped to throw out someone who had made the atmosphere insufferable with their jealousy scenes and twice I was the one to be thrown out. The last time it happened when I had a relationship with two vampires at the same time. After they had thrashed half of the hall, smashing a few precious vases and tearing a picture, I was evicted with the words "Don't you ever come back here!"

However, my reserved behaviour didn't mean I felt nothing towards them. Quite the reverse: I was attracted to Vincent although I knew that Yuri would be a better choice. Vincent had a pure and loving heart and if he got attached to someone, it was forever, whereas Yuri was a loner, just like me. Nothing – expect for ourselves – was eternal to us and we knew that sooner or later our company would drift apart.

xxx

Vincent and I were sitting on the roof. Because of the light pollution there were almost no stars in the sky, however, the dark sky looked beautiful anyway.

"What do you think? Do creatures like us have a soul?" Vincent asked.

"I don't know what to believe anymore. When I was still a human I had my Christian faith. I believed that a human being consists of flesh and soul. Soul is the intangible that leaves the body after death and goes to heaven... or hell. Be good and you'll reunite with God. Be bad and you'll end up in Devil's headquarters. That was easy. Then I became undead and suddenly things got complicated. I've gone through different stages. There was a time when I thought I had no soul. Then there was a time when I thought I had a soul but it's cursed. Then I went through a stage when I believed that my soul is safe, it's just stuck inside my body forever. But all that was ages ago. These days I don't bother anymore. I just seize the day, it seems like the best thing to do."

"Seize the day... Don't think... It's not the best way, Lucretia. It's the easiest one. It's tormenting not to know the truth." He paused. "Peace. I crave peace. Do you enjoy eternal life?"

"Yes, I do."

"But don't you ever feel lonely and depressed?"

"No. When I was still a human, I thought I couldn't live without close friends, family... I wanted to get married, I wanted to be a mother... But then a few years went by and I realised that I feel fine alone. When I wanted a company, I found it, but otherwise..."

"But haven't you wanted to be with someone?"

"I was in a relationship from time to time, but it never lasted for too long. I didn't want anything permanent."

"And Nigel? According to what you said, he loved you so much that he was ready to give up his human life..."

"Nigel... He was one of the nicest men I've ever met. Unfortunately, we met too late. Miss Westmoreland would have viewed him as a gift from the above and would have been with him until the end of her days. Miss Lockwood viewed him as a problem that needs to be solved. There was no other option. If Nigel and I would have stayed together, it would have brought no good. As a human, he'd age and die, leaving me with a heart full of pain. Pain that would never go away. If I would have turned him into a vampire, sooner or later we'd have split up and that would be even worse. And, the main point – I didn't want to be with him. I didn't want to share my life with anyone."

"How caddish a man must have been to turn a loving young girl's heart into stone?"

"Vincent, this conversation is pointless. I understand you, but you don't understand me. We are completely different.

You can't live without love; you need someone to care about. Me, I'm a loner. I enjoy such life."

I stood up and made a few steps. I tipped my head back and looked at the nightly sky, then glanced at Vincent. He looked more sorrowful than before. I sighed. I guess I had been too sharp. I sat next to him and gave him a hug.

"Vincent, I feel sorry for you. You are my friend and it's sad to see you like this. And... I'm sorry that I can't respond to your feelings. I'd be in your heart forever, but I'd need to leave you. It's just my nature."

Silence fell. Then I got up and walked away.

***

Vincent

"No, unfortunately I can't help you and lend some flour. I never cook at home. Yes, of course, it's a pity I can't help you, but you should ask other neighbours too. No, no, there's no need to apologise. Yes, have a good evening too," Yuri said in a suspiciously kind voice.

That didn't last long, though. As soon as he had closed the door he was back to his normal self.

"I'm so sick of it! What is wrong with Londoners these days? Don't they know the rules - don't talk to anyone on the Tube, don't know your neighbours, basically ignore everyone and always be rushing somewhere?"

"Maybe they've just moved here and haven't learnt the ropes yet," Lucretia suggested.

"And why is everyone suddenly a baker? Artisan bread? Are you kidding me? Sometimes I have a very strong desire to put up a sign saying "No food here, it's a vampire's flat.""

That made Lucretia laugh.

"In that case you won't stay here long," she said.

"I know, but sometimes the temptation is so huge. Besides, I haven't been truly nasty to anyone for a long time. All right, enough. Where were before we were interrupted?"

"We were discussing whether vampires can burn."

After we had discussed ourselves, we started to discuss our so-called species. We were spending evenings sharing what we knew: legends, assumptions, superstitions... We compared it to our experience, as well as discussed books and movies. Of course, given who we are, we could have chosen a more sophisticated topic but that would be boring because we'd be talking about things we've discussed a million times in the past one hundred years.

"As far as I know, vampires can be killed with a stake or a knife through the heart. I've never heard about fire. But...

who knows. I haven't met anyone who'd been in a fire," Lucretia said.

"All right, let's presume that fire does no harm to vampires. How do you think – can a vampire survive the explosion of a nuclear bomb?"

"Yuri, your questions are getting more and more bizarre, aren't they?" Lucretia exclaimed.

"I'm just curious."

"I suggest you think of the following issue: there are enough nuclear weapons on Earth to blow up this planet seven times. If an explosion happens and vampires survive, how would we feed? All our "food" would have turned into ashes."

"Lucretia, I like the way your mind works. You think outside the box."

"How about discussing something more reasonable?" I interrupted.

Yuri rolled his eyes.

"I see that we need to change the topic - Vincent is sulking again."

"Do I have to look happy all the time?"

"Not at all. No-one can be happy all the time, it would be a pathology then. However, Lucretia and I don't like to see you sullen and silent without a reason, do we?"

"No. Any proposals for the further conversation?"

"Have you read "Dracula"?" Yuri changed the topic so easily as only he could.

Lucretia said "yes", I nodded.

"I read it right after it was published in 1897. I consider it a masterpiece. I liked that it is written as a compilation of letters and diaries. It makes the story more interesting. You can see everything from different points of view, see presumptions and make conclusions before the characters."

"It left a strong impression on me too, but I read it somewhere in the 1920s. Unlike you," I pointed at Yuri, "I was not so much interested in Dracula and his world, as in the other characters and their relationships. It is a sad story on how different fates may interlace and how the whole life can change in a single moment..."

Whilst reading "Dracula" I had been making parallels to my own life.

"Mina's letters to Lucy... A heart-breaking contrast between her presumptions and reality. Mina thinks that Lucy is preparing for the wedding, but Lucy is dying of Dracula's bites... Her destiny truly touched me. Poor Lucy... Oh, I'm so sorry..." I exclaimed as I saw how Lucretia's face changed.

"You don't need to apologise, you didn't do it with an intent," she said, although she still looked upset.

Lucretia had told us how her grave was burst open and the circumstances in which she had found out about it. Many years ago, someone, talking about her sad story, said "poor Lucy" and now, because of me, she had experienced a deja vu. I knew that the name "Lucy" appeared only in documents, however, it was still her name and she responded to it. I imagined Lucretia listening about her death and the break in, hearing people talking about herself and in the end asking what she thought about it not knowing who's sitting in front of them. I couldn't picture how she was feeling then.

"Yes, the book is excellent. It took me a long time to read it. I think it was at the beginning of the 1930s and I was still living in Chicago at that time."

"You have lived in Chicago?" Yuri sounded surprised.

"Yes, for two years, from 1930 until 1932. Then I got into trouble with a local gangster and decided to flee to New York."

"We have lived in Chicago, too," I said.

Lucretia looked amazed.

"When?"

"I lived there from 1921 to 1937," I said.

Yuri's voice sounded different from the voice we had used to – the unexpected discovery had unhinged him.

"I arrived there in 1932 and spent two years in the city."

"I can't believe it! We weren't far from meeting each other already then!"

Silence fell for a moment. We all were thinking about the same thing. How many times our paths had silently crossed to finally lead to this meeting?

"By the way, why did you go to America?"

"Because of the same reason as you did," Yuri pointed at Lucretia. "To redeem the money I lost in 1929… and to earn more."

Lucretia nodded.

"I went there to have a fresh start," I said.

"Of course," he said. This time his voice sounded as usual.

***

Lucretia

Lately I have been spending more time with Vincent. One of the reasons why we bonded so well was the fact that neither of us needed much sleep and we could easily stay awake during the day. Yuri needed at least ten hours of sleep and struggled with sunlight. Recently he had started to sleep for fourteen hours when he had time for that. Yuri was going to make a large investment in real estate and had to spend a lot of time in meetings. He came back late and went to sleep immediately. At the moment I was seeing him for about fifteen minutes a day – in the mornings just before he left and in the evenings.

For me, six hours of sleep were enough, I could barely sleep for eight hours. Vincent, who had spent so much time among humans, could go to sleep at any time. Sometimes I had a feeling that he doesn't sleep at all – at least I had never seen him asleep. Vincent didn't care whether it was day or night outside. He had got used to sunlight. I didn't care about it much either, although I was not always able to stay in the sunlight for long periods of time.

Talking to Vincent I had noticed one interesting fact – he never used the word "vampire". He used various names to talk about himself and us, except for that one. Also, he reluctantly spoke about the grisly part of his life: hunting. Once he mentioned that he hunts twice a month and tries to attack only, as he said, mean-spirited men. In other words, criminals. I, too, preferred criminals. Yuri said he attacked people he didn't like but knowing him that could include anyone.

But those were rare confessions. Most of the time when Vincent and I were alone we discussed old legends. We were talking about eternal life and the few possibilities of how to end it. Vincent believed that he had a soul but it was cursed.

This thought was occupying Vincent's mind more and more, until one evening he suddenly said:

"I don't want to continue this. I want to end eternal life."

"What?!"

"I've been hapless and depressed for many years. If there's a chance to stop it and find the peace I crave so much..."

I tried to reason with him, I begged, I argued but nothing helped. Vincent had decided he wanted to die and asked us to help him. Yuri and I were adamant:

"No!"

Vincent didn't speak much about this subject anymore, but we felt that it was not for the better. Now he kept his thoughts to himself and that was even worse.

***

Yuri

One evening Lucretia stormed in and exclaimed:

"Vincent is completely out of his mind!"

"What happened?"

"After we refused to help, he decided to seek other ways to die."

"What has he done?" I asked in a tired voice that was characteristic to parents who wanted to know what kind of trouble their children have got in.

Lucretia held her breath as if she'd be thinking of what had happened.

"I just can't believe it... Vincent decided to walk around London hoping that someone would start picking on him because of his looks but no-one did. He got fed up and started upsetting people. It didn't take long until someone got a knife out. Vincent was stabbed in the stomach, then the police arrived."

"Where is he now?"

"He's talking to police officers. They wanted to take him to hospital, but Vincent convinced them it's not serious. He's a medic after all. I can't believe that he could act so stupid."

Lucretia sat down and held her head in her hands for a moment.

"We have no choice. We have to help him."

"No!"

We were now exchanging angry looks.

"I said we have no choice. Vincent has made his decision and nothing in this world can change his mind. We can help him to die with dignity, not on the street. Besides, what if his body turns into ashes after death? Would you want that to get into the media? Vampires exist and they are among us?"

I knew that she's right, but I didn't say anything.

"I know what you're thinking of. How can one give up what you value the most? How can one give up the chance to live forever? Me, I understand him. In the first few years after my transformation I was thinking about it too. But not anymore. Besides, emotions are Vincent's weak point. He can't be alone; he needs somebody to love. We're different. We need no-one but ourselves."

Once again, she was absolutely right. Vincent was very close to me and I knew how hapless he was. If death would make him happy...

"All right. Let it be. We will help him."

***

Lucretia

We were on our way to a cemetery. We had picked an old abandoned one away from tube stations and major roads. One thing that had always made London great was that it was a city that never sleeps. Sometimes it could be a serious disadvantage. Tonight, for instance. If anyone would witness what was about to happen it would be game over for all three of us.

Vincent had taken the lead; his steps were quick and we had to adapt ourselves to him. He was craving for peace this life was unable to provide and didn't want to linger. We silently followed him for we knew that it wouldn't change anything.

I was feeling very anxious. I was the one who had to kill Vincent – Yuri had categorically refused to do it. If everything happens as planned, Vincent will redeem his soul and it will make me happy, if not, he'll simply be dead and I will be burdened with guilt for the rest of my life. And eternity is a damn long period of time...

Vincent opened the gates of the cemetery and moved on. It looked as if he knew where to go. After a few minutes he stopped. We were standing at a family's burial place. It consisted of a large granite gravestone and a plate. The plate was at a desk height and reminded a coffin with a smooth surface.

Vincent turned to us, ready to listen to farewells. His face was still full of determination.

"You are crazy," Yuri said.

"It's not the first time when you're saying it to me."

"No, but it is the last one."

I went to Vincent and embraced him. I pressed myself to his chest, unable to believe that soon he would be gone forever. Apparently, Vincent guessed what I'm thinking of. He stroked my back.

"Lucretia, please don't be sad because of me."

Then he released himself from my embrace and laid down on the grave plate. I sighed and put a stake to his heart. I had deliberately chosen the stake. It was more acceptable to me than to stab Vincent with a knife, which would make me feel like a jealous wife or lover. No way. If Vincent wanted to die, it must happen in a more poetic way.

Vincent closed his eyes. I knew I only had one chance, so I raised the stake and plunged it down. The stake pierced Vincent's heart and a heart-breaking yell, a mix of desperation and relief, broke out. For a moment I thought what had I done, when suddenly I saw that Vincent's face changed. I had never seen him like that. His face was now full of peace and happiness and his lips contracted into a smile. I had seen this expression before. It appeared in the moment when the spirit left the body, all worries disappeared and the eternal piece set in. In Vincent's case it was *almost* like that. The next moment his body turned into ashes. "We made it! Vincent was right!"

Yuri looked shocked. I understood him. Vincent was one of the few individuals who were close to him. And now he, too, was gone.

Me, I was overwhelmed with relief. If not the happiness, which had appeared in Vincent's face in the moment of death, I probably wouldn't be able to forgive myself for agreeing to help him. But now...

I took a look around. It was two am and there was no-one else in the cemetery. However, I wasn't sure if someone hadn't heard Vincent's scream.

"Pass me my bag!"

Yuri froze. He was lost in thoughts and hadn't heard me.

"Pass me my bag!" I repeated.

"What for?"

"I have an urn there. Do you think that I'll leave Vincent's ashes on the gravestone?"

Yuri passed it to me and said:

"I was right about you. You always plan things through."

I quickly swept the ashes into the urn. Then we left.

xxx

"What shall we do with the ashes?" I asked Yuri. Two days had passed since Vincent's death.

"Well, I definitely won't keep them at home."

"I wouldn't like to bury them in a cemetery. It would be strange – a vampire among humans."

"Yes, it would. Forest is another option; however, I don't like the thought that the urn will be buried somewhere."

"Maybe we could scatter them somewhere?"

"I just thought of it too."

"Maybe in the sea?"

"Then we need to go outside London."

"We could go to my hometown."

"To Brighton? Why not. It's a great place where to rest."

"How did you... Nevermind."

A few days later we boarded a train to Brighton. I had a bag with the urn on my lap. I was looking outside the window, watching the changing landscapes. Decades had passed since I had last been this way.

We arrived in the early evening. Most tourists had already left and it wasn't difficult to find a quiet spot on the beach. The tide was out, the sea was calm and a light wind was blowing. We went into the sea with our boots on. I opened the urn and scattered the ashes.

"Goodbye."

After a moment they had already mixed with the water and wind. We stayed on the beach for a while.

Once we were back in London I realised I wanted to leave. Sooner or later it would have happened anyway. Yuri and I had grown apart. We were so different. It turned out that Vincent had been the glue that held us all together. Without him, we felt awkward in each other's company. I farewelled, moved out of my apartment and bought a one-way ticket to Paris.

The Flash

May 2006

"Two hundred thousand pounds. Does anyone bid more?"

I lifted up my auction number. This auction was for a painting. It depicted an idyllic scene from the 19th century: a young couple holding horses on the side of a winding road. There was nothing special in the picture, but I liked the colour scheme. It would look well in my new place.

The author of it hadn't succeeded in writing his name in art history, but there was something enchanting about the picture. No wonder that its price had gone up from ten thousand to two hundred thousand pounds. Several bidders had already withdrawn and currently I had only three rivals left.

"Two hundred thousand pounds. Does anyone bid more?"

The bids continued to increase. I really liked the painting but I had set my limit at five hundred thousand pounds. Currently, two hundred and seventy thousand pounds were offered.

"Three hundred thousand pounds. Does anyone bid more?"

Another bidder withdrew. Now I had to outbid only two people. At the beginning of the auction, there were ten of us.

"Three hundred and fifty thousand pounds. Does anyone bid more?"

The third bidder withdrew.

I offered four hundred thousand and hoped that my last rival would finally give up, however, it looked like he or she had other plans. And very deep pockets, too.

The sum had risen up to four hundred and fifty thousand pounds. I decided to see whom I'm trying to outbid. The same thought had come into my rival's mind. Our eyes met and... there he was. Yuri. He smiled and a metallic shine appeared in his eyes. It was clear that now the real auction would begin.

Ignoring my previous limit, I bid six hundred thousand pounds. Now I was driven not by the willingness to obtain the picture, but by ardour. I knew that so was he.

I offered nine hundred thousand, but Yuri outbid me immediately. I sighed. I liked the picture, but I wasn't going to pay millions for it. And that would inevitably happen if I'd continue to bid.

I participated in several other auctions, but didn't see anything I'd really like. After a few hours I decided to call it a day and headed towards the exit. As I was leaving the room, I felt that someone else left it too.

"Have you returned to London?" I heard the familiar baritone next to me.

"Almost. I have some unfinished business in Paris, but my current address is London, not Paris."

"What a loss to Paris, what an acquirement to London."

"Good day, Yuri."

"Good day, Lucretia," he said, kissing my hand and looking at me with his ice-blue eyes. "What a pleasant encounter."

"Mutually."

"You're very welcome to visit me if you want. The address hasn't changed."

I promised to use the invitation soon and we farewelled.

When I left London nearly four years ago, in September 2002, it was mainly because of Vincent's death. Fleeing seemed like the best option. I travelled around France, Belgium, Luxembourg and Italy, enrolled in a short art history course in Paris, and later decided to explore more of Central Europe by going to Prague, Vienna and Budapest.

There wasn't a particular reason for my comeback. I never stayed in one place for too long and when I felt the familiar restlessness it was time to pack and go.

A few days later I was already knocking on Yuri's door. It was a bit strange to return here. The apartment looked almost the same: black-out curtains, lots of books, and a mix of high-end furniture and antiques. Vincent's favourite red velvet couch was still in one corner. When Vincent was still alive there was usually a pile of books and a bag with few belongings under the couch.

The only new thing I spotted was the painting of one of the walls.

"It looks nice. Fits into the interior," I said. "However, it would look better in my living room."

"Remarkable, isn't it? A simple, even banal painting by an author that even art historians haven't heard of, has so much magic that it was sold for almost one million pounds. How much were you ready to offer?"

"Half a million, but when I saw that it's you whom I'm trying to outbid, I was ready to offer a million or two. And you?"

"As much as it would be necessary," he smiled. "When I want something, I get it. Changing the subject – what were you doing all these four years?"

"This and that, but mostly... nothing. And you?"

"Pretty much the same."

"Where are you staying?"

"Serviced apartments in Knightsbridge. I can't be bothered to buy and furnish a place at the moment."

I stayed until morning, having spent the whole night talking. I left only because Yuri wanted to go to sleep – it was physically difficult for him to be awake between six am and four pm.

When I was on the door-step, I suddenly asked:

"Are you still angry that I agreed to help Vincent?"

He looked surprised. Yuri hadn't expected such a question.

"No, of course no... I admit, I was dissatisfied when you stood on his side, but... You were right. Vincent would not have given up this idea, he would have continued to seek death and probably would have died in some ridiculous way. It was difficult for me to lose a close friend, but I knew that eternal life had no worth in his eyes. I don't reproach you anything, Lucretia. I'm the one who should apologise – you had to help him die, while I pretended not to have anything to do with it."

Now it was my turn to be surprised. I was used to dealing with Yuri-the-cynic, not Yuri-the-nice-guy.

"I'm speechless," I said.

"Lucretia, you did the right thing."

Yuri and I had got on well already before, but now we became great friends. It turned out we had more in common than I had previously thought. That and the fact we had no other friends. Yuri avoided humans and his vampire friends had scattered all over the world. Me, I preferred human company, but everyone close to me was dead.

Now I was visiting him several times a week, staying in the apartment until morning or staying overnight. Yuri joked that the red velvet couch had ceased to be his property - first it had been claimed by Vincent, now me. I didn't actually need to sleep on it. My body rarely felt discomfort. I could sleep on a bed of nails or a pile of bricks and still feel fine but I was an aesthete and preferred a bed. Usually Yuri went to sleep first, while I stayed awake for a while, checking out his coffee table books.

Sometimes I remembered Vincent's words that Yuri was not completely satisfied with his life - he wasn't very willing to adapt to this time, but neither could he continue to live in the old way. I was wondering if he still felt like that. I wanted to talk to him about this, but I knew I have to wait

– there were topics Yuri discussed rarely and reluctantly and only when he initiated them himself.

One evening we were strolling around London. It was night and many miles were behind us. I think we weren't even within the city boundaries anymore.

We were crossing a small bridge and I stopped to watch the calm water. It was an old habit of mine. Yuri stopped too.

"You know, I admire your ability to adapt. Everything you've told me... You have lived so many lives in so many places. You always try something new and are in step with time, while I tried to preserve the world exactly as it was when I needed only two digits to write down my age," he said.

"That's true and sometimes your attempts are almost absurd. Like it or not, but life isn't something still. Me, I couldn't live without changes."

"Lucretia, you're amazing and that's why I like your company. You inspire me. I've spent years wondering what to do with my life and how to end the stillness. I don't want to continue to live in the old way. I want to start a new phase in my life and I wish you'd join me. Could we be more than just friends?"

I knew that this was going to happen. Yuri fancying me was nothing new – it was the same four years ago, only then he viewed me as an addition to his collection of trophies. I don't want to pretend to be better than I am, so I'll confess that I viewed him exactly in the same way. But then we had Vincent between us and Vincent, too, had feelings towards me.

That night I didn't give an answer to Yuri, although I already knew it – no. It wasn't because I wouldn't like him, but because I didn't want to share my life with anyone. My last serious relationship had ended in 1973, when I divorced from Byron. Everything that came after it were just short affairs.

Solitude is a phenomenon with two faces: on the one hand, it can be frightening and may erode you from inside, on the other hand, with time one gets used to it and doesn't want to change anything. Solitude and the feeling of freedom and independence that came with it caused euphoria. And euphoria usually wasn't something one tries to end. I wasn't an exception.

It would have been better if Yuri would receive my rejection already then on the bridge, but unfortunately such traits as indecisiveness, hesitation to act and avoidance of dealing with unpleasant things, usually accompanied with escape – symbolic or real - were very characteristic to me. I started to avoid Yuri: I no longer visited him and didn't reply to phone calls. A few weeks passed.

xxx

One evening I received a phone call.

"Miss Westbridge? Your order is ready."

In 1997, when I got a new passport, I decided to take precautionary measures and changed my name to Simona Westbridge.

I let out a screech of ecstasy, but in the next moment I gained back my self-possession.

"Excuse me, monsieur Marchand. I can't believe that it has finally arrived!"

He gave a laugh – monsieur Marchand was my personal assistant. He was helping me to do business, looked after my real estates and simply was a nice man to talk to. Of course, he had no idea who I actually was.

I looked at my watch – it was too late to go to Paris tonight.

"I wish I could leave for Paris immediately! Unfortunately, I have to wait until the morning. Please meet me at the airport. I'll get the first flight."

He promised to do that, we farewelled and I hung up the phone.

I had six hours until the plane. Six very *long* hours. I started to drum my fingers on the desk, trying to figure out how to kill the time. It was no use to go to sleep, because I won't be able to sleep anyway – the excitement was too big. I took a book from the shelf and tried to read, looking at the watch from time to time. For me, it seemed that tonight the hands were moving slower than usual.

When the dawn finally came, I called a taxi and went to the airport. As soon as the plane had taken off, I became absolutely impatient – I was shuffling and looking out of the illuminator all the time, hoping to see Paris under me.

When I walked out of the Charles de Gaulle airport, I saw that Monsieur Marchand was already waiting for me. He had rented a car the size of a limousine.

"Miss Westbridge! I'm so happy to see you again!" he said as he hugged me and kissed on the cheek.

"Mutually."

We got into the car.

"How much time will it take?"

"About forty minutes."

I became peevish and he noticed that.

"Unfortunately, there's nothing we can do about it. Unless you know how to teleport," he smiled.

"No, I don't." What a pity, I thought. After all, it's a very useful skill.

"It's sad that you decided to leave Paris. If you wouldn't be English, I couldn't understand how someone can prefer London to Paris."

I gave a laugh.

"It's difficult to explain… I love Paris, I really do.. It's my favourite city. But I felt drawn back to London so I moved."

"You want to spend some time in the country of your birth? I can understand that. But the lack of cafe culture in

England... Where are you going to spend hours meeting friends and watching the world go by? You can't even get decent coffee there!"

That truly made me laugh. I had no idea what coffee tasted like in London as I hadn't drunk it since 1861. Good old Monsieur Marchand. He knew how to crack me up.

Finally, we had arrived. The chauffeur had taken us to my almost-ex-property and Monsieur Marchand opened the garage door. There it was. The purpose of my arrival to Paris – a replica of a black 1982 Pontiac Trans Am. It was the car I used in the 1980s, when I lived in America (yes, I was a fan of "Knight Rider", I confess). I fell in love with it from the first sight and now got it made to order. During a trip to Italy a few years ago I found a garage that specialises in custom made cars. I had a look at their ongoing and completed projects, chatted to the staff and ended up ordering a car. My car wasn't a 100 % KITT replica, though - it had the red scanner and the dashboard, but it also had seat belts and air-conditioning. Sunlight wasn't a problem for me, while heat still was. Originally I wanted to put my initials on alloy wheels, but then I remembered that my real initials didn't match my current ones. Plus, alloy wheels were easy to lose and custom made ones were expensive to replace. Oh, well, I'll always have time to do it.

My car had a manual gearbox - I wasn't a fan of automatic ones - and it was a left hand drive vehicle. When I ordered it I thought I'd spend some more years in Paris and intended to use it for travelling around Europe. I loved being on the road and the ability to go anywhere and explore places at my own pace.

I went to the car and put my head on its roof. My right hand was sliding over the roof, caressing it.

"Don't you want to test it?" Monsieur Marchand asked.

"Of course," I said. "What about petrol?"

"Full tank."

"You're at your best," I said and got into the car.

He gave me the keys; I started the engine and drove out of the garage. At first, I wanted to try it out on local roads, then go to Germany and try my car on German autobahns.

After my test-drive in the outskirts of Paris, I went straight to the hotel Monsieur Marchand had booked for me. Since I was in town, I wanted to stay for a couple of days and wrap up a few things. I didn't want to stay in the house, because it had a buyer and I didn't consider it mine anymore.

I left my Pontiac in the hotel car park and entered the building. As I walked in, I saw a familiar silhouette at the reception desk and couldn't believe my eyes. Yuri!

"What are you doing here?" I asked without any pleasantries and small-talk.

"Lucretia, what a pleasant surprise! You're in Paris too? I came here for business."

"Exactly at the same time when I'm here. What a coincidence." I didn't hide sarcasm in my voice.

"Indeed." He smirked.

"Just wondering... What's your room number? 317?" I asked. "Mine is 318."

"No, it's 320. So, we will be neighbours again. I'll be quite busy for the next few days, but I hope that we will have time to meet each other."

Then he farewelled and went to the lift.

I didn't believe a single word he had said and I was sure that his only business in Paris was me. Only... how had he found out that I'm here?

It was late evening when I left the hotel. I deliberately waited until dark so that the traffic would have died down and driving around would be more enjoyable. It was a nice August evening - not too warm, not too windy. It was still summer but I could already sense autumn in the air.

My destination tonight was Cologne's autobahns. I sighed as I pulled out of the car park. What was I thinking when I decided to move to London? I knew that my Pontiac would be ready soon. I had no need for a car in London. When would I use it? At night when I'd decide to circle around the M25? My car had a 5-litre engine but the national speed limit was only 70 miles per hour. Hardly exciting.

The car was gorgeous, though. I loved it almost as much as loved myself. It was easy to control and the ride quality was superb.

The first time I drove a car was in 1923. In those days, I didn't find driving exciting, but, as years went by and technologies developed, I became more and more keen on it and had owned dozens of cars. I had had even a Rolls Royce Phantom in my garage. I guess, I was under mass psychosis when I bought it – everyone had it, so I wanted it too. However, a few rides were enough to realise that this car wasn't for me and I sold it. I remember how Byron was making fun about it – at first, I had stormed into the room, delighted that I'd bought myself a Rolls Royce, but a few months later I said that I was sick and tired of that car and wanted to get rid of it. Rolls Royce was a small madness, but come to think of it, my whole life in the sixties was one costly madness when money was spent left, right and centre.

By breaking the speed limit, I, both wittingly and unconsciously, got to the territory of Germany faster than I had planned. It was close to midnight and finally I could drive at full speed. I accelerated and the speedometer was now showing 150 kilometres per hour. I felt great - to me, driving was one of the biggest pleasures in life. Even if this car was destined to spend a lot of time in an underground car park in London it was still worth having it. I increased speed to 180 km/h - the handling remained perfect. I remembered an incident many years ago when one of my cars, at the speed of just 110 km/h, had become ungovernable, ran off the road and crashed into a pole. Luckily, there were no passengers – for a human such crash would have been lethal, while I just got out of the car, took a look around, hoping that the incident had no witnesses, and decided not to buy a car of this model anymore.

Being lost in my thoughts, I didn't notice that the speed had reached 220 km/h. It was close to the car's maximum – 240 km/h. I took my foot off the accelerator and gently pressed the brake. I loved speed and this car was absolutely safe for driving fast, however, I decided to slow down. Although there were no official speed limits on autobahns I knew that the recommended maximum speed was 160 km/h. I looked at the speedometer, it was now showing 140 km/h.

I spent a couple of hours driving. It was early morning when I returned to Paris.

xxx

The British are famous for their love of nature and I wasn't an exception. Although the hotel had easy access to central

Paris, it looked like a country pad and had a golf course and stables. Although the speed that I could reach by horse wasn't even close to the one I could reach by car, horse-riding was still one of my favourite leisure activities.

When I had chosen a horse and taken it out of the stables, I noticed another flora and fauna loving Brit. Yuri noticed me too. We greeted each other.

"Nice evening, isn't it? If only it wouldn't be so sultry," he said.

"Yes, it is nice. And sultry too. Luckily, September is just around the corner," I replied.

"Are you planning to have a long ride?"

"Of course. I haven't been on a horseback for years."

"Me too."

Suddenly a thought came into his mind.

"Would you like to compete?"

"Why not? Do you see those trees? The distance from here to them is approximately three hundred yards. The one who finishes the last will have the opportunity to look at my back," I said.

"You're very self-confident, aren't you? In that case, I offer to make the race more interesting. How about a bet?"

"What do you suggest as the object of the bet?"

"An evening spent together. If you lose, we'll have a date. If I lose, you'll have a free evening."

"Don't you think you're overshooting?"

"No. You know what feelings I have towards you."

I didn't like the wager, but I was sure I'd win.

"All right. I agree. Only don't forget that you can't cheat by jumping off the horse and finishing, carrying him on the shoulder!" I joked.

He grinned. We took our places on the starting line.

"Ready, set, go!" I shouted.

During the whole distance my horse was alongside his. It looked like we could finish together. I tried to pinch and dash, but I couldn't. Less than 50 yards were left until the finish. I prepared for a draw, when I suddenly saw that Yuri's horse starts to run a bit faster and overtakes mine. The next moment we passed the finish line. Unbelievable! I jumped down the horse and furiously walked away down the road. There was an apple tree on the roadside. I went to the tree and punched it – I needed to get rid of the anger. I completely forgot how strong I am until I was hit on the head by a stream of half-ripened apples. I bawled and ran back onto the road. Yuri was standing a few meters away from me, laughing.

"I've never seen such a reaction when a woman gets to know that she's having a date with me."

"You rascal! You did it on purpose!"

"I could have overtaken you already at the beginning, but it wouldn't have been so interesting."

"You deceived me!" I shouted.

"You cannot stand defeat, can you? What makes you angrier: the defeat or the date?"

"Both!"

I went back to my horse.

"Be sure you impress me!" I said and rode away, trying to leave behind a big cloud of dust.

"Opera? I should have expected that..." I said, stepping out of the limousine.

Yuri didn't want me to see where we were going, so he had rented a limousine with the darkest tinted windows ever. Now I could finally see where we were – outside Paris National Opera.

"Not really. Look closer."

I looked at the programme. Sarah Brightman.

"How did you..?"

"You were born in the 19th century, so you like opera. However, you belong to the 20th century, so you prefer something more modern. Sarah Brightman combines both."

"And I already thought that our date would be accompanied by the smell of naphthalene... So far, so good."

Yuri pretended he hadn't heard sarcasm in my voice. I had to admit – he had amazing deduction skills. Sarah Brightman was indeed one of my favourite singers. I had seen her live a couple of times.

We went inside the opera house and took our seats. Although I had the habit to behave like I'd be a convinced modernist, in fact I truly enjoyed reading classics, listening to classical music, going to opera and ballet, visiting museums and stately homes… I knew Paris opera inside out. The building itself was so beautiful that it invited one to return here again and again.

The lights turned off and the concert began. I liked all Sarah Brightman's songs, but there were several that I especially liked. Opera and the music created a special atmosphere and, in the moment, when "Fleurs du Mal", my favourite song from the singer's repertoire, was performed, I was taken over by such a thrill that, if only I could cry, tears of joy would have appeared in my eyes. It was a wonderful evening.

xxx

"We should have done a car race. I'd be at the finish line before you'd have managed to turn the engine on."

"I can't drive."

"That's even better! I demand a revanche," I said as I walked into Yuri's hotel room.

The room reminded a huge refrigerator – air conditioning was on full blast. I had done the same in my room.

"Tell me place and time."

"Here and now. This is for you," I said and threw a velvet parcel to him. I wittingly did it as aimlessly and casually as possible, but he caught the parcel so easily as if my toss would have been the most precise in the world.

Yuri opened the parcel and looked at its content.

"Since when provision of foils is included in hotel services?"

"You can get whatever you want for a generous tip," I said.

We went to one of the fields that was used for horse-riding. I hadn't fenced since the sixties and Yuri hadn't practiced since Vincent's death. The first fifteen minutes were just a warm-up, during which I lost to Yuri, but later he lost to me.

Then the real battle began. He wanted to duel, not to beat me, while I kept in mind the shameful result of the bet. I didn't want to experience a defeat again. We fenced for several hours, until it became so dark that we couldn't see our foils anymore. This time the winner was… friendship.

I had spent ten days in Paris and it was enough to finish everything, which meant that I could return to London. But before that…

I knocked on Yuri's door. He opened it almost instantly.

"I'm going back to London tomorrow. If you have finished all your business in Paris, I can drive you back. I'm leaving at four pm."

"I don't have any business left here, so I accept your offer with pleasure. Where shall we meet? At the hotel entrance?"

"Yes. Then… See you tomorrow." I said and turned around to go to my room, hearing the door closing behind me.

What a coincidence! I was going back to London and he was about to leave too. Of course, I knew that it would be exactly like this.

Way back was much more pleasant than the outward journey – if I had to choose between plane and car, I always preferred the latter one. I never got used to the idea of being in a metal tube thousands of feet up in the air. I didn't like flying and I also found it incredibly boring. There was nothing much to see in the sky. Travelling by car was an entirely different matter. I could see so many different things and I was in control all the time.

As for this particular journey, I have to admit, now I had a better company too.

"You're a very good driver. Did you go to a driving school or simply bought the licence?" Yuri asked.

"I bought it. When I drove a car for the first time, driving schools didn't exist yet. Later, when they appeared, I was already such a good driver that there was no need for driving lessons."

Most of the route was already behind us and London was quite close. So far, Yuri and I had discussed various topics, except the one which interested me the most.

"Confess – you went to Paris because of me, didn't you?"

He gave me a mysterious smile, which could mean both: that I'll hear the truth or that he'll be lying again.

"Yes. You left London in such a rush that I decided to find out why."

"How did you find out that I'm in Paris?"

"It's useful to have good relationships with concierges, janitors, airport staff..." he smirked.

"You are impossible! But wait... Officially my name isn't Lucretia Lockwood. How do you know what's written in my passport?"

"In case you have forgotten, we used to be neighbours. On one occasion you were going through some documents in my flat. I noticed that you signed them as Simona Westbridge."

Impressive. He was also great at spying.

"Why are you so interested in me?"

"As I have already said to you, I'm trying to turn over a new leaf in my life. There's an emptiness I want to fill... When I met you, I realised that you are what I'm looking for. You're the one who can help me in this."

"So, you're trying to put your life in order at my expense? Excellent. Only... What's in it for me?"

"It sounded too selfish, didn't it? I think you know the answer."

We had arrived at Yuri's place and I had just stopped the car on the edge of the pavement.

"Thank you for the drive," he said. Then he got out and went into the building.

There was a saying that it's difficult to attract a vampire's attention, but even more difficult – to attract *my* attention. It was true. Making an impression on a human woman was relatively straightforward: restaurant meals, nights out, foreign travel, gifts and, of course, showing off money and status. In the vampire world, none of this worked. Vampire women were very self-sufficient and had plenty of money. Plus, they had seen it all before. There was only one thing that could make an impression on them: personality. In our world, everything was simple: if two vampires felt drawn to each other, they could become a couple and be together for decades. Unlike humans, we had less things to worry about, didn't have to build a career (an unwritten rule – vampires do not work, vampires receive dividends) and our biological clock had stopped years ago. Sometimes it seemed to be too simple, although it was quite logical. Besides, it needed to be taken into account that many of us were born in the 19th century or earlier and in that time, this is how things were done in the human world too. Relationships were far more transactional and rational in those days.

With me, things were more complicated. I preferred human company and most of the men I had been together with were humans. It put a seal on the relationship: I could never become too attached to anyone, could never tell the truth about me and the relationship couldn't last too long. Now there was someone who mesmerised me, someone who reminded me of myself, but whom I rejected. I had adapted myself to constant changes, but here something serious could develop and I wasn't ready for that. I liked my life as it was.

The trip to Paris changed Yuri's tactics. Before it, he had kept a distance, because he wasn't sure of my feelings towards him and didn't want to lose the friendship I offered. Now he had seen that I was attracted to him after all.

Someone rang the intercom. I had a delivery. I opened the door and saw a courier with a large but surprisingly slim parcel in his hands. Is that a painting, I thought? I signed for the parcel and brought it into the living room, where I unwrapped it immediately. Indeed, it was a painting, very similar to the one I tried to buy in the auction: the same painter, the same colour scheme, the same couple, only in this picture they were pictured on the bank of a river, watering their horses. "I'm sorry I didn't send you *that* painting, but I like it too much. I hope you'll like this one. Yuri." I was astonished – he had made a serious effort here.

The painting wasn't Yuri's only dispatch to me. Later he started to send me letters with poetry, aphorisms or quotes every week. They were always carefully selected and described me or Yuri. The letters were written on a specific paper – it was made in nowadays, but looked like paper that was used in the 19th century. Yuri used ink for writing and his handwriting was almost calligraphic. The letters never contained anything personal, not even a signature. It simply was a way how Yuri reminded me about himself.

xxx

"You decided to come?" Yuri asked.

"What are you talking about?"

"I mentioned this play to you a few days ago and offered to see it together," he said.

"Did you?"

We were at Her Majesty's Theatre and had met during the intermission. I had decided to have a night out, enjoying culture.

"Indeed…" I said. Now I remembered. Yuri had offered me to see the play "The Sunset Boulevard", but I had declined.

"Anyway, I'm glad to see you. Did you receive the painting?"

"Yes. It is very beautiful. You probably worked hard to source it."

"Yes, but it was worth it. Special persons deserve special presents."

We were standing in the middle of the foyer and I noticed that people are looking at us with interest. It was not only because of our outfits – coincidentally, we were both wearing 19th century inspired clothes with a modern twist - but also because of ourselves. There was some serious chemistry between us and people could sense it.

We looked in the mirror. We would be a beautiful couple and there was something similar in our physical appearance. But... relationship meant frankness and trust, feelings from which I had broken away a long time ago.

"We look good together, however... It doesn't take much to make an impression on someone," I said and looked at a young man on the opposite side of the room. The effect was stronger than I expected – the poor guy became so mesmerised by me that he almost ran into the door.

"No, it doesn't," Yuri said and gazed at a woman who was standing near us. His look made her knees shake.

The first bell rang.

"Right, the theatre in the foyer is over," I said. "We have to go back to see the actual play."

A few days later I received another parcel. I was looking at it, trying to guess what is inside it. I unwrapped it and saw… alloy wheels with initials "LL". In my mind I turned over every single word I said to Yuri while driving us back from Paris – I was absolutely sure I didn't tell him that I wanted such alloy wheels. There was a note in the parcel: "I noticed that your car is missing something. Yuri."

For a moment, I became speechless. Maybe I should call him and thank him for the gift? But then another thought came into my mind – no, I'll better put the alloy wheels on my car instead. I grabbed the parcel and went to the underground car park.

After giving me this present Yuri did something very nasty – he disappeared. No calls, no letters, nothing. At first, I didn't care, but later I couldn't stand it anymore and did exactly what Yuri wanted me to do: I went to see him.

"Listen, what have you found in me? Please don't tell me that you started to fancy me because of my brains."

"Of course not. It was your physical appearance. I think your beautiful legs were what I saw first. Then – your lovely face. And also, you have a fantastic backside."

"So do you," I said.

"Already when I saw you for the first time, I thought that you're one of the most beautiful women I've ever seen. But the looks alone wouldn't mean much to me. You have an incredible ability to change your life at a moment's notice. You can mingle in London's high society for years and then suddenly go to Switzerland to train animals in a circus."

"Mmm…I've worked in a circus not only in Switzerland, but also in France. I was training tigers, lions, leopards, elephants and bears and invented many daring tricks. Those were ten wonderful years of my life – from 1895 to 1905."

"That is what amazes me. I can't do anything like that."

"I can teach you how, but we won't have to become a couple to do that."

"I'd like to know why you are holding back your feelings towards me. At first you yearn for me, then you reject me. This evening is not an exception."

"What are you talking about? Can't I simply visit you? We're still friends, aren't we?"

"Lucretia, it's two am. If this would be a friendly visit, you'd have come here much earlier."

Once again, he was right.

I had sunk into my thoughts, so I didn't notice when Yuri had left. I looked at the clock – it was five am. The bedroom door was open. I went in and saw him sleeping. Usually both humans and vampires, while sleeping, lost their masks and looked vulnerable. But not Yuri. Even asleep he looked as powerful and charming as he was awake and radiated the same attractive force. Yuri was lying on his stomach; his long black hair was covering his shoulders and half of the back. I had never seen before that someone could be so charismatic while asleep. I felt hypnotised.

I went closer to him and sat on the bed-side. Before I realised what I was doing, my hand had already touched his face and caressed it. The hand slid over the shoulders and ran through his hair.

Suddenly Yuri opened his eyes and looked at me. I froze. Vampire's sleep usually was very deep and I didn't think that we'd wake up.

"Lucretia, you don't want to reject me, do you?"

My answer to this question was still "yes" and "no" at the same time.

"If watching me sleeping is so pleasant, you're very welcome to join."

Yuri stretched his right hand and gently touched mine. I knew that when he offered me to join, his words had no other meaning. This charming Reynard was too smart to act like he really wanted to: pull me towards him and kiss so passionately that not only all my thoughts, but also memories of previous ten years of my life would fly out of my mind. Then he'd undress me with the lightning speed and make me forget some fifty more years of my life. The only thing I didn't like in this thought was the fact that I would have nothing against it. In my thoughts, I groaned. How had he managed to leave such an impression on me?!

I laid down next to him, so I could see his face. Yuri closed his eyes and fell asleep again. I continued to watch him until my eyes became heavy and I fell asleep too.

When I woke up, Yuri wasn't in the bed anymore. I went into the living room and saw him sitting behind his desk, reading something.

"Are you already leaving or will you stay for a while?" he asked.

"I think I'll stay. Do you often sleep with your clothes on?"

"Sometimes. I have such a habit, while you have a habit to sleep with your make-up on."

"How do you know that?"

"Just a guess."

"Is there anything else that you know about me, although I haven't said it to you?"

"Yes. I know that I need you more than you need me."

It seemed that after this episode our relationship should change, however, it didn't happen - I made a step back again. I have no idea how long it would have continued like that if one evening, when I had gone hunting, I wouldn't have accidentally met him.

"Good evening, Lucretia. I'm so glad to see you, given your extremely busy lifestyle."

"You sound like we hadn't seen each other for years, although it's been only two weeks since we last met."

Of course, I knew what was the subtext of his words – Yuri was mocking my avoidance of him.

We were in a rough part of London. It was a chilly November night, it had been raining and the streets were almost empty, so hunting took more time than usually.

"How long will we play this cat and mouse game?" he asked.

Yuri's behaviour was so annoying sometimes. He could beat around the bush and then suddenly ask a direct question.

"Which one of us is the cat, and which one – the mouse?"

"I think we turn the tables from time to time."

I sighed. I knew where this conversation would lead – Yuri will ask me the question I didn't want to answer.

"Lucretia, why can't we at least try? If it doesn't work out we'll go separate ways."

The last three months for me had been sealed by an inner struggle. On the one hand, I wanted my life to remain as it was, on the other hand – I wanted to be with Yuri.

When one is in a relationship, one doesn't belong only to themselves anymore and loses a part of their freedom and independence. I'd preferred to ignore the next thought, but I couldn't silence my inner voice – in a healthy relationship, there's always time for yourself and opportunities to be alone.

"If only you'd know how desperately I want to turn around and run..." I said.

"You can do so if you want. I won't try to stop you. I just asked you a question to which I hope to hear the answer someday."

I looked at Yuri. His face was absolutely calm. What a pity that I couldn't see his emotions – he was really good at hiding them.

In a sudden attack of frankness, I shouted:

"Do you realise what mess you have created in my mind? I don't want to be with anyone, but neither can I live without you. Whatever I do, I think of you!"

After I had said that I felt anger. Anger towards myself. There were two things I couldn't stand: defeat and losing control.

"I've got to the stage when I don't even know what to answer to you. If I say "yes", I'll be unhappy, if I say "no", I'll be unhappy too!"

"Then it looks like you have to choose the least of two evils."

"How can you be so calm and understanding?! You treat it as if it wouldn't be about me and you, but about me and someone else!"

"And how should I react? Lucretia, you mean a lot to me and I want you to be happy. If you think that you'll be unhappy with me, say it and I will accept it."

Amazing! He needed me more than I needed him, but he was caring more about me, not himself. This man was worth keeping around. Oh no... what did I just think?!

"Do you realise that together with my beautiful face and great mind will also come my impossible character?"

"Don't worry, I'm not a piece of gold either. Does it mean that you have made the decision?"

I nodded.

"All right, let it be. My answer is "yes"."

Voice of Blood

I walked out of the hotel and saw that the taxi was already waiting for me. The driver gave me a curious look. I gave him a smile. I knew that it was difficult *not* to look at me. Nice make-up, permanent waves, a costume that fit me perfectly, high-heeled shoes – given my age, ninety years, I looked perfect. How else if I didn't look my age? Officially I was 25 years old and two months ago I had celebrated my birthday by organising a lavish party. It was the talk of the town for weeks.

I got into the car and, as usual, ordered the driver to go to the club-restaurant "Metropolis". Tonight, I had a meeting with Bernard, my business partner and also lover. He was cold hearted and narrow minded and I wasn't particularly fond of him but this way it was easier to keep an eye on what he's up to. Bernard, too, was with me only because of convenience. Actually, I had suspicions that he was pocketing my money, but I didn't have any evidence.

The taxi driver accelerated and the car tore along the streets of Chicago. The year was 1931 and I had reinvented myself once again.

I walked in the restaurant and glanced over the hall, seeking for Bernard. He was sitting at the table with his usual – disinterested – facial expression. He was in his mid-thirties and had blonde hair and blue eyes. If not Bernard's menacing look, I could call him handsome. I noticed that today he was not smoking and considered it a small victory. I was sensitive to cigarette smoke and always coughed when someone was smoking - it turned out that there was at least one thing vampires and humans had in common.

I went to the table and sat opposite him.

"Good evening, Bernard."

"Good evening, Lucretia."

A waiter came to us and I made an order. Bernard smirked about my choice – as usual, I had ordered a small portion of fish – but didn't say anything. I couldn't feel the taste of any human food and, since my body couldn't digest it, it made me feel bad. Thus, the less I ate the better I felt. It was part of the game "human life" and I was impeccable in my role.

"Our income from gambling has increased by thirty percent in the last two months," he said.

"Thirty percent? Impressive."

"Luca, I think you bring luck to me."

I smiled. Bernard had given me this nickname saying that it reminds him of the word "luck." I said I don't agree with him, but he ignored that.

"I have something for you."

The next moment I saw a velvet lined box in front of me. I opened it and saw a beautiful emerald and silver bracelet – Bernard knew that I don't like gold. Contrary to what I had expected it was gold not silver that burnt my skin. The bracelet was very fine and, beyond doubt, very expensive.

"It will suit your eyes."

I immediately put the bracelet on, thinking – had Bernard bought it to celebrate the success or had he stolen from me and bought me a gift using my own money?

"Thank you, it is wonderful. Do you realise that now you will also have to buy me a necklace and earrings?"

"I do, however, do not expect it to happen soon. By the way, you already have a necklace."

"Yes, a *sapphire* necklace."

"Well, but that doesn't change the fact that it's a *necklace*."

Instead of a reply I gave him a coquettish smile and we focused on another topic.

"What about other businesses?" I asked.

"Our liquor business is stable, although the situation can change during the next few months – new rivals, Sammy Black and Co, have appeared. They are new ones in this area, so at the moment I don't know much about them."

"We need to collect information. Have they worked elsewhere?"

"Yes, in Missouri."

"Ahm."

"As I said before, currently the business is stable, but I have a feeling that we'll be facing big changes in a year or two, and not because of our rivals."

"You think that the government might reconsider their decision to prohibit liquor?"

"Exactly. So, we should keep our eyes open. If we need to leave the game, I want it to happen without big losses."

"So do I."

"Then we should succeed. Luca, you and I are a great team."

"You're flattering me." I found it difficult to accept compliments from him. I never believed he actually meant it. It showed how little I trusted him.

"Am I?"

The waiter came and brought me my order. As he left, Bernard finished his report.

"Last but not least - there are no significant changes in our smuggling business. That's all for you."

Indeed, it was. I took part only in some of Bernard's deals.

It all had started less than a year ago. I considered myself to be well educated in finance, however, I couldn't predict the financial crash of 1929 – it was something the world had never experienced before. Since part of my money was invested in the States, I decided to deal with everything by myself and came here. It didn't take much time for me to realise where the money was circulating now and I adapted myself to the new environment. Now my money was invested in various illicit deals. The new environment had another advantage – the "food" was always around me. I didn't like the thought that I'd need to kill innocent people, thus for many years I was hunting only criminals and other shady people. Fortunately, the proverb "you are what you eat" didn't apply to me. I hadn't turned into pond life. I admit – I was tough and had a caustic tongue, but I was generous, caring and sympathetic to those who deserved it.

A few days later I was at "Metropolis" again. As I saw Bernard, I realised that he has good news.

"Your smug face must have a reason," I said as I sat down.

"You're right. The police accidentally discovered a floating gambling-house at Lake Michigan." He smirked. "Now we have one rival less."

"Are we talking about Casey Spade? It was predictable. He had become too revolting. I wonder who betrayed him?"

I smirked, too. It was our job, of course.

Bernard soon left, but I decided to linger. I had moved from the restaurant hall to the bar and was drinking whiskey with soda, which, at the moment, was my favourite drink. Actually, I had to be cautious with alcohol use because already small doses had a strong impact on me. It didn't cause drunkenness, only a bad feeling. However, whiskey was different. Even bigger doses didn't cause hangover and it was the only drink whose taste I felt. Not much, only a little bit, but still... In addition, whiskey made a strange calming effect on me. I had no idea how that's possible, but because of these reasons I sometimes drank it even when no-one was around.

I was a bit bored, so I took a look around and saw the same old faces. "Metropolis" was a gangster bar and ordinary people didn't dare to come close to this place. And, despite complete disregard of the Dry Law, the police were never seen here. Blackmailers, smugglers, thieves, murderers and their girlfriends and lovers – those were the regulars of "Metropolis".

However, from time to time new faces appeared. I noticed a young man whom I had never seen before. He had a baby face but the serious look and behaviour showed that actually he was close to thirty. He noticed that I'm watching him, glanced at me, then turned away.

Gary, one of my acquaintances, came to the bar. In my opinion, he was one of the deftest smugglers in the country – when watching him at "work" it seemed that import or export of any goods was a child's play. He was pleasant as a person, too. Unlike Bernard, who's true face was revealed quite soon, Gary had created an image of a simple, witty man, not of a powerful gangster, whom he, beyond doubt, was.

"Hello, Lucretia. Are things so bad that you need to be here alone? Could it really be that there isn't a company you could join?"

"Hello, Gary. What's so bad about solitude? Actually, I'd like to play poker, but no-one wants to see me at the table anymore."

"It's because you always skunk everyone."

"I know. Sometimes I try to let someone else win, but then I get carried away and forget about it."

"And that's why guys start to panic when they see you walking up to the poker table," he laughed.

We chuckled. It wasn't far from the truth. Poker was one of my vices. Now I didn't play anymore, so gangsters could get their self-esteem back.

"I noticed a new face among us. Do you know him?"

"Yes, I do. Cedrick Faraday. He first came here six months ago and then disappeared somewhere for a couple of months."

"Is he local?'

"No. He speaks with a British accent. Cannot tell you more, Cedric doesn't say much about himself. As far as I know, he's looking where to invest money."

Gary ordered himself a drink and farewelled. I decided that I've got enough of "Metropolis" tonight and went back to the hotel.

xxx

"Shut up!" a hysterical voice shouted.

"It is difficult to argue with a person who's pointing a gun at you," I said in a calm voice.

When I returned to my hotel room, I was greeted by a gangster's girlfriend and a Luger that was pointed at my chest. Of course, it could do no harm to me. One moment and I would have made it unworkable. I could even try to tie its barrel in a knot as I once did with a rifle, but I knew I can't afford such tricks tonight.

"Confess: did you have an affair with Jerry?"

"Of course, no. Why do you think so?" I said, meanwhile trying to remember the truth. Maybe yes, maybe no – my memory was too short to remember all my affairs.

The pistol was shaking in her hands and anger didn't disappear from her face. I hoped she wouldn't shoot. I really didn't like to kill someone without a reason, but I couldn't let her go if she'd cause an injury that was life-threatening or fatal to humans.

"Sarah told me."

If I'd manage to calm her down Michelle would save her own life.

"Sarah? That Sarah who alleged that blue pelicans are flying at "Metropolis" after she had drunk too much absinth? That Sarah, who tried to put one of her lovers in jail, so she could be with another one?"

"Yes."

"And you believe her? Today she'll fabricate something about me, tomorrow she can do the same to you."

I noticed that my words have had an effect on Michelle. She looked indecisive already before my speech, but now she started to doubt even more.

"Did she present any evidence to you?"

'No."

With every moment Michelle became more and more fickle.

"Maybe you'll take that gun down? It may accidentally shoot. And then you'd get into trouble..."

I gave her such an honest look that Michelle couldn't endure it and turned away. The next moment she really took the gun down and sat in one of the arm-chairs. I let a few moments pass in silence until I spoke. It was time to show some empathy.

"You probably feel terrible. Can I offer you a drink?"

I was impressed with how my voice sounded. Tonight I had achieved new levels of faking something.

Michelle looked awful: smeared make-up, red eyes and tousled hair.

"Can you make it a double?"

She took the clip out of the gun and put it on the table together with the pistol.

"Of course. It looks like it will be good for you."

Michelle stayed for about an hour. While sipping whiskey, she suddenly opened up: it turned out that she was sick and tired of all this environment, intrigues, Jerry's non-stop affairs with other women and the feeling that her life has no purpose. She apologised to me and said she's sorry about her stupid behaviour. I walked to the taxi with her and said that I hope things would get better for her. At that moment I was sincere.

xxx

"Bad luck!" Bernard said as he put away the newspaper.

Once again, we were having dinner at "Metropolis". Of course, only he was eating. I was drinking whiskey while reading the newspaper. Huge headline on the first page said "Police Confiscate Enormous Amount of Alcohol". There was a photo under it: a warehouse, full of boxes from floor to ceiling, and a very proud police unit.

"The police arrived at the warehouse just one day after a cargo of alcohol was delivered. Chicago police can celebrate."

"Yes, with a box of confiscated whiskey," he laughed. "By the way, how did you manage to find out when the cargo arrives?"

"I have good informants," I smiled. This, too, was our job.

I glanced over the article again, when suddenly an angry shout sounded across the restaurant:

"I cannot stand your lies anymore!"

Everyone's look focused on the table in the mid section. Mary had pulled out a revolver and pointed it at Franky, her boyfriend. No-one seemed to be surprised. Something like that happened quite regularly. A revolver in a lady's bag was a staple, just like a powder-case and a mirror. Even I had it although I never needed a gun to solve my problems. Let's say that I was following the local trend.

Everybody was watching what would happen, but no-one interfered.

"I'm sick and tired of you wasting money on lovers, your non-stop binge and the fact that you pay no attention to me! I'm not a bijou that can be left neglected whenever you want!"

Franky's face was absolutely calm. It wasn't the first time they washed their laundry in public. Mary and Franky had been together for so many years that none of them remembered when exactly they had become a couple.

Mary continued to bawl for a moment until someone had enough of this and two gangsters ran and disarmed her. Mary objected to such a turn and started punching them. Finally, Franky, too, was tired of the scene. He grabbed Mary and pulled her out of the restaurant. Later he came back. Alone. Apparently, Mary was sent back home.

Mary didn't show up at "Metropolis" for a while. After her return, she treated as if nothing had happened and called Franky "darling" again.

I felt that someone was watching me and turned my head. For a moment my and Cedrick's eyes met, then he turned away. It wasn't the first time when it had happened. There was something strange in Cedrick's look. It wasn't the look that was characteristic to men who were interested in me, nor the look which men who tried to involve me in their deals had. It seemed that Cedrick had some specific interest in me, but I couldn't understand why. Besides, he always kept a distance – Cedrick had never approached me even for a small talk. It was confusing me. I finished my drink and left the bar.

"Do you really need to smoke so much?" I said and with a gesture pretended to disperse the smoke.

"Absolutely! It is the only way to keep you away from the poker table," Barney said and gave a loud laugh.

I had come to Barney and his company's table. Barney was involved in so many deals that it was easier to say what he wasn't doing. I had worked with him a couple of times. The company had just finished a game and Barney had won. A huge roll of bills was laying in the middle of the table. I looked at the cards, thinking that I'd love to play at least one game, but I knew they wouldn't let me – no-one wanted to deal with Lucretia Lockwood and lose all the money he had on him plus a wrist-watch and cigarette case. So, instead of playing, I sometimes joined Bernard and pretended to be his talisman.

"By the way, Luca, it's allowed to smoke here. Get used to it."

"If that would be in my power, I'd forbid smoking inside "Metropolis.""

The men looked shocked. After a short exchange of banter, Barney said:

"I suppose, you didn't come just like that?"

"No, I didn't."

Gangsters left, so I could talk to Barney in private.

"I'm at your service," he said.

"I just made big money with gambling and I want to invest it somewhere. I suppose you have some good suggestions, haven't you?"

"You have attracted someone's interest; did you know that?" Gary said. After the conversation with Barney I had gone back to the bar. Gary's facial expression showed that he had been looking for me.

"Not until you told me," I said in a nonchalant voice. "May I know that person's name?"

"Cedrick Faraday."

It didn't surprise me.

"What does he want to know?"

"When did you come to America, what are you doing here, with whom you're friends with... I don't like that."

"Neither do I."

"Cedrick is suspicious. I think he's working for someone. I decided to warn you."

"Thank you. I appreciate it."

Gary left. I was thinking over what he had said. Could it be that someone whom I didn't know was interested in me? If so, why? Cedrick Faraday, who are you and who is behind you?

The next few days were quite eventless, until one evening... I had just come into my hotel room when I realised that something is wrong. A hardly perceptible fragrance was in the air. Eau de cologne. Housekeepers definitely weren't using men's perfume and I never brought anyone here. It meant that someone had sneaked into the room. I listened carefully but I didn't hear anything and checked the rooms quickly. Whoever had broken in here had already left. It was clear that people don't do a home invasion just like that, so I checked my belongings – nothing was missing. I stored documents and everything else I considered to be important in a bank safe and always had the key with me. All jewellery was still in my jewel case, but even if something had been stolen, I wouldn't care – it had never meant much to me. Anyway, who and why had sneaked in here and rummaged through my belongings? I had one suspect.

Later that night I had to go to "Metropolis". As I entered the hall, I saw Cedrick. He gave me a quick, disinterested look and walked straight past me. I inhaled the air around him. I knew this fragrance. Cedrick was the one who, in my absence, had ferreted around in my hotel room!

I hadn't been so furious for years. I was sitting in the darkest corner of the restaurant, considering what to do. Cedrick's behaviour and the fact that I didn't know anything about him made my blood boil. Several times I had asked about him to various gangsters, but no-one could tell me more than Gary. I guess the only option was to use Cedrick's own methods and spy on him.

I was about to open the door of my hotel room when I suddenly felt that I'm not alone.

"Good evening, Lucretia," I heard Cedrick's voice behind me.

"What do you want?" I hissed as I turned to him.

"I need to talk to you."

"And for this purpose, you definitely needed to choose such a moment."

"I wanted to meet you when you're alone."

"It sounds suspicious, doesn't it?"

"Won't you invite me in?"

"I'm not in the mood for that."

Although I realised that this an appropriate moment to finally talk to him, I wanted to show that it's not so easy to approach me. He sighed.

"I guess we could continue like that all night long… All right, I will tell you the purpose of my visit. Lucretia, I am here because we have something in common."

"What are you talking about?"

"I'm one of Nickolas Westmoreland's grandchildren."

With a gesture I called him in, meanwhile taking a quick look around in order to make sure that there was no-one in the corridor who could have heard us. Suddenly I understood everything. I understood why Cedrick had looked at me like that, why I, when looking at him, had felt strange, confusing feelings. Visually he didn't resemble my brother, but something in his gestures and moves reminded me of Nickolas. All right, Cedrick had recognised me as one of the Westmorelands. Only... Did he know who exactly I am?

"Whiskey?" I offered.

Cedrick nodded and I went to the buffet.

"I guess, I'll have a drink too."

"And I thought that vampires drink only blood."

I froze.

"Now I really need a drink."

I made whiskey with soda and ice for him and a neat one for myself. I gave the glass to him and, after I had sipped a bit of my drink, said:

"I see that the family secret is being passed from generation to generation."

"At first grandfather, his brothers and my great grandfather agreed that the secret would remain a secret, but he changed his mind in 1871, when Doris, my mother, was born. He was looking at her in the cradle – so tiny and vulnerable - and swore to protect her from a destiny like yours. Elias had three children then – two sons and a daughter – and he supported grandfather. Later great grandfather gave his consent. By the way, at first grandfather wanted to name my mother after you, but then changed his mind... He was afraid that it could affect her fate."

"It's all right, I understand him."

"Therefore, your sad story is known to everyone in our family. My brothers and sisters know it, my cousins know it, my aunts and uncles know it. It changed the Westmorelands. We've been taught not to trust people much. And we all stick together – if one Westmoreland has a problem, the whole family will help. We've been raised to be polite, sympathetic, great-hearted and friendly, but to keep a distance between us and people who don't belong to the family. Our trust must be earned."

What I just heard saddened me. Of course, I wasn't so naive to believe that what had happened to me won't leave any impact on the rest of the family, however, I was afflicted by the thought that Westmoreland children were taught to beware of people since early childhood and to trust only members of the family. Each new generation passed it to the next one and would continue to do so as long as the family would exist...

"How did you recognise me?"

"At first I didn't. I've seen a picture of you, but you look completely different now. But then I found out that your name is Lucretia and you're from England. I thought – what if... I started to observe you."

"Also, you started to collect information about me and broke into my hotel room."

"I'm very sorry about that. I was looking for evidence that you really are Lucretia Westmoreland, my aunt."

"Aunt? No-one has ever called me like that." I chuckled. We looked like peers.

"Grandfather often told me about you. He said he was your favourite."

I nodded.

"I loved all my brothers, but I loved Nickolas the most."

Besides Nickolas, I had two other elder brothers – Michael and Elias. Michael was ten, Elias – two years older than me.

"Is Nickolas still alive?" I asked although I realised that it's not very possible. Nickolas was five years older than me and only one decade separated me from being a century old.

"No, he died at the age of eighty, being surrounded by his seven children and countless grandchildren."

"And Elias?"

"He died when he was sixty-six years old. He, too, passed away happy. Elias had five children and many grandchildren."

"And Michael?"

For the first time I heard a sad note in Cedrick's voice:

"Michael died young, at the age of thirty-six, and had no family. A fire started in a neighbouring house. Everyone hurried there, including our family. When they realised that one of the neighbour's children was still in the house,

Michael ran into the flames and tried to save her. He found the child but, on his way back, the ceiling collapsed right above them, crushing them."

I didn't say anything for a moment, then asked:

"And my father... How did he feel? He lost two children within five years..."

"At first he was devastated. At first you, then Michael... Besides, Michael was the one who was supposed to take over great grandfather's deals... After his death, everything was divided between my grandfather and Elias. But, unlike the case with you, great grandfather got over Michael's death, because he had died doing a good thing."

"I didn't expect him to recover."

"Grandfather told me that during the first years after your... hmm... transformation, great grandfather was very depressed; nothing could delight him. But, when Elias and grandfather got married and grandchildren were born one after another, he felt happy again. Of course, bitterness about your fate always stayed in his heart, but he died with a smile on his lips. He believed that you're doing well.'"

Since that day I started to go to "Metropolis" less often and spent most of my time with Cedrick. I asked him about my family, while Cedrick was interested how I have lived all these years. Of course, he also wanted to know what it's like to be a vampire.

"How old are you now?" he asked.

"I celebrated my ninetieth birthday on the twenty-ninth of January."

"You look excellent for your age," he smirked.

"Do not banter me, all right? By the way, what is your age? When were you born?"

"On the twenty-seventh of October nineteen-aught-three."

"So, you're twenty-seven years old now. I already thought that you're older than you look. Do you still live in Brighton?"

"No, I moved to London when I was seventeen," he said. A moment later he had already returned to his favourite topic. "You don't age, do you?"

"No. I stay exactly as I was at the moment of my death. The only things that may change are eyes and facial expression. They may change depending on lifestyle and emotions. When vampires are satisfied with their life you can see it in their face and vice versa. Thus, even if the face doesn't age, it still may change."

"And other things? For example, what would happen if you'd cut your hair?"

"It would grow back within a few months. Or years. Depends on the cut. By the way, my hair grows very slowly, while nails grow very fast. I'd prefer it if it would be the other way around."

"What would happen if you'd dye your hair?"

"And what do you think? It would change colour."

"What are the differences between a vampire and human body?"

"Well... I can bend iron with bare hands and run one hundred yards in six seconds. Vampires barely feel tiredness, don't feel cold, their skin is colder, sunlight causes dislike... Most biological processes have stopped...

Some have remained – for instance, my heart beats, but very slowly."

"Is your skin really cold as ice?"

"Touch it," I said and outstretched my arm to him.

"I had imagined vampire skin to be different. I thought it's icy and harsh. Yours is only a bit colder than human's and very soft."

"It is icy only on the hands."

"And what about human food and drink?"

"Well, it is the same as to fill a car with water instead of petrol. There will be an outcome, but not the one you need. I have to eat and drink something in human company. All right, I can always say that I'm on diet and avoid food, but I still need to have a drink or two... Another problem is smoking. Smoke always causes a cough. Usually no-one smokes in my presence, but it's difficult for me to be in restaurants and bars where the air is fully covered by blue smoke… Alcohol… Usually already a few glasses cause terrible hangovers, but whiskey affects me differently…. I can drink a lot of it, especially if I dilute it with soda. Wait a minute, is this some kind of an interrogation?"

"I'm just curious."

There was something I really wanted to know. I was waiting for Cedrick to speak about it, but he didn't. So, I asked.

"Do you know something about Jack's fate?"

"Didn't I tell you? I can't believe I forgot to do that! Jack married Cornelia, but the marriage wasn't happy. Jack fell in love with her, but Cornelia had no feelings towards him. She had one affair after another, and, after their second child was born, said that from now on she would not sleep with him anymore. Jack started to drown his grief in alcohol. After Cornelia ran off with a lover, Jack became completely devastated. He died lonely and grief stricken. Although great grandfather had forbidden that, grandfather and uncle were cheering – finally that bastard had got what he deserved! Grandfather even said that on the day when he heard of Jack's death, he and Elias emptied a case of champagne between them."

I guess I should have felt satisfied, however, I wasn't.

"You know, I actually feel sorry for him."

Cedrick gave me a surprised look.

"Did I hear you correctly? You feel *sorry* for him?"

"Yes. Of course, he was a liar and he used me, but I, too, am responsible for what happened to me."

Cedrick was so thunder-struck that he didn't know what to say.

"If I wouldn't have taken his betrayal to heart so much, I wouldn't have died and turned into a vampire."

"Did I understand you correctly – you blame yourself for the fact that Jack, when he started a relationship with you, hid that he's engaged and that you suffered when you found out the truth?"

"I'm not justifying him. I'm just saying that what happened to me was my fault too. I was too sensitive."

xxx

Although I enjoyed Cedrick's company, I knew that this was not the right place for him.

"You should leave, preferably – go back to England. You're my relative and I worry about you."

"Don't worry, I know how to take care of my own security," he smirked.

"There's something you don't know. Vampire bravos are working in the city. Good-looking young boys and girls who get rid of people fast and clean. A meal they get paid for," I said ironically. "Of course, they don't say who they are and what methods they use."

Suddenly Cedrick's face wasn't so relaxed anymore.

"Sounds impossible, doesn't it? I didn't believe either until I saw them "at work.""

Cedrick and I were at "Metropolis". I wanted to show him the bravos but none of them was here yet. However, sooner or later they would show up. I saw at least two or three of them every time I was here.

I was right. In less than an hour these birds of a feather started to arrive one after another. Apparently, they had recently woken up.

"Take a look around. Can you recognise vampires?"

Cedrick was silent for a moment, then pointed at several men and women. I nodded.

"Very good. However, you missed four."

I showed him those vampires. They were bravos, too, but less conspicuous. They behaved more freely, sipped their drinks as if they'd feel their taste, but, still, their look betrayed them. I could fool nearly everyone, while it was impossible to fool me.

"If you wouldn't know that they're vampires, would you pay attention to them?"

"To some of them."

"And what would you think?"

"That they're junkies. Unsettled, icy look, torn moves. They become nervous in human presence."

"You've got impressive observation skills. However, I hope that you'll never need to use this knowledge. In theory they are a danger to everyone, because you can never know who perceives who as a threat. So be careful."

xxx

"You know, there are rumours that you and Cedrick are a couple," Mandy, some gangster's girlfriend and a huge chatterbox, said. She had sat at my table and her look was full of curiosity.

"We're not lovers," I said and pressed my lips together. Sure, I anticipated that rumours would start to spread about Cedrick and me.

"Does Bernard know?"

"Bernard doesn't need to know because I have nothing to hide from him."

I gave Mandy a look that said "I-won't-tell-you-anything" and she left, completely disappointed.

Although me and Cedrick tried not to arrive at "Metropolis" together and we were cautious when visiting each other, we couldn't hide our friendly relationship. Cedrick didn't like the rumours either, but there was nothing we could do – revealing the truth would have blown our cover. I was Lucretia Lockwood, an orphan with no relatives, while Cedrick pretended to be a simple Londoner who had nothing in common with the Westmorelands.

It was very late when I returned to the hotel. I was too lazy to remove my make-up and change and went straight to bed. I was slowly falling asleep when suddenly I felt that I'm not alone here. I opened my eyes and saw a flaming look and sharp teeth. Rachel, one of the bravos! The next moment I had already shaken her off and jumped on her, pinning her to the floor. She tried to break free, but realised that it's useless – she couldn't measure swords with me. Now she was the one who was looking at a flaming look and sharp teeth. Rachel's face had completely changed, surprise and fear was visible in her eyes.

"But… How? You don't look like one of us."

I gave her a smile that said "oh-you-naive-one" and, for a bigger effect, gave her another icy look before I spoke.

"Rachel, how could you make such a terrible mistake? I realised who you are when I first saw you."

"But… you look like a human; you behave like a human…"

I sighed. Apparently, she was a new-born and so was the whole bunch of bravos. There was no other way to explain that no-one had noticed that I'm a vampire too and warned her. Usually vampires didn't kill each other. The unwritten rule was that if you have cheated death and made it this far you are to be left alone.

"You needed to be more observant. Nearly seven decades have passed since my transformation and I've spent most of them among humans. I've adapted. Unlike you."

It was true. Rachel's unsettled look and nervous moves betrayed her. So did her skin, which was too pale, and bad make-up – transformation into a vampire didn't mean acquisition of unbelievable beauty. Some, like me, had stunning looks, while others looked like the living dead.

"And now tell me: who sent you?"

The answer didn't surprise me much.

"Bernard."

"Who else is on the list?"

Rachel looked so scared that she probably would tell me anything just to get away from here.

"Johnny Richards."

I knew him. Average gangster with a long list of crimes. I won't miss him.

"Jacky Jones."

A lurcher. It won't be a big loss.

"Tracey Scott."

A smuggler and a big player in the liquor business. Another person I won't miss.

Rachel told me a few other names. None of them paid my attention, until...

"Cedrick Faraday."

I hissed and, taken over by anger, unconsciously squeezed Rachel's hands harder.

"Did he tell you the reason?"

"No. Bernard never does that."

I stood up and pulled Rachel up with me. Now I was holding her with only one hand, but it was enough – in a one-to-one fight she couldn't endanger me.

"Now listen. You'll go straight to Bernard and tell him that the plan has failed and me and Cedrick must be left alone. The reason is up to you. I want him to understand that whatever he plans against us will not succeed. Is it clear to you?"

Although Rachel was afraid, curiosity awoke in her.

"But why? Why do you protect your lover so much?"

How I hated to hear these words!

"He's not my lover! That's all you need to know. And now get lost and never come back. If I ever see you or anyone else from your gang trying to attack me, I'll destroy all of you!"

I kicked Rachel out and slammed the door. I lived in a five-star hotel, but the recent events made me feel as if I'd live in a barn with the door wide open – anyone who wanted to get into my room did it so easily as if there would be no concierge and doors!

It wasn't the only reason that made me so angry. Bernard! I unconsciously touched the emerald bracelet. Not so long ago he told me that I brought luck to him, now it turned out that he wanted to get rid of me. Traitor! His fate was clear – Bernard must die. Betrayal was one thing I never forgave.

I went to the phone and dialled Cedrick's number. He picked up after the twelfth beep.

"Are you alone?"

"No."

"I need to talk to you. Immediately."

I felt some kind of disaffection – apparently, he had other plans for this evening – but he realised that I have something very important to say.

"All right, come."

"I'll be at your place within half an hour."

When I arrived, Cedrick's guest, whoever she was, had already left.

"Cedrick, you must leave as soon as possible. And it's not a suggestion."

"Someone has "ordered" me?" he gave me a serious look.

I nodded.

"But you're not the only one who was "ordered". I was on the list too."

He frowned.

"What do you mean?"

"Rachel, one of the bravos, "visited" me today."

Cedrick was truly surprised.

"Visited you?"

"Rachel is quite young; she didn't notice that I'm a vampire too and tried to kill me. I threw her out of my hotel room, but before that I got some information from her."

Cedrick flew into a passionate rage.

"Who?!"

"Bernard."

Cedrick reacted just as I expected. He started up, expressed his feelings with the help of some swear words and promised to tear Bernard into pieces. Despite his age Cedick was still full of adolescent ardour.

"What shall we do about it?"

"Not we. I. *You* will board the first ship to England. I will deal with Bernard."

"You think you can remove me just like that? So easily? In case you haven't noticed, I'm not a child!"

A long Cedrick's monologue followed during which he explained why he's not going to leave Chicago. I understood his stubbornness – for him, immediate leaving looked like a cowardly escape.

"Cedrick, do I often ask you something?" I looked into his eyes, not letting Cedrick avert. "In fact, I've never asked you anything. I can deal with Bernard. I can deal with Rachel. I can deal with anyone. But I can do it only if I have no weak points that could be used by a foe. I won't be able to act if I would have to worry about your safety."

"Now you sound like my mom."

"I tried."

For a moment Cedrick tried to argue, but then he raised his hands showing that he's giving up.

"All right. I'll do as you say. But… Why were both of us on the list? Was it really because of the rumours?"

"I don't think so. In that case Bernard would rather have tried to scare, not kill, you and dealt with me himself. Bernard wanted to get rid of me because he had laid hands on my money. You... It's hard to understand. Have you invested money somewhere?"

"Yes, in gambling."

"You must have worked with one of Bernard's rivals then. He's really protective of that business."

I took Cedrick to New York Harbour. It was sad to separate, but I felt that I must send him away from the States, otherwise an idea to secretly come back to Chicago could come into his mind.

We embraced and he asked:

"Will you visit us when you're in England?"

"Well... I don't know... Don't you think it would be strange? You're the only Westmoreland I know. Besides... Wouldn't it be traumatic?"

"No, not at all. You're the reason why our family is so strong. They love you although they've never met you. Visit us and you'll see."

"I will think about it."

"And... If you ever decide to come back... I want you to know – you have a home where you'll always be welcome. The Westmorelands take care of each other."

Cedrick's words started to make an impact on me. It was nice to know that I still have a place to call home and a family.

Cedrick had to go. On the way to the ship he turned around and hailed one more time:

"We love you, Lucretia! You're always welcome at home!"

When he was already on board, Cedrick went out on the deck and waved at me. I waved back. The opportunity to return home and visit my family was so alluring... However, serious doubts were oppressing me. Maybe it would be better to leave everything as it is? The ship turned on the engine and lifted the ropes. For a moment I was watching it departing, then turned around and went out of the harbour.

The Return

Landscapes replaced each other, but I was viewing them without interest – during the past few years, I had seen them often enough. The locomotive was sweeping forward and I felt elated. I was on my way to Brighton, my hometown, and I was going to visit Cedrick.

When we separated in Chicago in 1931, I thought that I saw him for the last time. Back then I thought that it would be better if we would not meet again. But right after I had moved back to Great Britain, I realised how much I miss him and reckoned that it would be silly to ignore him if we live in the same country.

Of course, many years had passed since the day when I took Cedrick to the port until the moment I returned to England. As soon as Cedrick had left, I went to deal with Bernard. I could forgive him pocketing my money - I'd have demanded it back and then pretended that I've never done any business with him - but Bernard hadn't contented himself with that only, no. He didn't consider my money to be enough for him, he decided to remove me and sent a bravo to me. Even after that my reaction was quite peaceful. I became furious only when I found out that Bernard had ordered to kill Cedrick too.

The revenge turned into a huge mess. I guess the Devil himself was on Bernard's side and he stayed alive. As if that wouldn't have been enough, now he knew that I had tried to kill him and knew that I knew about his plans to kill me. A war started between us. Both of us had to change the tactics, but everything we tried to do to each other failed. What was the worst thing, because of me and Bernard everyone else suddenly remembered about their grievances and turf wars and then... People started to disappear one after another and vampire bravos started to decline jobs – because of countless orders, soon they weren't even able to look at people. I guess they had filled themselves up for the next few months. Left without their assistance, gangsters returned to old methods. Shots started to ring out more and more often. Due to all this bustle I had no time to deal with Bernard anymore because sudden attempts on my life followed one after another and I had to defend myself.

The first attack took place on an evening. I had just left my house and was about to get into the car when a storm of bullets was sent to it. And, what is important to mention, it came from machine guns, not pistols. My only weapon was a revolver with six bullets. I always had it with me – just in case. If anyone witnessed this episode, then it looked quite unbelievable how a woman with a revolver defeated two gangsters who were armed with tommy guns, however, it would have looked much more unbelievable if I'd had faced my opponents like a vampire – by going through the storm of bullets and dealing with them with bare hands.

After this attack, several more followed. The most splendid episode took place in a club basement. I was invited to a private poker game. Cards, money, whiskey, conversations – everything was as usual. I sipped more whiskey, when suddenly I noticed how everyone's facial expression changes. They were staring at me with horror and disbelief. Something was wrong. I smelled the drink carefully. Light odour of almonds. Cyanide! In a hundredth of a second, I had already turned into a beast of prey – my eyes lit up in anger and I hissed. I spilled the content of the glass into the face of the person who was sitting opposite me, shouted "Bastards!", reached out my right hand and hit three of the gangsters. All of them fell on the floor with no signs of life. I had broken their necks.

The others tried to run away, but I couldn't allow that to happen. I could somehow explain how I managed to survive in all those shootouts, while this had no plausible explanation.

I could move faster than anyone else and soon two more corpses were lying on the floor.

"Great," I thought. Now I had to set this place on fire in order to hide what had happened. Five dead bodies and arson in one evening.

As I had done it, I was standing outside watching the flames taking over the building. It would never end, I thought. Things were getting worse with every day and there was no time for revenge. So, I left Bernard for others to tear into pieces and left. Soon I was viewing the panorama of New York City from the Statue of Liberty observation deck. I stayed in New York until 1956 when I decided to return to the British Isles.

That's when Cedrick and I met again. We hadn't seen each other for twenty-five years. Cedrick had become 52 years old; he was married with six children and already had several grandchildren. He had moved back to the family house, which once used to be my home. A few wrinkles had appeared in Cedrick's face and his hair had become slightly grey, but he still was radiating energy and his smile could make clouds disappear in an overcast sky.

In my life, nothing had significantly changed – I lived alone, spending my days doing whatever I wanted and invested money here and there.

Cedrick was in raptures about my arrival whereas Marie, his wife, wasn't. During my visit, she was giving me looks full of fear. Cedrick had told her the family secret many years ago, before their wedding, but she never thought she'd actually meet me. But, since she was a lady of fine breeding, her behaviour was impeccable.

I had arrived at lunchtime and Marie had prepared some food. She tried to be a good hostess and said in a shy voice:

"Maybe you want something... We could kill a chicken."

"No, thank you. I'm not hungry," I said in my most polite voice.

I appreciated Marie's effort. I knew that she's scared and that being in one room with me was stressful to her. I really wasn't hungry but, even if I would, I'd never drink chicken or any other animal blood in her presence. I looked like a human and if Cedrick wouldn't have told her who's coming Marie would have no idea that I'm actually a vampire.

So, there I was, sitting at the kitchen table with nothing in front of me while they were having lunch. For Cedrick it wasn't anything new, while poor Marie felt uncomfortable and barely touched her food.

After lunch Marie left us alone. We stayed in the kitchen and Cedrick couldn't wait to find out what had happened in Chicago after his departure. I briefly told him about the chaos I had accidentally caused.

"You know, you did right when you sent me away from Chicago. I would have returned," he said.

"I knew that. That's why I insisted on your return to England."

"Back then I was so full of youthful zeal... and also stupidity... I thought – I'll show to everyone what the anger of Cedrick Faraday is! Now, when I look back, I see how childish it was. I have a wife, children, grandchildren. I've lived a wonderful life. I'd have nothing of what I just mentioned if I'd had thrown myself into the whirl of revenge."

"And what was I trying to explain to you all the time?!" I laughed. "I was doing it only for your own sake. You had your whole life ahead and I didn't want it to come to a sudden end because of a hasty decision."

"Don't think that it was the only time when I exposed myself to danger!" Cedrick said.

"Of course, of course," I nodded. "The adventurous spirit of the Westmorelands!"

"By the way, what were you doing all these twenty-five years?" he asked.

We got so carried away talking that we didn't notice how the time passed. It was late evening when I decided to go back to London. Cedrick offered me to stay overnight – at that moment I could hear Marie's heart skipping a beat – but I said "no". One thing was to visit the house, which I was forced to leave nearly a hundred years ago, another thing was to spend the night here. Also, I didn't want to stay because of Marie. She had been very brave during the day and deserved to have a rest.

During one of my next visits I asked Cedrick to take me to my family crypt – I felt I must do it. Cedrick agreed without saying a word and went to get the keys.

We went into the crypt. The air was wet and stale and there were spider webs on the walls. The last time I had been here was in November 1862 – on the day when I woke up from the dead. The crypt was built after my mother's death. My father and brothers were buried here too. While building the crypt, my father had intended a place for himself, his wife and children. Of course, he never thought that two of his offspring would die before him.

I went to a sarcophagus and caressed it. The next one was painfully familiar to me. My fingers slid over the epitaph on its side. "Lucy Lucretia Westmoreland. January 29, 1841 – November 19, 1862"

I turned to Cedrick.

"Is..."

He nodded.

"They decided that it would be safer to leave the chambermaid's ashes in the coffin. They're still there."

It was weird to look at my own tomb, but it was even more weird to realise that there was a stranger lying next to my family. However, I understood why my brothers and now Cedrick had decided to keep her ashes in the coffin – just in case a local fan of vampire legends, willing to break into the crypt, would show up.

There was Michael's sarcophagus right next to mine. Next to him, Elias and Nickolas were buried. My family. I was supposed to be among them, but I was still alive and would never join them. I knew that being here would cause sad reflections, however, I had to come. More than ninety years ago I had to leave home, farewell from my loved ones and break with the past, now I could return to the place where I had spent my human life.

I had a final look at all six sarcophaguses, then turned around and went out of the crypt.

xxx

Eight years had passed since that day and my life had significantly changed - I was a boho now. In the 1950s, I was a lady in a Chanel suit with a pearl necklace and gloves, now I was wearing typical 60s stuff. Couture was out, miniskirts, bright colours and bold prints were in. Today I was wearing a purple tunic with golden embroidery and a faux-fur gilet. The hair that once used to be tied in a perfect knot was now tousled. My name had changed too. I wasn't Lockwood anymore. Now everyone knew me as Mortensen. Mrs Mortensen.

Only one thing had remained the same – despite the fact that I owned several cars, including a brand-new Rolls Royce Phantom, I was still going to Brighton by train. I guess the reason behind that was my unwillingness to deal with bad roads and potential breakdowns.

In London, I used every possibility to drive a car. My ardour with cars started in the 1940s and had only increased over the time.

The train entered the station. Cedrick was already waiting for me standing on the platform. He had aged very little in the last decade and was still full of energy.

"Lucretia!" he shouted even before I had stepped out of the train properly. "I'm so glad to see you again!"

We hugged. During these years we had become so close that the thought that there used to be a time when I believed we shouldn't meet again seemed completely unimaginable now.

"What's new in London?" he asked.

"Nothing new: youth revolution, rock'n'roll and bohemian lifestyle."

"How's Byron?"

"Good."

"I've never met Byron and probably never will, but I think that he's a wonderful man. He has a good impact on you. You look so joyful and that makes me happy."

I smiled. What Cedrick just said was absolute truth. During my vampire life, I had never felt such easiness and happiness as now, being with Byron.

We went on foot to Cedrick's house. Cedrick loved long walks and so did I. I could walk many miles without any rest.

"Welcome back!" Cedrick cried lively while opening the front door. As I stepped in, I saw Marie coming to us.

"Lucretia, I'm so happy to see you!" she said and gave me a hug.

That was another thing that had changed. Marie had got used to my presence and wasn't afraid anymore.

I liked to look at them. Marie and Cedrick were a wonderful couple. They completed each other; Marie was a live wire Irishwoman who understood Cedrick's adventurous nature and always managed to stop him in time, before he had done something stupid. Cedrick loved his wife's hot temper and wisdom. For some six children would be too much, but Cedrick and Marie said that they would have wanted even more children if only they hadn't been so busy raising the existing ones. It was clear that this couple would be together until death does them part.

Marie's attitude wasn't the only change in Cedrick's house. The house had become more lively – from time to time, but especially in summers, some of Cedrick and Marie's or Cedrick's siblings' grandchildren stayed here. Cedrick's children visited the house very rarely, usually only around Christmas time. None of them lived in Brighton, so Cedrick was truly delighted about every family gathering. At the moment, two teenagers, grandchildren of one of Cedrick's sisters, were here.

Cedrick always presented me as one of the Westmorelands, without any further explanations. No-one ever had any questions because there were so many of us. While other people were around, Cedrick always called me "Luca". He wanted to tell everyone who's returned to the family, but I had begged him not to do that. I knew that my arrival would cause furore: the whole Westmoreland clan would gather at Cedrick's house and stare at me as if I would be a museum piece or a circus monkey and I didn't want it.

I wasn't afraid that someone could recognise me, although there was a picture of me in one of the rooms, among pictures of my parents and brothers. I could stand right under it, but no-one would think that I'm the girl from the painting. Lucretia in the painting was sweet and innocent and had a timid smile. She was sitting in a chair with a large vase of flowers on her left and wore a pale pink dress with a flower pattern. Lucretia who was looking at the picture was tough, strong and a party animal.

From outside the house almost hadn't changed, while the inside had been redecorated a lot. Growing up there I had never realised the true size of it. To me it was simply a nice house with plenty of room for us kids to run around. I knew we had a few apple and pear trees in the orchard and had a lovely garden but it was only when I first visited Cedrick that I saw the true size of my family home for the first time. It was an estate. The house was huge. The "little" orchard occupied a few hectares. The garden was only slightly smaller. The family also owned lots of land nearby.

I came from a merchant family. My great-grandfather had bought this estate in the 18th century from an old but penniless family. They couldn't afford the upkeep of the place anymore and had to sell.

Back then merchants were frowned upon. Old families, even if they were broke, were accepted everywhere whereas my ancestors had to wait for invitations. A family name was all that mattered and The Westmorelands weren't yet posh enough. Luckily, by the time I was born attitudes had changed and I was welcomed in most places.

When my family purchased the estate it was a Georgian house. Later they kept adding to it, mostly useless bric-a-brac, to keep up with the Victorian fashion of putting stuff on any piece of furniture possible. Most of it was gone now.

The interior of the house reflected the different eras and owners. The entrance and stairs still had the dark wooden panels I remembered from my youth. The library looked almost like it did on my father's day but the furniture had to be changed at the turn of the century because the original pieces had started to disintegrate.

Someone had once decided to turn the house into an art deco place but hadn't got any further than the dining room and one of the reception rooms. There was also a 1930s reception room and I even spotted some 1940s utility furniture. Cedrick had no idea how it got there. He reckoned someone must have bought it after the war or exchanged it for something. The family had no need to buy more furniture during the war. No-one lived here full time in the 1940s, Cedrick and his many cousins came and went, mostly to check if the house was still in one piece. It was only in the early 1950s when a family meeting was called to decide what to do with the house. Cedrick was keen to move in and look after it. He wanted to preserve the family history. Also, as he once revealed to me, he never gave up hope that one day we would meet again.

During one of my early visits Cedrick showed me the room that once used to be mine. I recognised it only by the view, no original furniture had remained. It was now a simple guest bedroom decorated in an Edwardian style. Cedrick explained that while my father was still alive this room had a status of a memorial museum – nothing could be changed or thrown out. When father died, Elias and Nickolas started to give away my belongings; their children who were managing the house after them gave away the furniture. Even the piano in the main reception room wasn't mine.

The only thing that indicated that a girl named Lucretia Westmoreland had once lived here was my picture.

"They didn't do that because they wanted to forget you," Cedrick had said. "It was because the presence of your belongings made them very sad."

I was now comfortable with staying overnight and often visited Cedrick and Marie for at least 2-3 days; I usually stayed in one of the bedrooms that had once belonged to my brothers.

xxx

Cedrick had bought a new piece of land and wanted to show it to me. He hadn't yet decided what to do with it and said that in case he wouldn't figure out something else he'd set up a pasture for horses there.

We were walking along the road, talking about this and that, when suddenly I asked:

"Are you afraid of death?"

"Have you been pondering about life and death again? The answer to your question is "no"," Cedrick said in a very sure voice. "I believe that people have a soul, which is immortal. That means that I will always exist – in one form or another."

"Just like I. What a pity that we will be on different sides of eternity."

"Lucretia, don't think about what you can't change. And don't look at me as if I'd be seriously ill. I'm in good health. Besides, I'm only sixty years old. I'll be around for at least a decade or two," he smiled.

"I'll take your word," I said. Cedrick's smile was contagious – I smiled too.

"By the way, here we are," he changed the topic. "So, what do you think?"

We were standing near a big enclosed field. At the moment it was covered with long grass, but the location was good and it was big enough to be used for various purposes.

"I like it. Only I have no idea what to do with it."

"Neither do I," Cedrick sighed. "Apparently I'll set up a pasture for horses here. Or… I'll talk to Marie. Maybe she has some good ideas."

Today's was a short visit and after a couple of hours at Cedrick's I returned to London. Now the place I called home was a split-level flat close to Regent's Park. Truth to be told, the first floor was actually the attic, which we had turned into our bedroom. Byron had bought this flat a few years ago, before he met me, and renovated it. On the ground floor, there was a kitchen, two rooms which we used as living rooms and libraries, and a bathroom. The first floor was occupied by our bedroom only. The house had a sloping roof and skylights. During the day the room had plenty of natural light and a beautiful view, at night we could stargaze.

A bed with a baldachin was placed next to one of the walls. Usually it wasn't made because Byron had a habit to spend most of the day in bed. There was always a tower of books near the bed, which we had taken from our ground floor libraries.

In the middle of the room, there was an easel with empty tubes of paint around it – Byron liked to paint landscapes and, watching him painting, I became interested too. Byron offered me to show how to use brushes and paints and did it with pleasure.

Near the wall on the skylight side we had a record player and a shelf with tons of vinyls: Chuck Berry, Buddy Holly, Elmore James, Muddy Waters, Howlin' Wolf, other blues and rock'n'roll artists... Byron kept his belongings scattered across the whole flat (but, at the same time, he always knew where to find something if such a need appeared) and I had fallen into this habit too.

We didn't have a real wardrobe. There was a big desk in a corner with a pile of clothes on it. Byron usually rummaged there and found something that suited his mood. It was another of Byron's habits I had fallen into. Overall, our bedroom looked like an artist's workshop.

Byron and I met in 1960 at a party. He was a descendant of an old family, his parents could trace their ancestors back to the Middle Ages. Parents had named him after their favourite poet, but Byron himself preferred the poetry of John Keats. Byron had dark blonde, medium length hair and blue eyes. He radiated peace and warmth, which, in addition to his intelligence, was the reason why I fell in love with him. We became a couple in 1961 and married in 1963. For us the marriage wasn't important, but Byron's parents didn't like the fact that we were simply living together and insisted on marriage. The ceremony was very simple. Besides us, only two people participated in it – our friends, who were the wedding witnesses. When the rest of our friends and acquaintances found out about the wedding, they were a bit upset that we hadn't organised a big party for everyone. Byon's parents found out about our marriage one week later when Byron called them and said nothing about the humble ceremony. I guess they were happy that

Byron had informed them about what was going on in his life.

Byron loved beauty: in art, people, nature, architecture... He was a natural born aesthete and called his lifestyle The Big Exploration. Byron wanted to broaden his consciousness and try as much as possible. In order to achieve this goal, he used wanderings, meetings with different people, literature, music, cinema, as well as LSD and mescaline. The only thing that didn't go into the Exploration were women. Since Byron and I got together he stopped paying attention to other women. I, too, had become monogamous.

Byron was in his usual place and was reading a selection of poems by John Keats. I had the impression that soon he'll be able to recite the whole of "Endymion".

Byron didn't know whom I actually was. I think, even if he would, it wouldn't bother him much. He'd simply be curious about my world, but I preferred his and wanted to stay in it.

I walked up to the bed and opened the baldachin.

"Hello," I said.

"Hello."

I sat on the bed and kissed him.

"There's a party at Marcela and Winston's place tonight. Would you like to go?" he asked.

"Sounds interesting. At what time does it start?"

Marcela and Winston were our friends. Their parties gathered a really motley crowd and were always worth attending.

"What do you think of John Keats poetry?" Jane asked. I was at the party and we had just met.

"His poetry is very beautiful, however, my favourite poet from the Romantic era is Percy Shelley," I replied.

I liked my new acquaintances – all of them were well-educated young people with a wide range of interests, willing to explore the world and live a life, full of impressions and events. They thought about the future, but respected the 19th century. I could tell them a lot, however, I had to be careful and remember not to fall into details.

"Yes, mine too. Also, I like William Blake and William Wordsworth. And Byron of course."

"Oh, yes. Byron…" I said ambiguously and smiled.

My Byron was somewhere near and was participating in a lively discussion about art.

"I don't think that a nail, driven into a wall, can be called a piece of art. In that case, my whole house is a piece of art," he said.

"But Byron, your house *is* a piece of art," someone replied to his remark.

"Byron, this is called the modern art," Winston, the starter of the discussion, objected.

"If that is modernism, I'll better stay old fashioned."

Winston sighed and shook his head as if he'd be saying "no". Winston preferred cubism, dadaism and anything abstract.

"I think that art at least partly should reflect the effort that was put in it. When we view Renaissance paintings, we know that they weren't made in an hour. They were painted for months, sometimes even for years. Besides, they're full of nuances that reveal gradually."

"In that case – what do you think of cubism and surrealism?"

"I prefer impressionism."

"But how can art develop if artists don't search for new directions?"

"I'm not against the development of art, not at all. I'm just saying that not everyone can be an artist and not everything that is created is art."

"While listening to you I start to think that you were born a century too late."

"Maybe I was."

Our circuit could be divided in two groups: the futurists and those who preferred the past. The first ones were enthusiastic about each new art direction and shape and tried to imagine how the world would look in the year 2000, while the latter preferred aesthetics of previous centuries. Byron, of course, belonged to the past lovers, while I was somewhere in the middle.

xxx

"Parents..." Byron sighed as he hung up the phone.

"What did they say this time?" I asked in a sympathetic voice.

"They mind that I spend my days in idleness away from them. They'd like me to idle at their house," he said ironically.

Byron's parents didn't like his lifestyle at all. They'd prefer if Byron would listen to their advice on how to live and, just like his three brothers, would have a "decent and regular" life, which they could follow. Byron's parents didn't like even his looks – his favourite clothes were beige trousers,

Hessian boots and replicas of shirts from different decades of the 19th century.

If only Byron's parents would know about their son's experiments with drugs and marriage with a vampire... They'd immediately take him away from me.

At the moment we were staying in one of Byron's country pads. A few days ago, we had a party here. The last guests had left yesterday and the house wasn't cleaned yet. It looked like after a hurricane. The garden didn't look better – it was full of arrows and foils. In places like this I could turn to two of my old hobbies again: fencing and archery. Byron and our friends were also interested in fencing, so quite often impromptu duels were held. I have to admit: I had made Byron a very strong antagonist.

So far, Byron didn't consider cleaning important – he airily stepped over all the litter that was on the floor and went straight to the garden to paint.

I went outside and watched him painting, when suddenly sadness took me over. Right now, we are happily together, but a few years will pass and we would have to break up. There was no other way. What a pity. If there was someone with whom I'd like to stay together, it was Byron. Unfortunately, eternity was a too long period of time and I couldn't take him there with me.

I enjoyed vampire life, but sometimes, for instance, in moments like this, I was craving to be a human. As a vampire I had immortality and eternal youth, enormous endurance and I was immune against all diseases. I had a wide range of interests, including medicine, and once, after reading a book about various illnesses, I thought – how great that it doesn't apply to me anymore. I could do dangerous things without thinking about the consequences. However, human life meant a certain cycle: youth, maturity, age, human life was so precious because it could end any moment. Many things could be experienced only once in a lifetime and it made everything special. Me, I could postpone everything because I had plenty of time.

Humans could believe in such things as eternal love. Vampires knew that it didn't exist. As a human I could join Byron in his wanderings to Morocco and other countries with hot climates. As a vampire I couldn't do that. Already + 80 °F was too hot for me.

As a human I could be with Byron until the last breath – his or mine.

It was strange that such thoughts had come into my mind now. I had Cedrick and now Byron and I should be happy and not be thinking about life and death again. But maybe everything was quite logical? In the past I lived only for myself, now I had two people that were close to me, but whom I'd lose someday.

Byron was painting a scenery. When the picture was half-finished, he stopped painting for a moment and took a look at his work.

"Luca, what do you think of it?" Byron asked as he turned to me.

"I think that the proportions of the trees in the foreground need to be retouched, otherwise it's very good," I said. "By the way, you were so into the painting process. How did you notice my presence?"

"Luca, it's impossible not to notice your presence," Byron said and gave me one of his beautiful smiles.

After a few days in the countryside we returned to London.

"Are we going out tonight?" I asked.

"Yes. To a concert."

"Who's playing?"

"The Rolling Stones."

"Never heard of them. What do they play?"

"Rock, blues, a lot of covers. Amazing band – they generate more energy than a nuclear power plant! They'll get into the history, you'll see." Byron's voice was full of admiration.

The Rolling Stones gig was fantastic. Their music and behaviour on stage made people lose their mind. The concert ended in a chaos and intervention of the police. When we got out on the street I noticed that Byron's shirt is torn and my dress is damaged. We had the same thoughts about the concert.

"That was fantastic! I definitely want to see them again!" Byron said.

Embraced, we were walking along the pavement.

"Wait," I said and stopped. "I left my car on the opposite side of the street."

"I know, but the night is so beautiful and I'd like to have a walk. You can come after your car tomorrow; nothing will happen to it."

I agreed. In fact, even if something would happen to the car, I wouldn't care. I could afford to buy myself another Rolls Royce. Or two.

xxx

"Happy anniversary," Byron said as I opened my eyes.

Byron was lying next to me, but he was fully dressed which meant that he's been awake for a while.

It was March 31, our first wedding anniversary. I was a bit surprised – I had thought that Byron would ignore this date. After all, the only reason why we had married was the parental pressure. We didn't even wear wedding rings.

Byron took a small box out of his trousers and gave it to me. I opened it and saw a massive silver ring with a huge amethyst.

"It was made to order especially for you."

"Thank you. It is wonderful."

I took the ring out of the box and put it on my forefinger.

"Are we going to celebrate tonight?"

Byron shrugged his shoulders.

"I don't know. We can go and listen to some jazz bands if you like."

"All right. You choose the venue," I said. Then I leaned towards him and we kissed.

xxx

"Have you read Borges?" Ashley asked. He was a new character in London and was currently fighting for a place in it by organising one party after another.

"Yes. Borges is one of my favourite authors."

"Fantastic writer. His works are timeless. I read stories written in the 1920s and I have a feeling that they were written now. Those who will read them after ten, twenty years will feel the same."

"Exactly my thoughts."

Ashley had gathered a big crowd: Winston and Marcela were here too, as well as a bunch of unknown people. Chuck Berry's music was playing and, to all appearances, the party was successful.

A little way from us a discussion about who actually started rock'n'roll was held. There were several assumptions, but everyone was lacking arguments.

Marcela go tired of it and exclaimed:

"Whatever! It's not important who started rock'n'roll, the fact that it exists is what matters!"

These words were followed by loud applause and whistling.

I went to get myself a drink and made whiskey with soda. It wasn't the only non-vampire thing in my life – living in this circuit, I had tried LSD and hashish. I was curious to see if my body would react to them. It did: LSD caused unpleasant hallucinations, while hashish raised my spirits. Sometimes I wondered what would happen if I'd meet a vampire explorer – he or she would probably be shocked about my lifestyle.

"You're very lucky that you have such a man as Byron," Cheryl, one of my acquaintances, said. She had just come to the drinks table and was pouring punch in her glass.

I heard envy in her voice. It wasn't anything new to me – there were many women in London who were mourning the fact that Byron is taken.

"Yes," I agreed. "I'm really lucky. He's special."

"But..." Cheryl asked. "Sometimes Byron can be so self-contained and people don't know how to treat him. Doesn't it bother you?"

"No. Byron requests a lot of privacy for himself, but he allows other people to do the same. It's very easy to be with him."

I wasn't exaggerating. We really were a perfect couple. Byron didn't try to break into my territory, I didn't try to break into his. He never argued because we didn't have a reason for that. We understood each other from half-a-word. Quite often, we didn't need words at all.

xxx

I came home after a three-day party. Byron wasn't there. To all appearances, he hadn't been here for a while. I usually let him know about my absence, while Byron had the habit to disappear without a warning.

I went to the kitchen and opened the fridge. The only food there was a half-empty bottle of milk. I noticed an empty bread packaging and an empty can of tuna lying on the table. Lack of food was normal in our place – the fridge was filled only when we were preparing for parties. Byron mostly ate out. Come to think of it, during these three years I had seen him eating only a few times. What was his usual food? If I wouldn't know for sure that Byron is a human, I'd start to think that he, too, had a dark secret.

In other circumstances I'd find that annoying, but in my case Byron's absence was an opportunity to have the place for myself and be a vampire. It was especially handy if Byron wasn't here when I went hunting. Then I didn't have to spend ages in the bathroom cleaning my teeth in order to hide the taste of blood in my breath.

One thing I really liked in Byron was that while being mysterious himself, he allowed others, too, to be mysterious. However, sometimes his mysteriousness reached unbelievable extents. For instance, I didn't know Byron's age until our wedding day. Now I know that he was born on March 20, 1938 and currently was 26 years old. Byron didn't like to celebrate his birthday, so we simply spent the evening at a local blues club.

After a few days on my own I became bored and went to Brighton.

This time I walked to Cedrick's house alone – during our phone call, he had apologised that he couldn't meet me at the station. He had to be at the house until late afternoon because of ongoing construction works.

I opened the front door and stepped in. Today the house resembled an ant-heap, workers were walking back and forth. Initially it was Cedrick's idea, he wanted to make some improvements, get rid of collapsing pieces of furniture and carry out routine maintenance work. Marie had joined in, deciding that she wanted to reshape the garden, and hired a landscape architect who was walking across the yard with his assistants planning how and where to plant trees and flowers. Loud music could be heard from upstairs – one of Cedrick's elder sisters had sent her 16-year-old grandson Emil to stay here for awhile.

"Lucretia! You're already here!" Cedrick exclaimed when I came into the hallway. He was giving instructions to one of the workers. "How pleasant to see you! I'm desperate to escape from this madhouse!"

"You started this madhouse!" Marie shouted. She had just come out of the kitchen – her apron was covered in flour.

"And you continued it!" Cedrick shouted back.

"Hello, Lucretia! It's crazy here at the moment. Besides, it's lunch time... I need to call everyone to the table," Marie said and went out to the garden to invite the landscapers to have a meal.

By using the lunch break, Cedrick sneaked out of the house and we went on a short walk. I knew that something had happened – Cedrick was anxious.

"Will you share your concern with me?"

Cedrick sighed.

"My fourteen-year-old granddaughter is pregnant."

"What are you going to do?"

"Support her, what else. The Westmorelands help each other no matter what," he said.

Of course, Cedrick didn't like the situation but he couldn't imagine acting differently.

It was the most characteristic quality of my family – mutual support. Everyone was raised to help others. If my father had helped me to start a vampire life, then conscience didn't allow others to turn their back on someone when something less serious happened. Sure, the Westmorelands had inner conflicts and arguments, but when it was about the interests of the family as a whole, everyone could forget their grievances at least for a moment and work together. This is why the family was so strong.

I had planned to stay in Brighton for two days when a force majeure occured.

It was evening and Cedrick and I were sitting in the living room, discussing what came first – the chicken or the egg, when one of his neighbours arrived to tell us about an incident he considered to be important.

"Several animals, mostly sheep, were bitten to death in the last few days. What is strange, none of them is torn and everyone was bit in the neck. No-one knows how that happened. It's probably some wild animal."

Cedrick paled. I'd pale too if I could. We looked at each other – we had no doubts who the "animal" was. A vampire had appeared in the neighbourhood.

As soon as the neighbour had left, Cedrick asked me:

"Lucretia, could you stay for a few extra days?"

"Of course. But I'll need your help. Firstly, warn everyone not to stay outside after eight pm or, in the worst case, not to stay outside alone."

At least ten people were staying in the house at the moment: Cedrick, Marie, Emil and some of the workers.

"I'll need a reason for such a warning."

"Tell them that there's a suspicion about a wild beast or other nonsense like that…"

"What about Marie?"

"It will be better if we do not tell her anything at this point."

"She's witty, she'll soon realise that there's something in the wind."

"I know. And then she'll reproach us for not saying anything to her," I grinned.

"What shall we do?"

"I'll guard the yard, while you keep your eyes and ears open. It's not very likely that the vampire has originated from another vampire. Probably someone has turned into a vampire after death. If you could get a list of persons who have recently died… We could try to figure who it is."

He nodded.

"I'll try. It's very important to act inconspicuously. The locals haven't forgotten the old legends and it doesn't require much to make everyone get their pitchforks out."

"I know. And I really wouldn't like it to happen. I'm the only one who can face the vampire without risking my life."

"And what do you plan to do?"

"I don't know. It depends on the situation."

On the next day Cedrick gave me a list of everyone who had died during the previous month. I crossed out everyone who was older than 30 or had died in an accident as they were less likely to transform. In the end, I had narrowed it down to six people: Mary Farrow, 26 years, died of tuberculosis; William Stanforce, 27 years, died of a tumour; Emily Huntington, 22 years, died of congenital heart disease;

Dolly Sanders, 28 years, died of leukaemia; Seth Hoxton, 26 years, died of a tumour; Lesley Smith, 25 years, died of liver disease. Any of them could be the vampire.

I settled in the living room, near the window, and kept a constant eye on the yard.

I suspected that it's only a question of time until locals would realise what is happening and, armed with stakes and other weapons, will comb local forests and keep watch on their houses. I had one big advantage – I had no trouble being up at night. Nothing could distract me and I didn't need any rest. Besides, I had excellent night vision.

I didn't have a plan – I was simply protecting my family. Vampires could start with animal blood, but later they switched to human blood. I knew it from my own experience.

A few days passed. The vampire showed up in the neighbourhood again, but not in our house. It was the evening and I was in my "post", talking to Cedrick, keeping an eye to the yard. There was no-one there and everything seemed to be alright, however, I was feeling uneasy. I looked at the yard again, trying to see anything suspicious. Cedrick noticed it.

"The vampire is here?"

"I don't know," I replied. "I can't see anyone, but my gut feeling is saying that something is about to happen."

I stood up and went to the window. Suddenly I saw movement. Emil appeared from nowhere and crossed the yard.

"Emil is there," I said.

"Emil?! I told him not to leave the house in the evenings!" Cedrick exclaimed in an angry voice and went to the door. "I'm gonna go after him."

My eyes followed Emil and I didn't notice the moment when a silhouette slid out of bushes. It quickly approached Emil and grabbed him.

I threw open the window and jumped out of it.

"Get your damn fangs off him now!" I shouted, running to Emil.

The vampire was female. As she heard my voice, she lifted up her head and I could see Emil's neck. She had already bitten him, leaving two small bloody wounds.

I grabbed the vampire and threw her at least twenty feet back. Cedrick had jumped out of the window too and rushed to Emil.

Not taking my eyes off the vampire, I said to Cedrick:

"Take him indoors."

My look was full of fury and I slightly opened my lips, showing teeth with barely visible razor blade sharp fangs. When my antagonist realised that I'm a vampire too, she decided to flee.

Within a few seconds she had already run to the flint wall and climbed over it. I had never seen a vampire who could move so fast. I had to put on the pace if I didn't want to lose her from the sight.

I climbed over the wall too. The distance between me and the vampire now was at least a hundred yards. There was a forest path behind Cedrick's house that led to a field.

When I had run through the forest, I realised I'd lost her. The field was huge and spear-grass was reaching my chest.

There was another forest on the opposite side of the field, but I didn't think that she had managed to get so far. Spear-grass didn't move, which meant that she had hidden somewhere near.

"Although you just tried to suck my relative's blood, I won't do anything bad to you," I said. Nothing happened. "I won't leave until you come in sight."

A little way from me the spear-grass moved and the vampire stood up. She looked completely different now. Puzzled. Scared. She was very young, maybe in her early twenties.

"What's your name?"

"Emily."

"Have you attacked a human before this night?"

"No."

"Unfortunately, that is inevitable."

"I'm so confused... Just three weeks ago I was in hospital, close to death, but then I found myself in a cemetery, looking at my own grave... In childhood I often heard legends about vampires and now I've become one of them..."

These words made me look at Emily with brand new eyes.

"Your story reminds me so much of my own story..." I said as I sat on the ground. Emily sat too. "Same events, same feelings... Puzzlement, confusion and no clue about what to do next."

She looked at me with brand new eyes too.

"You are Lucy Westmoreland!"

"I *was* Lucy Westmoreland," I corrected.

"But how… Your grave was burst open once and your ashes were found there…"

"I don't want to get into details… What I can tell you is that my family loved me so much that they were ready to accept me as a vampire and helped me to escape."

"Tell me… How it is… To be a vampire…"

"The beginning is very difficult. Nothing is the same anymore. You're forced to leave behind everything that used to be your life, to leave your relatives and run. After that… Everything is up to you: whether or not you'll be able to adapt."

Silence fell. I don't know for how long we would have stayed there if both of us hadn't heard a noise. I pricked my ears up. Human voices and heavy footsteps.

"Keep up with us! If the vampire is somewhere near, it's dangerous to fall behind!" a man said.

"The locals!" I exclaimed.

Emily looked terrified.

"If you want to live, run and never come back!" I said.

Emily sprang to her feet and like lightning crossed the field. I ran back to the forest. Hiding behind the trees, I tried to see a silhouette. The locals were about sixty yards from me. I counted twelve people.

They all were armed with rifles, stakes and even dung-forks and were moving very quickly.

"Two days ago, the vampire was seen in this area. Maybe he or she will show up again."

Young vampires had to hunt more often, two to three times a week. Later the need for blood reduced and it was enough to hunt four to six times a month.

The local vampire hunters went to the field. Emily probably was already quite far from here. I didn't want the hunters to notice me, but neither did I want to linger here in the forest, so I was inching away, moving almost without a sound. When I was far enough from them, I started to run and, in a minute, I was on the path near Cedrick's house. There was no-one around, however, I decided to enter the yard through the fence, not by climbing over the wall.

I went back to the house. Emil was in his room, which used to be Elias's room once, and Cedrick was with him. Marie, as it turned out, had fallen asleep while watching TV and knew nothing about what had happened. However, tomorrow we'd have to tell her everything. Luckily, all workers had a day off today and had gone to the pub, so there were no witnesses of the incident.

"Emil, you were told not to leave the house in the evening," I said. Although my voice sounded strict, my facial expression wasn't harsh.

"Cedrick already told me off. Everything ended up fine, right? Besides, I'll have something to remember for my whole life!"

I shook my head.

"Typically Westmoreland – no matter what happens in life, it will be considered as exciting!"

We all laughed.

"You're aunt Lucretia, aren't you?" Emil suddenly said.

"Did you realise that yourself or did Cedrick tell you?"

"I realised it. When you ran after her, I understood that you're a vampire too. Why should a vampire protect me against another vampire? There's only one explanation: you're family. But, in fact, I knew from the beginning that there's something odd about you... Your and uncle's relationship... I had a feeling all the time that you know each other for many years."

"You're right," Cedrick said. "Lucretia and I first met each other more than thirty years ago."

Emil livened up – it was obvious that we wanted to know more.

"Luca, vampire's bite isn't dangerous, is it?" Cedrick asked.

"No. Transformation happens only if one has drunk vampire's blood. Only a bite without serious loss of blood isn't dangerous."

Next afternoon I went back to London. Emil was so excited that he had met aunt Lucretia that he didn't want to let me go. Cedrick and I stayed in Emil's room until the dawn when tiredness took him over and Emil finally fell asleep. Before my departure I made him promise that he wouldn't tell anyone about me. Emil seemed very upset, however, he made the promise. I slightly softened and allowed him to share the story – but only after many years, to his children and grandchildren.

When I came home and entered the flat, I stopped for a moment and listened. Complete silence. That could mean both: that Byron was at home and that he was out. I went upstairs to our bedroom and opened the door slowly. Byron was sitting on the bed, reading a selection of English Romantic poetry.

"Hello," I said.

"Hello."

Byron usually didn't ask where I had been and what I'd done, even if I came home after more than a week's absence. It was another of his qualities I liked.

I sat next to him and rested my head on his shoulder. Byron put aside the book and caressed my face.

"Something is pressing you, isn't it?" he asked. Although Byron showed his own emotions quite rarely, he felt the mood of others very well.

"A bit. I was thinking about life and how things can suddenly change. Why does everything happen the way it happens and not in any other way?"

"I've thought about it too and never found an answer. I can only tell you that life is an amazing process. We pay for our mistakes and become awarded for right decisions.

Sometimes it doesn't matter where life throws you. What matters is how you deal with it."

I was thinking about Emily a lot on my way back. What will happen to her?

"Would you like to tell me what you are thinking of?"

"No, I've already thought enough about it. I want to purify my mind a bit. How about some poetry?"

Byron didn't even open the book – he could recite many poems from memory. Sitting next to him and listening to his voice, I understood one more time how attached I've become to him. I didn't know how many years together we have left, but I knew that this will be the time I'd always remember with warmth and love. But for now… I closed my eyes and smiled.

Revelry

London, 1829

The brightly lit ballroom was filled with music. The room was crowded, the dance floor was full of waltzing guests, however, there were more people sitting at the table, with a generous amount of food and drink in front of them. Small talk, latest gossip, closing of deals and tales about adventures and heroic deeds that were spun out of thin air – tonight's reception wasn't different from any other.

I had just come into the room and for a moment I watched everything from aside. Nothing had changed over the years: London's high society still consisted of hypocrites, libertines, liars, easy life seekers, people whose lives were destroyed by the decisions of others or those who had tried to escape from their surroundings, but failed, day-dreamers, old maids and naive ladies who were foolishly left without supervision by their husbands who, because of the age difference, were old enough to be their father. Luckily, from time to time someone who was genuinely interesting wandered in. Although I never accepted any other truth but mine, I liked to listen to different opinions. One of such persons was Lord Grishill, but tonight I didn't see him here. Probably he was still mad at me because our last conversation had ended with an argument. I guess I'd have to send him a little gift as a sign of a conciliation offer.

Despite tonight's boring guest list, I knew that there are at least eleven like minded individuals at this reception – other occupants of this house.

"Count Rokosovski!" I heard someone calling my name.

It was an old lady who mistakenly thought that she was still in the spotlight. The only reason why I knew her name was because she was unbelievably annoying.

"Lady Godridge!" I said and pursed my lips.

"Count Rokosovski, how pleasant it is to be in your house again! The reception, as usual, is splendid!" she was chatting, at the same time trying to embrace me. Knowing how difficult it is to get rid of her, I managed to grab her hands.

"Everything is wonderful: the food, the music, the atmosphere. How do you do that?"

"That's not only my credit."

"Indeed. This reception is the result of joint effort," Arifay's voice sounded next to us. "Yuri, do you have a moment?"

"Excuse me, Lady Godridge. I'll be back soon."

She looked disappointed - evidently, I wasn't the only one who had got rid of her company this evening.

"Did you really have something to discuss with me or you just decided to rescue me?" I asked as soon as the doors of the ballroom had closed behind us.

"I came to your rescue. That old hag is a real meddler. She belongs to the kind of people who are annoying both sober and drunk."

"Remind me – why do we keep sending invitations to her?"

"I have no idea. Actually, it would be an appropriate time to show her that she is way past her prime."

"Good idea. So, from now on we will not invite her anymore."

"Well, I'm not saying that a sixty-year-old can't go out anymore. After all.. You and I are way older yet we're still charming."

We both laughed.

"Did you save anyone else from Lady Godridge's company tonight?"

"Yes. Konstantin is also rambling around."

"I'll go and find him."

"And I shall rejoin the reception," Arifay said.

He went back to the ballroom, while I went upstairs to the first floor. Konstantin was in his room, this time – alone. He was sitting on the window-sill, looking out of the window.

"Are you preferring solitude tonight?" I asked.

"Temporary. Some idiots made it impossible to stay downstairs."

Konstantin was the "youngest" inhabitant of the house – he arrived here one year ago from St. Petersburg - and fitted in perfectly. He was an adventurer, a celebrator of life, a ladies' man, a great storyteller and also a great liar.

"Your visit has a purpose, right?"

"Yes. Do you remember Lady Kelsworth? You had an affair with her recently."

"Of course I do. It's impossible to forget a woman like that – young, charming, but destined to a boring life with her husband who is as interesting as a stone block."

"You see, the Lady got very excited and told her friends about the affair. Be careful, these revelations shouldn't reach her husband's ears. Old Kelsworth can be very nasty when angry."

"You could search the entire world and wouldn't find a woman who hasn't got imperfections, because all of them have at least one…" Konstantin sighed. "So, the Lady likes to share her private things with others? I'll have to talk to her..."

The day after a reception always started with cleaning. We hired servants only for receptions, cleaning was always done by us. There was an agreement between us – everyone takes part in it. It was a way to show that we were all equal and respected each other.

When I went downstairs and entered the ballroom, I saw that I was not the first one there. Sibyl, Melisa and Beatrice were already clearing the tables.

"Good afternoon, Yuri! You haven't missed anything, we just started a bit earlier," Beatrice said.

"Yes, I had a weird insomnia today and there's plenty to do here," Melisa explained.

"Have you already decided who's doing what?" I asked.

"No. At the moment we need to throw away leftovers, then someone must clean the ballroom and wash the dishes," Sibyl said.

"Has anyone checked the house?"

It was one of the most important things to do. Sometimes we happened to find sleeping guests in the rooms, the basement or even out in the garden. Of course, we called a carriage, farewelled and, as soon as they had left, dropped our masks and stopped pretending to be humans.

"Yes. The air is clean. There no-one else but us in the house," Melisa replied.

"Amazing! What a mess!" Arifay said as he came into the room. "Please remind me: why are we doing this?"

"Because we're a bunch of bored vampires," I replied. "Besides, where else will we have the opportunity to see such a circus?"

Arifay grinned and joined us.

"By the way, when is the next reception?" he asked.

"In three days," Melisa said.

"What about food reserves?" I asked.

"Almost finished. Marisa and Francis will go to the market tomorrow," Beatrice said.

Marisa and Francis were the only vampire couple in the house and virtually inseparable. I think they even hunted together.

"Remind them to buy Barnaby's wine," Melisa shouted from the opposite corner of the room.

Arifay frowned.

"Barnaby's wine? I thought we had five bottles left."

"We had, until Lord McGray crawled into the basement and drank them all."

"Five bottles in one go? What a boozer!" he exclaimed.

"Five bottles in one night? So, he was the one who vomited in the basement!" Konstantin's voice sounded behind us. "And I had to clean it! I'll remember that. The next time we play cards together he will owe me even his underwear by the end of the night!"

No-one doubted that Konstantin would indeed do it - he was one of the best players in town, although the rest of us were quite good, too.

After Konstantin had expressed his wrath, he rolled up his sleeves and joined in. One after another the others appeared and in less than an hour everything was done.

xxx

"Good evening everyone!" Konstantin shouted.

He was on the first floor, near the stairs, and had just gained everyone's attention. He was impeccably dressed, with a flower in the buttonhole, "carelessly" tied neckerchief and he was smiling. Konstantin was holding a bottle of wine in one hand and two glasses in the other. He jumped on the banisters and slid down to the ground floor, where the guests of tonight's reception had just started to arrive, and landed airily. In the next moment he was already approaching a young woman.

"My dear Isabella, how pleasant it is to see your face again!"

Of course, he didn't actually mean it.

He freed up one of his hands so that he could kiss Miss Isabella's hand. This theatrical behaviour made her blush. I had seen this happening so many times before. In a few months, if not weeks, time Konstantin will be saying compliments and showing attention to someone else.

Konstantin gave her another beautiful smile and invited her to go to the ballroom. Another celebration of hypocrisy was about to start.

"Lord Grishill is still resentful," Francis said as he sat next to me.

"Really?" I asked sceptically. At least two months had passed since our discussion. "In that case, he's taking everything to heart too much."

"He didn't like your critique of his views of political processes in Western Europe in the eighteenth century."

"I know. However, my arguments were much more precise than his. Unlike Lord Grishill, I was talking about things I had partly experienced myself."

"Of course, but you can't say that to him. Actually, you could have spoken in a more polite manner," Francis uttered.

"Never!" I was adamant. "I cannot stand if people try to avoid a disagreement. If you have a discussion without a row you're not doing it properly!"

Tonight's reception turned out to be much more interesting for me than the previous one. Already at the beginning of it, when I was examining the guests, I knew that the evening wouldn't be wasted.

"Have you heard about the tragic happening when two young men died because of love? Both fell in love with the same girl and were ready to fight for her heart, so they became rivals. The rivalry ended with a duel where both of them died," Lady Douglas said. Her voice was full of romantic enthusiasm and sentiment.

We were sitting at the table and besides me and Lady Douglas there were a few more people here.

"Tragic indeed," I said. "Apparently the youngsters didn't know such a mathematical operation as division."

"Count Rokosovski! Shame on you!" she exclaimed indignantly.

"I just said my thoughts."

"You're disgusting."

"Yes, I am, but at least I'm sincere."

Moments like this made the hassle of organising receptions worth it.

I had just stopped chatting to someone, when Beatrice came to me. She had a few grapes in her hand and was pretending to eat them. No-one would suspect that she didn't feel their taste and that actually this kind of food was harmful to her.

Beatrice pressed her back against mine.

"Are you searching for a company for this evening?" I asked.

"I guess so," she said thoughtfully.

"Are you eyeing anyone?"

"Yes, that charming young man," she said and pointed at a man near us.

"Oh, young Cheltham. Good choice. But bear in mind that looks can be deceitful. He looks shy, but actually he spends more nights in brothels and bars than at home."

"Excellent." Beatrice smiled. "It will save me some time."

"That's the biggest advantage of an angel's face – you can do devilish things and no-one will suspect you."

Beatrice laughed in a hollow voice.

"Speaking about an angel's face..." she said. "Look there."

She pointed at the McAndrews family: Mr McAndrews, his wife and their teenage daughter. They were talking to a lady and her son at the moment. The McAndrews had decided that it is time for their daughter to get married and were looking for a suitable groom.

"Every time I look at them, I have the impression that they are trying to get rid of that girl," she sneered. "There are rumours that she is pregnant."

"In that case they don't have much time left," I smirked.

xxx

"Have you heard about the incident that happened at Lady Rantley's house last week?" Sir Harris asked.

"Sort of," Sir Bromley replied. "But your tone makes me think that you're very well informed."

"You're right. Can you imagine: robbers broke in there at night! Lady Rantley woke up from the noise they were making and went downstairs to see what was happening. She caught them putting her silverware into bags. She wanted to scream to wake up the servants, but one of the robbers took a candlestick and hit the poor lady in the head.

It was pure luck that she stayed alive!" Sir Harris was infuriated.

"Shocking," Sir Bromley said. "I understand that one can be attacked on the street, but in one's own house..."

"Burglars and silverware – that's classic," I said.

"Count Rokosovski, how can you be so cynical?"

"Easily: if one wants to live in London, this is something that needs to be taken into account. One can never feel safe here: not on the street, not at home."

"That's because the penal system is not harsh enough!" Sir Harris exclaimed.

Not harsh enough? Was he really considering such punishments as hanging, drawing and quartering and pouring hot iron down one's throat being gentle punishments? Unless, of course, Sir Harris was a sadist the world hadn't seen yet.

"I'm for the severity of punishment and public punishment," he said.

"That works only if it happens rarely. Only then it has the right effect," I objected. "If there's too much violence and it's always in front of one's eyes, people get used to it and the idea loses all sense. For instance, the public cutting off of a pickpocket's arm has become a form of entertainment, like street theatre. Do you know what is happening in the crowd? While people are watching how a pickpocket loses his arm, pickpockets who haven't been caught yet empty pockets of the audience."

After I had said that I looked straight into Sir Harris' eyes. He had nothing to say.

Of course, discussions, arguments and gossip weren't my only entertainment during receptions. When I came out of my room, I saw that Arifay was in the corridor. He had leaned against the wall and smiled as he saw me.

"Yuri, it's the third time this evening. You're insatiable."

"Actually no. But what can I do if I've literally been dragged into the bedroom? How would it look if I'd say "no"?"

"Since when do you care about what others say?"

"I don't. I'm talking about how I would look in my own eyes. It's stupid to reject something that falls right into your arms."

Arifay passed me a bottle of wine. I sipped a bit and immediately spat the wine out onto the floor. It was part of our theatre, otherwise it would be difficult to explain how it's possible that we drink wine so often but have no alcohol in our breath.

"I think I'll go downstairs," I said. "There are a few people there I haven't upset yet."

As I returned, an elderly lady approached me. She and her company – a bunch of coffin-dodgers – were talking about the circle of life, paying great attention to youth. It wasn't surprising that they spoke to me. Many people in London were interested in how I had managed to retain my good looks.

"How old are you now? the lady asked.

"I'm thirty-eight."

"So, you were twenty-six when you arrived. You haven't changed at all since then."

"I have, but only a little."

"What is your secret?"

"I never worry. Also, I don't drink much alcohol. Nothing damages the face more than hasty decisions made while being drunk."

They laughed.

"Yes, that's a good method. However, it won't work for me," one of the men said. "I'd give a lot to get my youth back and never lose it."

Upon hearing these words, I decided to tell them some truth.

"Why? Eternal youth is quite a useless thing. What is youth? Time full of foolish enthusiasm and wrong decisions. Maturity – that is what I consider to be a value. Young face, complemented by a mature mind – that's the ideal to achieve."

This conversation made me think of things I didn't want to discuss with anyone, so I left the room. Twelve years... Twelve years of my life had passed in this house. When I bought it, I thought I'd stay here for five, maybe eight years, but things worked out differently. I liked this place and I wasn't hurrying to leave it. The house looked the same as on the day I bought it, the only thing that had changed was its inhabitants.

For a human such period of time, spent in one place, wasn't much, but for a vampire it was a lot. Arifay and Beatrice kept reminding me that I've been in London for too long and it's time to leave. I couldn't object anymore and, unwillingly, had allowed Arifay to sell the house.

xxx

"Are there any news from Vincent?" Beatrice asked.

She enquired about him from time to time.

"No. The last time I met him was some six months ago. I've sent several letters to him, but he hasn't replied. The only thing I know is that in one moment he may be seen at almost every reception, then he disappears for months."

All three of us were in the drawing room. Another day had started in our house. We had no receptions planned this week, so the house was quite quiet and everyone was minding their own business.

"Poor boy. Everything was going so well..." Arifay said sadly.

"... until he married Elisa," I finished the thought.

"That was his fatal mistake. Vincent will never recover from that."

"He was such a sweetie… If he would have been with me, nothing like that would have happened," Beatrice said as she was playing with her hair.

"Beatrice, let me remind you that there was time when you couldn't stand Vincent."

"So did you," she snapped back.

"In the beginning, no-one liked Vincent," Arifay reminded us.

"And there was a reason for that! A vampire from the gutter who suddenly arrives at our house!" I said.

"Who, though, turned out to be a charming and intelligent young man," Arifay reminded this fact too.

"And that's why I regret what happened to him," I said.

Beatrice sighed.

"It's sad that Vincent avoids us."

xxx

Receptions had become such a natural part of our life that the longest period we could bear without them was one month. Of course, they cost us a lot of money because humans, unlike us, needed food and drink, but we didn't care about that. Each of us had enough money to party for decades.

I was going to the basement to get more wine when I saw Arifay coming out of there, followed by a young lady. Her cheeks were suspiciously red and the dress – slightly crumpled. As she saw me, she immediately hung her head - apparently, she thought that I hadn't noticed her face – and rushed away.

"I'm pleased to see that you're not as passionless as I had thought."

"I know, I know... Everyone perceives me as a shy intellectual, pure and innocent," Arifay's voice was full of sarcasm. "But the truth is, I like entertainment too. After all, there are twenty-four hours in a day. Eight of them I spend asleep, the remaining sixteen must be filled with something."

In the last few years Arifay had become more and more cynical. He wasn't that Arifay whom I met fifteen years ago anymore. Back then he was a quiet man with a sad look who never told anything about himself, but often asked questions about the meaning of life, the changing nature of feelings and so on. I could see that he carried a lot of pain inside him, however, I never tried to question him. One evening Arifay told me everything: how he had given up his human life because of love and how badly it had ended. It turned out that there was no such thing as eternal love, there was only eternal life which now had lost any meaning. Arifay never spoke about it anymore and I could only guess if the changes in his personality were real or it was just a mask.

When I returned to the ballroom, a pleasant surprise was waiting for me.

"Count Rokosovski! Good evening!"

"Good evening, Oliver! Is it only my imagination or you really weren't here half an hour ago?"

"I've just arrived," he explained.

Oliver appeared in this circuit quite recently. He was a young aristocrat who hadn't been corrupted by life and people yet. Oliver's views were full of naivety and idealism and it seemed that he had no idea what kind of world he was living in. That is what made me notice him. It turned out that Oliver, unlike many others, wasn't willing to settle down as soon as possible and make his life boring and predictable. Quite the reverse: Oliver wanted to leave England and travel around Africa, India and South America. He believed that people there lived differently and that he would experience things that could not be found anywhere else. Oliver tried to be as open-minded as he could and never interrupted me even if he disagreed with me. Because of all that, I was always happy to meet him. Oliver, too, liked my company, although sometimes it wasn't easy – assuming that I may be a bad influence, people tried to "save" him from me. Tonight wasn't an exception. We had just started a conversation when some lady came to us and, naming a childish reason, literally pulled Oliver away.

Unfortunately, those people didn't know one very important thing – Oliver didn't want to be saved. Less than twenty minutes later he was in front of me again.

"Once again, people advised to beware of you," he said.

"I hear it all the time - that I'm mad, bad and dangerous to know, but can anyone actually recall the last time when I have corrupted someone?" It was a rhetorical question. "I presume that you don't like it if someone is trying to teach you, nevertheless, I'll give you advice. Avoid people who seem to be exhibiting their high moral standards and who throw stones at someone because of a tiny sin. Such people are the biggest sinners who criticise others about things they do themselves. Or at least would like to do... Don't avoid people who're followed by bad fame and who don't deny sins that are attributed to them. Such people have so much behind them that now they're pretty harmless."

"How can you stand all this?" Oliver asked. His voice was full of disgust.

"What exactly?"

"This so-called cream of society. It is so sour that it should be poured down the drain immediately. The whole room is full of boring people who, because of unknown reasons, have decided to vegetate, not live. They've chosen to be regular and obedient and have given up everything that could have been their life."

"Oliver, do you realise what nonsense you just said?"

Sometimes his naivety was unbelievable.

"Nonsense?"

"Yes. Nonsense. Your words show lack of information. Do you really think that this room is full of regular and boring people? Quite the reverse. Look at, for instance, Lord

Dowergates and Lord Jeffrey who're talking so freely to each other. Lord Dowergates pretends he doesn't know that Lord Jeffrey has an affair with his wife, while Lord Jeffrey pretends he doesn't know that Lord Dowergates recently sabotaged one of his deals thereby causing big losses. As soon as Lord Jeffrey will have left this hospitable house, he'll start to plot the revenge. Or... look at Mrs Barlow and her sister, Miss Stephany Field. Mrs Barlow is really looking after her thirteen-year-old sister, she likes to take her to receptions..."

"Yes, they're very close."

"No-one doubts it. Only... Mrs Barlow is Miss Field's mother, not sister."

"*Mother*?"

"Yes. At the age of fifteen Helena gave birth to a baby. The name of the father... and also the location of his grave... are unknown. Helena's parents decided to hide everything. Stephany became the youngest child of Mrs Field, while Helena was married off to Mr Barlow a few years later. If we continue the topic... Mr and Mrs Hadgeworth. They arrived, smiling happily. At the moment Mr Hadgeworth is going to say hello to a lady, who, actually, has been his lover for years. Mrs Hadgeworth, too, saw an "acquaintance" and at the moment is engaged in a small talk. Rest of the evening The Hadgeworths will spend in the company of their lovers and, if they abide by their tradition, soon all four will disappear from our sight for a moment. And these are just a few examples. Do you see it now?"

He made no reply.

"Everything I just said is true. Oliver, nothing here is as it looks."

"Isn't there anything pure and true in the whole of London?"

"Why do you confine yourself only with London? Do you think that outside it everything is better? I'll have to disappoint you. There is so much pretending and so many masks in the world that one has put a lot of effort to find something real. But… is it necessary? For instance, I'm more interested in lies and secrets. Why do you think I'm organising all these receptions? I love to watch this theatre and to reveal everyone's true face step by step."

During our conversation I was watching how Oliver's face changes. Now it was full of anger.

"What you just said to me is disgusting," he said, then turned around and left the room.

Poor Oliver. I had given him the first lesson in life and he didn't like it.

xxx

I was woken up by a loud noise - someone was persistently knocking on the door. It was two o'clock in the afternoon and in our house no-one usually woke up before four. I quickly got dressed and went downstairs where I saw that Beatrice had already opened the door. Two police officers came in.

"Good afternoon, we would like to speak to the owner of this house," one of them said.

"That would be me."

"We were informed about the disappearance of a person. The last time when he was seen was three days ago in your house. We would like to speak to you and everyone else who lives here."

The police were in our house for a few hours, mainly because most of us were still sleeping and struggled to get out of bed, and also because there were only two officers dealing with all twelve of us. However, we couldn't provide any useful information. The description of the missing person: around 40 years old, with pale hair, medium height, wearing a grey suit was attributable to one third of our guest list for that night, while his name – Harry Wolton – didn't ring any bells. If Mr Wolton wouldn't have disappeared we wouldn't even know that he was at the reception – his name wasn't on the guest list.

"One question: do we have anything to do with this?" I asked as soon as the police officers had left.

Everyone shook their heads, which could mean both: that none of them was to blame for Mr Wolton's disappearance or that someone simply had a short memory.

Beatrice wasn't hiding her dissatisfaction:

"The police... And why was it established? We managed just fine without them."[1]

"I have a feeling that this is not the last time when we see them," Francis said.

"They may come back to search the house," Arifay presumed.

---

[1] There was no police in London until 1829.

"And we need to be prepared for that," I said. "We need to immediately hide everything that shouldn't be seen by outsiders."

Konstantin chuckled:

"I already thought that it's useful to store my belongings in a safe."

"What safe?" I asked. "There is no safe in your room."

"I made it."

"May I know where?"

"Don't worry, it's under the floorboards. At first I wanted to make it inside a wall, but later I realised that it could collapse."

"Konstantin, may I ask you to notify me the next time you decide to commence any construction works in my house?"

Hearing my venomous tone, others started to giggle.

"Of course, of course," he replied. I didn't believe him much.

"Shall we start now?" Arifay asked.

"Yes, we can," I said. "Since Mr Mikhailov has less to do than others, he could check the basement and the attic one more time."

Although the police's visit was an unpleasant surprise to us, no-one was really worried about it. People did go missing in our house from time to time. It was a play with fire and we were willing to take the risk. Besides, we didn't have much time for contemplation – we had a reception tonight.

xxx

I examined the crowd one more time, looking for Oliver, but he wasn't here. There could be two reasons for that. Either he was mad at me or needed time to accept the fact that his previous opinion about the society was wrong. Oliver was naive and that was dangerous in this circuit. Here indeed nothing was as it looked. And the sooner Oliver would realise it, the better for him.

In my case, nothing could surprise me anymore. I had seen all possible kinds of dissoluteness and rascality in my life. Sometimes I wondered what would happen if it would be possible, at least for a moment, to see everyone's true face. Probably the room would immediately be covered with mould and the guests would turn into unholy creatures who would remind walking corpses.

Tonight, a truly crafty set had gathered here. For instance, Lady Hastings, a lovely looking twenty-five-year old. At the age of nineteen she was wedded to Sir Hastings who was in his forties then. The marriage didn't last long – three years later Sir Hastings suddenly died. Circumstances of the death were so unclear that no-one doubted Lady Hastings had poisoned her husband. No-one spoke about it aloud because of lack of evidence and Lady Hastings was still welcomed everywhere. Many women didn't hide that they were envious of her. The Lady had everything: youth, beauty, money and freedom.

Or, for instance, Mrs Chatters, the second wife of Mr Chatters, a caring wife and step-mother. Mrs Chatters had been a close friend of Mr Chatters for many years and when he married, she made friends with the first Mrs Chatters. When Mr Chatters became a widower as a result of a terrible accident, she was always by his side to comfort and help. Mr Chatters appreciated it and soon married his faithful friend. Of course, he had no idea that his second wife had killed the first one.

Or the young Craven. A year ago he came to know that his grandfather had made a last will, in which he left most of his money to him. Mr Craven was truly excited and, probably showing his gratitude, killed grandfather. The only reason why he was still around us was lack of evidence. However, this money had brought nothing but bad luck to him – he had already lost one third of his fortune to settle gambling debts.

Theft, murder, sabotage, machinations… The people here were an example of how to reach their goals by destroying others.

xxx

Francis had been right – the police returned.

"This is very, very weird…" Sibyl said thoughtfully.

We were standing on the stairs watching how fifteen police officers were carrying out a search.

"I have no idea who Mr Wolton is, but someone really wants him to be found," I said.

The police officers spent most of the day in our house and their faces showed that they have found absolutely nothing. Before they left, one of them, probably feeling guilty, finally told us more about Mr Wolton's case.

"You see, Mr Wolton was a solicitor who was executing Lord Greyscot's last will. One of the heirs, Mr Buttersby, was very worried when suddenly Mr Wolton was nowhere to be found. Apparently tens of thousands of pounds are at stake."

I couldn't not share such news with others. I waited until everyone had returned home and then gathered them in the ballroom, where I briefly reported what the police officer had told me.

"Mr Buttersby wants to find the last will so badly that he will leave no stone unturned."

"Oh, what a skunk... Not so long ago he was smiling at us, drinking our wine and wanting to be our friend. What a hypocrite!" Melissa was fuming. "I suggest not to invite him here anymore."

"Why? Let's invite him... for *one last time*," Beatrice sneered.

"It's tempting, but... no. We already have enough problems with one missing person," I said.

xxx

"Be merciful to the young Parker. He's such a lovely boy, but you want to corrupt him," Lady Rosewood said.

XXX

Oliver had appeared on the horizon again and at the moment he was sitting at the table in the company of several so-called gentlemen.

"Do I? May I know how, if it's not a secret?"

"Admit – your company is not the best. Parker should spend his time in a more respectable company. Like the one he is in at the moment."

"You mean Lord Graceland who recently became a father of his seventeenth illegitimate child and Mr McGuire who is very proud of bankrupting the man who was considered to be his best friend? Lady Rosewood, I must say that you have a very extraordinary opinion about what is respectable."

"I have to apologise for my behaviour that night," Oliver said as he was walking up to me. "You tried to open my eyes and show me my delusion but got a scolding instead of gratitude."

"You don't need to apologise. Your reaction was quite natural."

"You know, I've started to listen more to what people are saying, to their conversations. And I don't like what I hear. I can't believe how blind I was. Conspiracies, lies, betrayal... People are bragging about them as if they would be some kind of heroic deeds."

"Don't you find the company of me and my friends revolting yet? Most of the things people say about us are true."

"I'm sure they are. However, for some reason I think that you and your friends are way better than the others because you're not hiding your true nature and you have some kind of integrity," he said. "Now I have to say farewell. I'm tired and I want to go home."

xxx

Lord Greyscot's case had quickly become the favourite topic in London's high society. Every day we found out more and more.

"Today I had gone to town to play poker when I ran into Sir Melwood and he told me the latest news in Mr Wolton's case," Francis said. "Not only Wolton, but the last will too is missing. No-one knows its content, except for Lord Greyscot and Mr Wolton."

We looked at each other – there were no doubts about the poor solicitor's fate.

"Do you know the net worth of the estate?" Sibyl asked.

"Eighty thousand pounds."

Konstantin whistled. For that amount of money we ourselves wouldn't mind getting our hands dirty.

"From what I've heard, in the beginning there were four heirs and each of them inherited twenty thousand, but old Greyscot made a new last will shortly before his death, excluding one or two heirs from it," Francis continued.

"So, someone sent Wolton to glory in order to hide the content of the last will?" Melissa presumed.

"Or to change it. I think soon the last will be found, but… will it be the same last will?"

"Exactly my thoughts," I said.

xxx

"Tonight, I have a very important announcement," I said and raised my glass.

I could read my guests like an open book. Most women thought that I'd announce either my own or a housemate's engagement. Most men expected me to tell them about a once-in-a-lifetime deal I've recently closed. And then, of course, there were people who were expecting that I'd finally announce my departure from London.

"My friends and I will soon leave London and this house will become empty."

As I had thought, a few people couldn't hide their delight, but most of them were shocked.

"And when will you come back?" a lady asked.

"Maybe never. We want to see other places. Cities. Countries. Travel outside Europe."

"What a pity," she said.

"We're leaving London with heavy hearts, however, we've chosen changes."

"You make it sound like a funeral, Yuri," Arifay uttered. He, too, raised his glass. "All good things come to an end. That's life. But memories, the memories of the good times, they stay with us forever. So tonight we will eat, drink and be merry. And we'll dance till the morning comes. Cheers!"

"Count Rokosovski, when you said you have an important announcement, I thought that you'll finally announce that you're getting married," Lady Chainsberry said.

"Judging by the faces of many of my tonight's guests, you weren't the only one."

My announcement had changed the atmosphere. One after another everyone had realised that serious changes are on the way. My departure meant the end of an era.

"You defied my expectations."

"I don't need to fulfil anyone's expectations but mine."

"Have you really never thought of marriage?"

"No. Based on my current observations, I can say that the woman I'd like to be together with hasn't been born yet."

The atmosphere in the house had changed too. Most of the vampires were packing their belongings with enthusiasm and were sharing their travel plans. Austria, Germany, the Netherlands, Switzerland… Only Konstantin and Arifay were staying in England. I had chosen Ireland as my destination although I didn't want to go anywhere.

xxx

Suddenly I heard that someone slams the door and runs upstairs. I heard loud shuffling of drawers in one of the rooms and other noise that evidenced that someone was packing his belongings in a hurry. Everything was accompanied by loud cursing. I listened. Sounded like Russian.

"What happened?" I asked as I went into Konstantin's room.

He had squatted down and was getting documents out of his "safe".

"Kelsworth!" Konstantin said this name in a voice full of hate. "He checked some of my deals and found things I wouldn't like to come into light. I must leave. Immediately."

"Are you leaving London?"

"Not only London. I'm leaving Great Britain and going back to St. Petersburg."

Less than ten minutes later he was gone.

Tonight's reception was the most splendid one: the rooms were decorated more than usual, tables were full of exotic and unseen dishes and champagne was flooding. This was our farewell to London. Even the people who couldn't stand me had arrived. They didn't even hide that they're celebrating my departure.

The only person missing was Vincent. I had sent him an invitation although I knew very well that he would neither respond, nor attend.

"Have you heard the news in the Greyscot case?" Sir Bromley asked.

"Depends on what you mean with news. If you have anything that is fresher than what I heard three days ago then I'm all ears."

"My news is less than five hours old. Mr Wolton's body was pulled out of the Thames this morning. It looks like someone made him unconscious or drugged him and then threw the body into the river."

"This case is getting more and more exciting. What a pity that I won't know how it ends."

"Leave me your address and I'll continue to inform you."

"I won't have a permanent address for a while because I've decided to travel around Central Europe," I lied. "But thank you anyway."

"What a pity that you've decided to leave. London will lose a great host and a wonderful conversationalist."

I had heard these words quite often in the last few weeks. I wanted to stay in London, but unfortunately it wasn't possible – the fact that I don't age could not be hidden any longer.

"Once again – I have to ask you: how can you stand all this?" Oliver was still trying to work out certain things.

He was not keen on going out anymore but he had to be here tonight.

"Very simple: I like it. This is my environment, my world."

"You like it? You like to be surrounded by lies, hypocrisy, back-stabbing and double-standards? Wouldn't you like to live in a world where everything is true and people are not trying to pretend to be better than they actually are?"

"Never! I praise hypocrisy and double-standards. Life would be unbearably boring without them. But, speaking about you... I suggest you leave this circuit as soon as possible. Don't let them destroy you."

XXX

The sale of the house was being finalised and everyone except me, Arifay and Beatrice had already left. I had asked them to stay and move out of the house with me – I didn't want to be in an empty house. I found it ridiculous, because, after all, I had spent most of my life in solitude, but I couldn't make this strange feeling disappear. Arifay and Beatrice found it funny too, however, they agreed to stay with me for a couple of days.

Shortly before the departure, Oliver visited me.

"Could... Could I join you?"

"What do you mean with "us"? There is no "us" anymore. As you see, this house is almost empty."

"I meant something else... You see, I've been a quite regular guest here and I've watched all of you. You're different. You have something that attracts me. I have a feeling that you have something that stays hidden for everyone else. I felt very good in the company of you and your extraordinary friends and it's sad that I will have to lose it. So… I would like to go with you. But, if you say that everyone has already left, then… Count Rokosovski, will you allow me to join you?"

I had expected this would happen. Of course, I had to decline the request. I didn't share my secret with humans.

"No. Oliver, believe me, my lifestyle is not for you."

"Why do you think so?" he said and I heard a grievance in his voice. "You don't know me well enough to judge about me like that."

"Have I ever declared that I know you?"

"No, never."

"In that case what you just said makes no sense. But tell me, Oliver, why do you think that you will do better in my company than without it?"

"Because I feel trapped. I want to live, not spend my life in boredom, obey strict rules someone else has created and get criticised just because I'm different. You live following your own rules and you don't care what others say. I would like to be so independent too and I want to learn it from you."

"I wish you luck, however, you'll have to achieve this goal without my help."

"I don't ask much from you."

"My answer still is "no". It's not because I wouldn't like company, it's because your lifestyle won't fit with mine."

"Why do you think so? I can learn to wake up at five in the afternoon and go to sleep in the morning."

"You know that my lifestyle is something more than that."

"I know," he said and suddenly something strange appeared in his eyes, something I had never seen before. By making his request, Oliver didn't want to join me as a human.

"Oliver, I suppose that you have a clear vision about what to do with your life?"

"I'd rather call it approximate."

"As you wish. Tell me, do you want to marry and be together with this special woman until death does you part?"

"Yes."

"Do you want to have children to whom you'd try to teach your values?"

"Yes."

"Do you want to travel around the world, visiting various exotic places, such as shores of Africa or South America?"

"I hope to see these places someday."

"Well, that is the answer to your question. None of it will be possible anymore if you become like me. My lifestyle means solitude and inconstancy. I never stay in the same place for too long and I know that nothing is permanent in my life. There are no rules in my world except for those I've made myself. I chose such a life deliberately because human life wasn't for me. With you, everything is different – if you become like me, it will be your biggest mistake."

"Why do you think so?"

"Because I have living examples around me. Have you heard of Vincent Styles?"

"Yes, I have."

"He was a good friend of mine. He still is although he has cut all ties with us... he became what you want to become and paid for it dearly. Do you want such a fate too?"

"No," Oliver said in a silent voice. He finally understood.

"Oliver, despite the public opinion, I've never wanted to do anything bad to you and you know it. I hope that you will have the life you want and won't become part of what you hate. But you can't go with me. Everyone has his own way in life and my way is not for you."

"Thank you. Will you ever return to London?"

"Definitely. After a few decades."

"Then maybe one day we'll meet again?"

"Possibly. It will be very easy to recognise me – I'll look exactly the same."

"What are you?" his voice was full of curiosity now.

"It will be better if you don't know that. You'll be able to sleep better at night," I smiled.

The departure day came and a carriage was waiting for me. Beatrice, Arifay and I got our travel bags and went outside. Unlike me, they were happy to move out.

"I hope to meet you again someday," I said.

"We will meet again. Life is long, but the world is small," Beatrice said.

"Yuri, is that melancholy I can hear in your voice? You're not as cold as I had thought then..." I could hear slight sarcasm in Arifay's voice. "I know what's happening. Every now and then there will be a particular point in time when everything clicks together perfectly and you enjoy yourself so much you wish that time would stop and you could stay in that moment forever. But that's not possible and it makes you feel as if you'd found your own little paradise only to be kicked out of it. It's happened to me, it's happened to Beatrice and now it's happened to you. Anyway, I'm in a bit of a hurry. If I miss my coach I'll have to walk to Oban."

"You're off to the Hebrides then?" I asked.

"Temporarily. Before I settle in Yorkshire. I haven't been to the Highlands and islands for a long time. My heart is craving natural beauty."

"You old Romantic... Send me a postcard from Staffa."

"Sure. I'll get it delivered by puffin post."[2]

"Boys, I'm in a bit of a hurry too. I've got a ferry to Holland to catch," Beatrice reminded us.

---

[2] Staffa is an uninhabited island on the West coast of Scotland, famous for its puffin colony.

"It would be a pity if you missed it. We wouldn't want you to swim across the English Channel!" I said.

"In this dress? Never! It's the finest silk money can buy!"

We all laughed.

"I'm glad to see you're feeling better, Yuri," Airfay said.

He and Beatrice embraced me and we farewelled.

Conciliation

What to do when you're tired of life but there's eternity ahead? What to do when you realise that you've made the biggest mistake in your life and cannot alter it? What to do when you realise that you cannot stay where you are, but neither can you move forward because you don't know where to go?

Such questions were occupying my mind during the first years after Elizabeth and I separated. When I left our house and went to London, I had no plans, no aims. My heart was full of bitterness and sadness and I was in the state of trance. I spent my days pondering over my life, trying to decide what to do with it. All this time I was completely alone.

Things changed in 1814 when I met Yuri Rokosovski. He never lived alone and invited me to join him and other vampires. I agreed. That's how I met Beatrice who later became my close friend. In 1817 Yuri, Beatrice and I moved to London. It was interesting to live together with others, to listen to their stories, experiences and opinions. I started to socialise again. I have to admit, during those years I did a few things I'm not proud of now, nevertheless, it is the time I remember with delight. However, nothing lasts forever. In 1829 Yuri sold the house and everyone dispersed – Yuri went to Ireland, Beatrice moved to the Netherlands, I stayed in England but moved out of London.

I was on my own again and had to think how to fill my days. The years spent with vampires had done good to me. I had partly regained the passion for life and, by chance, found an occupation I really liked. When Vincent joined us in 1820, I was asked to educate him. I taught him everything I knew. Sibyl, who was originally from France, taught Vincent

French. The beginning was difficult because Vincent had never learnt anything before and it took time until I saw first results. However, once he grasped something he became unstoppable. While teaching him I realised I've found something I would do with gusto in future, too.

In the early 1830s I got a job as a teacher in a boarding school in the country. I liked to share my knowledge, to teach something new to others. If necessary, I explained everything again and again to my students and never lost my temper.

Unfortunately, I didn't stay there for long because I had a Nicholas Nickleby worthy argument with the owner. Before he had managed to fire me, I quit the job myself.

Before I left the school forever, I wrote a complaint, as well as sent letters to the parents of several students. As I later heard, an investigation took place, but since the owner had good connections he got away lightly. He simply promised to eliminate faults. As far as I know, the school still exists.

Later I found a new job in another boarding school, but didn't stay there for long either. I liked to work with children because they were full of joy and life and the school itself was a nice location, however, I realised how physically difficult it is to play a human. Firstly, I had to be awake during daytime, not night, without a chance to get proper sleep. The next big problem was food. Hunting didn't cause any difficulties because there was a forest close to the school and many farms were located in the neighbourhood – back then, I had switched to animal blood. There wasn't much difference between animal and human blood, although human blood tasted a bit better. But since I had to keep this in secret, I had to join everyone at the lunch table. Human food was harmful to me and I always felt bad after eating.

Sometimes I could avoid meals, but those were rare exceptions. Also, I had to remember that I cannot move too quickly and can't demonstrate my actual physical strength. It exhausted me and I was forced to leave.

I moved back to London and became a private tutor. I had my own flat and refused to accept any job offers that required me to live at the student's house because it would mean the same life I had at the school. My students were very different. Children. Young girls from noble families who were receiving good education before they were given away in marriage. Elderly ladies who had suddenly decided that knowledge in arts or philosophy is more useful than knowledge in latest gossip.

Money wasn't important to me. Of course, I didn't work for free, but my life didn't depend on how much money I'd manage to bring home by the end of the week. I had earned a fortune during my years with other vampires and now could afford not to think about finances. One of the advantages of my life was that I had almost no expenses. I spent money only to pay the rent and buy books, and, when necessary, bought myself new clothes. Vampire "food" didn't cost anything and I had no needs.

That's how I had lived for nearly four decades. I couldn't call myself happy, although I was quite satisfied with my life. At least it had a meaning now.

It was an evening and I had gone out to take a walk when I saw a silhouette that looked familiar although I couldn't see the person's face.

"Elizabeth!" I exclaimed.

"Arifay!"

Of course, we recognised each other instantly although we looked different now. The look in our eyes had become warmer and facial expression – friendlier.

We looked at each other and the first thing that came into our minds was our break up sixty years ago, in 1807.

"What a surprise!" I said.

"Surprise indeed."

This meeting was so unexpected that we didn't know what to say and how to behave. Elizabeth made a step, but I caught her hand unconsciously.

"Wait... Please don't run. I feel as bewildered as you."

"We have a reason for that, don't we?"

We averted from each other for a moment.

"Did I scratch you badly then?" she asked, breaking the silence.

"No, I managed to grab your hands. And I... did you injure yourself after I threw you across the room?"

"A bit. I landed heavily on the side."

"I'm sorry for that."

"Don't worry, I forgave you years ago. After all, I started that row."

Silence fell again. This conversation was so odd.

"It looks like you're doing well," Elizabeth said.

"Yes, I am. And you... you look happy although your eyes are a bit sad. I would guess that the source of your happiness is always accompanied by sorrow."

Instead of making a reply she closed her eyes and slightly nodded.

"If we've met so unexpectedly…" I started.

"…we should say more than a few sentences to each other," Elizabeth finished the thought.

"Yes."

"Probably… but not tonight," she said.

From her tone I understood that it's not because she wouldn't like to have such a conversation so soon, but because someone or something was waiting for her.

"Are you hurrying somewhere?"

"Yes."

I gave my address to Elizabeth and we farewelled.

Elizabeth visited me quite soon, just three days after our encounter. I have to confess - although I had sometimes thought about her, I never cared about her fate nor I had deliberately wanted to search for her.

There were no signs of former extravagance in our looks. I got rid of my flamboyant clothing soon after moving out of Yuri's house because I had no need for it in my new life. Elizabeth, she had stayed in my memory as she was on the day we separated – wearing an expensive dress and jewelry. Now she was wearing a simple cotton dress and a faded grey cloak.

This evening we felt more comfortable because we knew what we wanted to say to each other. I briefly told her about the years with other vampires, but avoided mentioning debauchery that was part of our lives then. I always said that Yuri's house was a cesspool of depravity but Yuri never agreed. He said it was not the house that affected people, it was the people who affected the house. Yuri enjoyed every moment there while I preferred company of like-minded vampires or humans and tried to stay away from all that corruption. I don't remember when I succumbed. But, when telling about my life as a tutor, I got really carried away and had to apologise to Elizabeth for talking too much.

After I had told her everything I considered to be important, I finally let her speak.

"I work in a workhouse," she said. "Do you remember how much I dreamed about a child? Since I cannot have my own I decided to care about the children of others. I started as a nanny in wealthy families, but I felt it wasn't the right place for me... Those children are often spoilt or taught to be reserved since early days. I quit and went to an orphanage.

I mothered those who would not experience much joy and happiness in their lives. And, you know, in this darksome place I found happiness again. A few years ago, I started to work in a workhouse and mothered the children who were born or lived there. Sometimes I take care of old people and I'm with the ones who're lying on a deathbed. I can give love to those who lack it."

While listening to her I realised that I was starting to feel deep admiration and respect towards her. I could never imagine that she could choose such a life. I had never been in a workhouse, but I had heard terrible things about them. It was the place where the poor, the old, the sick and orphans often had to go. Workhouses gave food and shelter, however, people had to work very hard for that. In fact, they were exploited. It was difficult for me to imagine Elizabeth there, trying to ease the suffering of innocent people.

Since that evening Elizabeth became a regular visitor. Both of us had thought that her first visit would also be the last one, but everything changed when we saw how much our lives have changed for the better since the breakup. It turned out that Elizabeth had felt guilty for what she had done to me. It surprised me. Elizabeth had changed so much. She reminded me of that lovely girl she was during her human life, only now it was complemented by a mature woman's wisdom. It was hard to believe that there used to be a time when we made money from break-ins and the sale of stolen goods. Back then we only cared about ourselves and lived following our desires.

This is why I was so interested in Elizabeth's new life. How did she feel about working in a workhouse?

"Of course, it's difficult. To hear all those stories... I had never imagined that there can be so much cruelty and inhumanity in the world. There used to be time when I pitied myself – oh, poor me, I'm destined to be a vampire forever. But it is my fault, I made myself like this! I gave up everything I actually wanted in life. And by doing that I also ruined your life. That's why I want to apologise. I had no right to change your life like this."

"I said "yes" to vampire life, didn't I? I have to admit, I held a grudge against you for years for that, but then in one moment I realised that it's not right to blame only you for that. I'm guilty as well. I've forgiven you, but not myself."

"I can't forgive myself either," she said and went quiet for a moment. "You know, I'm delighted that we've met and buried the hatchet."

xxx

"Would you like to see where I work?" Elizabeth offered.

I agreed. It was late enough for most of the occupants to be asleep, so my appearance wouldn't be noticed, but it wasn't night time yet.

Elizabeth brought me into a room. It was wet and badly illuminated, the air was stuffy and there were many beds placed next to each other. I looked at the faces of women lying in them - they were covered in wrinkles regardless of age and sadness and suffering was visible in their eyes. Some of them were awake and looked at me with distrust.

Elizabeth went to one of the beds and sat on it. By seeing her, the old woman who was lying in it smiled and stretched her arms towards Elizabeth. Elizabeth held the woman's hands and in a voice that sounded soft as a caress, said:

"I'm here, Mrs Hester."

"Elizabeth, my dear child, if only you'd know how much you mean to me."

Tears appeared in Mrs Hester's eyes. She quickly wiped them, but then burst in tears again.

"Don't cry," Elizabeth calmed her and touched her cheeks brushing the tears away.

Mrs Hester noticed me and her look became cautious.

"He's a friend of mine. We haven't seen each other for years. I just wanted to show him where I work," Elizabeth explained.

"Will you tell me a story tonight?"

"Of course."

She started to tell a story about a far and exotic land where an astonishingly beautiful princess lived. Because of her beauty she was desired by many, but the King did not rush with giving her away in marriage. Once upon a time the king of a neighbouring country whose proposal the King had rejected abducted the princess. The King promised an award for her safe return. A bravehearted soldier from the King's army went after the princess and, having surmounted many hardships and fought many battles, brought her back. During the time they spent together, the princess and the soldier had fallen in love with each other and after the return the soldier asked the King the permission to marry the princess. The King said that it was out of the question, although he appreciated the young man's bravery. The lovers decided not to give up and, not seeing any other solution, ran away. The King sent half of his army after them. The runaways were caught and the princess was ready to give up her title if that would allow her to be with her loved one. Seeing how strong their feelings were, the King capitulated and blessed the marriage. The story, of course, was banal and the ending – predictable, but Mrs Hester truly enjoyed it. I knew why. When one has spent the whole life fighting poverty, difficulties and dealing with human cruelty, they want to hear stories with happy endings otherwise bitterness fills the heart and poisons it, killing faith in humanity and destroying the soul.

After hearing the story Mrs Hester fell asleep. Elizabeth got up very carefully and we left the room silently.

"Mrs Hester has been here for two years," Elizabeth said. "At the moment she's very sick and I think she hasn't got much left. Mrs Hester's life has been very hard – when she was very young, she started working as a chambermaid. Her employer's son seduced her and she got pregnant. The family didn't want a chambermaid with a child and threw her out on the street. Mrs Hester started to live in the slums and tried to find work. As soon as pregnancy couldn't be hidden, no-one wanted to deal with her anymore. The child was born on a night when Mrs Hester was absolutely alone. She couldn't do anything else but to beg, taking the child with her. One day she met a brick burner's wife who felt sorry for Mrs Hester and took her to her place. Meedy her name was. Meedy promised to help take care of the child if Mrs Hester finds a job and gives part of her wages to pay the rent and buy food. In addition, she introduced Mrs Hester to a lonely brick burner. His name was Morris Hester. Meedy proposed – why don't you get married? And they did. For a moment Mrs Hester's life seemed to be settled. Unfortunately, it didn't last long – her first child died of short commons, the next three pregnancies ended with either a miscarriage or a still-born child. Mister Hester turned out to be a difficult man. Mrs Hester gave birth to five children, but only two of them survived infancy. That's how she spent her life: in poverty, trying to feed her children and bearing with husband's violence. The children grew up and left home. The son works on a farm somewhere in the countryside. The daughter almost repeated her mother's fate. When Mr Hester died some years ago, Mrs Hester couldn't afford to pay the rent anymore. She was too old to find a job and was forced to go to the workhouse. Her story touched me. I started to tell her various tales and stories about a different, happier life. I do that every evening. I want her to have at least some happiness and ease at the end of her life."

"I respect you more and more every day," I said.

Elizabeth went to a door and opened it. This room was as darksome as the previous one. Here, too, many beds were placed next to each other, only they were baby cots. All the babies were asleep. Elizabeth stopped near one of the beds and said in a very quiet voice:

"Look at these children... They are so lovely and unprotected. Do they surmise what life expects them? What's the difference between them and the ones who were born in wealthy families? Clothes? I've been thinking a lot about it here. Why do people get sealed from the moment of birth? What gives someone the right to decide about the lives of others? These children didn't have the luck to be born to rich parents, but are they worse than the offspring of noble families?"

"There's no difference between them and people know that very well," I said.

"Yet they don't want to change anything in the existing order." Elizabeth sighed. "I take care of them with pleasure because I know that this will be the only care they will receive during their short life."

"They are so little. Do you think that they will remember it?"

"My inner voice says that they will."

Elizabeth caressed the face of the sleeping baby.

"How do you think – will a time come when one's fate won't be determined by their origin?"

"I don't know. But I'd like to experience that."

The workhouse was as disgusting as I had imagined it, although Elizabeth had said that things had improved since her arrival. The occupants adored her while some of her colleagues hated Elizabeth and tried to get rid of her. They ordered her to do the most difficult and dirtiest tasks without knowing that Elizabeth would work for hours in the rain, snow or a damp basement. All attempts to maltreat her failed.

"Of course, it's possible to do that if you know how," Elizabeth laughed. We were sitting in my kitchen because for some strange reason it was the most homely place in my flat. "They've tried to sabotage me so many times but never succeeded. For instance, they've poured something in my tea and then couldn't understand why nothing happens. Well, probably because I never drink it. Oh, and once they asked me to clean the snow from the yard after they had hidden my cloak. It was one of the coldest days of the year, by the way."

Life had made Elizabeth a warrior. She constantly tried to improve things in at least her workhouse, especially for children. Elizabeth remembered with a smile an old scandal that arose when she asked the cook how come that quite good groceries were sent to the workhouse, but the food made of them always tasted disgusting. The cook became angry, started to swear and tried to hit her with a big ladle. Elizabeth responded by such foul language that the cook blushed and grabbed the ladle. What was left of it was later picked up with a dustpan and brush. Curiously enough, since the incident food had started to taste better. Elizabeth's aspirations had improved sanitation and hygiene too. She believed that occupants of the workhouse should have a chance to wash and brush up and wash their clothes regularly. Those who were dissatisfied with Elizabeth's activities had complained about her countless times, but it didn't bring any results because there were many people who were on Elizabeth's side, besides, workhouses were lacking employees. Who would dare to fire Elizabeth, a person who never avoided a task and was faster than anyone else?

Although I liked Elizabeth's company and she liked to spend time with me, we knew that this would not continue for long. We had met and reconciled with the past. It was time to farewell.

I walked with Elizabeth to the workhouse. We walked slowly because we didn't know how many years or centuries would pass until we would meet again.

At the gates, we stopped. Elizabeth hugged me and we wished luck to each other.

She was about to enter the gates, but then turned around and said:

"Arifay, I'm sorry that the story of us had such a sad ending. I really loved you and believed that we'll be happy together. Forever... But there were so many things we didn't know. And I'm really sorry that everything ended as it did. Then, when I said that I cursed the day when I fell in love with you… Anger and disgust towards myself had taken me over that moment. I didn't mean it. I've never regretted that I fell in love with you. I regret only that I convinced myself and later you to make a decision that seemed to be an exit, but turned out to be a mistake. As humans we would have been so happy and had been together until death would do us part. What a pity that such a chance was never given to us."

Disappointment

There's a saying that when one door closes another one opens. Not for me. Doors closed one after another, but no other door opened instead.

I usually didn't put my thoughts on paper. I didn't like it. I preferred to merge memories rather than to remember what happened when. There was a time when I kept diaries but I stopped doing it when I noticed one unpleasant thing – my thoughts and feelings stayed the same, the only thing that ever changed was the date.

Over the years I started to feel disgust towards myself. It had turned out that the life that once seemed to offer so many opportunities actually forbid me so much. I felt trapped and lonely. I looked in the mirror, but didn't see my face. I still looked like I'd be in my early twenties, while, in fact, I was more than a century old.

My life was easier than human life, but it was lacking purpose. Since I had unlimited time and excellent physical shape, I decided to do something useful and help people. I turned to medicine. During the First World War I worked in field hospitals.

In 1921 I went to America. Now, three years later, I lived in Chicago and worked as a hospital porter.

I liked to take care of others. Sometimes patients became eccentric or sharp, but I never took it to heart. The hospital environment was unusual for them and it was natural that they felt confused, edgy or scared.

I couldn't not think about how much medicine had developed over the years. Many disease agents and new medication were discovered. Many lives were saved simply by following basic hygiene: clean wards, fresh air, regular cleaning. In the field hospitals many soldiers died not of injuries but of infections and diseases caused by insanitary conditions. It wasn't anything unusual on a battlefield, but just a few decades ago the same conditions had existed in most peace-time hospitals. I remembered London from my adolescence. It was a true nest of various diseases then. In families of the poor, children died one after another. Those who survived often had serious health problems for the rest of their lives.

I liked to see people recovering. Of course, it would have been better if they hadn't got admitted to hospital at all, but I felt joy every time when someone was discharged and returned home. I was especially delighted when a doctor had done a complex surgery or tried a new treatment. I believed that this was just the beginning and in future mankind would experience unbelievable medical progress.

However, every coin has two sides and my work didn't consist of positive things only. Not everyone recovered. It was especially sad when children died. They were so little and fragile, with eyes full of fear. They, unlike many old people who often felt tired of life, were scared of death and didn't want to die. Parents who were grief stricken tried to restrain themselves while they were with their children and tried to solace them, saying that death is not the end and that after death everyone goes to a new, wonderful world that is free from illnesses and sorrow. I had seen many parents of sick children and I never had a feeling that they really believed what they were saying. I had the impression that they *would like* to believe it.

Yet my life was incomplete. My heart was craving for love. And that caused a dilemma. After Elisa's death I was afraid to become so close to someone again, but I couldn't be alone. I knew that there was no happy end in my life, but still... I gave myself away to feelings although I knew that everything would end with a break up or disappointment. I didn't want to hurt any woman, but I was ready to suffer myself.

I met Susan in 1922. An accident had happened in the factory she worked at and Susan was among the injured. It wasn't anything dangerous, but she had to spend a few days in hospital. Later Susan said she could never have imagined that a leg injury could be so pleasant.

Susan had a 7-year-old son, Sammy. When we first met, Sammy examined me from head to toe and already two minutes later announced that he likes me and thinks I'm better than any other man Susan has dated. Susan blushed while I realised that Sammy and I have found a common ground.

A few months later our relationship had become serious enough to start to think about living together. Since she didn't want to move and I didn't care where to live, I moved into Susan's apartment.

xxx

"Vincent, what do you think – if I have homework that is assigned to the day after tomorrow, should I do it today or tomorrow?" Sammy asked.

It was the morning and I was in the kitchen making breakfast for Sammy. Susan was already at work, Sammy had to go to school, while I had some hours left before the start of my shift.

"I think it's better to do it today."

"I already thought that you'd say so. But why?"

"Because it's not good to do things last minute. If you do your homework today, you'll have more free time tomorrow. You won't need to worry that there's so little time and so much work that has to be done. Besides, sometimes you write something and later realise that you can express the same thought better. Have I answered your question?"

"Definitely!" he exclaimed.

I smiled and passed the omelette to Sammy. He ate quickly, then grabbed his bag and ran out of the apartment.

Susan said she admired my patience – I willingly spent time with Sammy and I was never tired of teaching him something new. It never troubled me. Sammy was unbelievably inquisitive and witty. He was interested in science and often asked, for instance, where does electricity come from or how an engine works. In the evenings, before sleep, I read him different stories instead of fairy tales. I was very surprised when one day he brought "Oliver Twist" from the library and said he's going to read it because he liked the extracts I had read to him. He really read the whole book.

Although Sammy was reading a lot, he wasn't a bookworm. He spent a lot of time outdoors playing with other children. They played hide-and-seek, touch-last, football and did running competitions. Sometimes they went to the river to put wooden boats in the water and then watched which one would reach the finish line first. If we had a picnic, Sammy managed to climb on almost every tree in the park. When he came back, he usually told us about the birds or animals he had seen or the facts he knew about them and asked questions if something wasn't clear to him.

I knew that I probably wouldn't be around anymore when Sammy would go to university and had decided to leave money to fund his studies.

My patience wasn't the only thing that surprised Susan. She was also surprised that after two years of living together I still looked at her the way I did on the day we met.

Susan was 34 years old and so far, life hadn't had much mercy on her. She grew up in poverty, married very young and became a widow soon. Sammy's father was killed in action in 1916 when Sammy was a baby. Susan had some distant relatives in one of the southern states but she couldn't rely on any of them.

Poverty and fighting for survival had toughened Susan. Many people had said that Susan has no manners, even people I worked with. It was unpleasant for me to hear that. Those people didn't see the real Susan. Yes, she knew how to swear and could be difficult to handle, but circumstances had pushed her to that. I remembered myself during my human life - I was a primitive creature back then because my hard life didn't leave space for anything else. In Susan's case things weren't so bad, nevertheless, there were many things she was forced to give up.

"As a young girl, I loved to read: poetry, fiction... Sometimes I read several books at the same time. Now... I haven't even opened a book for years. I've just lost interest," she once said to me.

I tried to bring back at least part of what she had lost, for instance, by taking her to the theatre, cinema or dancehalls. Sometimes I met Susan after work and we went home together. On the way I used to recite poetry or tell her about a book I thought she could enjoy. A few times Susan surprised me by asking what do I think about this or that author. My presence had awoken knowledge that had remained in her mind for all these years, waiting for the moment when it could be used again. I fell for her even more.

"Checkmate!" Sammy exclaimed. The next moment his face had already become thoughtful. "Wait, you didn't let me win, did you?"

It was the evening and all three of us were in the living room. Susan was sitting on the couch doing needlework, Sammy and I were sitting on the floor playing chess.

"No. You really beat me," I said.

It was true. I really didn't notice Sammy's clever moves. He was not only very witty, he was also a very considerable antagonist in chess, draughts and other games. Because of that others, both children and adults, avoided playing against him. I was glad that no-one had introduced him to card games yet. I had no doubt that Sammy would have excellent results there as well.

At least once a week we gathered in the living room. If Susan joined us, we played various board games. Sometimes Sammy read something for us. I had bought him an encyclopaedia recently and Sammy didn't hesitate to share his newly acquired knowledge with us.

"Vincent, can you suggest a good book?" Sammy asked as he cleared the chess board.

"I can suggest quite a few books. It depends on what you want to read."

"A book where the main character is a child and which has many adventures in the storyline."

"Have you read "The Adventures of Huckleberry Finn" by Mark Twain?"

"No."

"Search for it in the library. You'll like it."

Sammy nodded. During our short conversation he had managed to put all figures back on the chess board and we started a new game. Susan looked at us and smiled.

xxx

"Sammy, haven't I told you – stop being a piglet!" Susan exclaimed, throwing a pair of Sammy's trousers into his room. Sammy mumbled something, but Susan had already rushed away.

It was Sunday and Susan had decided to tidy the place up a little bit. Since my moving in here the cleaning was quite symbolic because I took care of almost everything. I washed floors, dishes and clothes, dusted, chopped wood, kindled fire and did anything else that needed to be done. It was nothing new for me – I had done the same when I lived with my family and later when I had lived alone.

Susan had a two-bedroom apartment. Given her wages, it could be considered a luxury but actually living there didn't cost much. The house was old, poorly maintained and located not in the best area and the landlord used low rent to attract tenants.

No repairs had been carried out in the apartment for years and it was modestly furnished, but it had a special aura. It was pleasant to live here or just to pop in. Susan liked handicraft and all the rooms and the kitchen were decorated with mats, table-napkins and table-cloths she had made. Susan's favourite motives were flowers and birds. She loved colours. Of course, it was Susan and

Sammy's presence that made this apartment truly nice. They never complained about anything, never felt insecure about the future. "You have me and I have you," they often said to each other. And, while Susan had Sammy and Sammy had Susan, nothing could scare them. Now I had appeared in their life and they had accepted me completely. I was a shoulder they could lean on, while they were the family I had longed for. People whom to love and protect.

Although I worked long hours, I never really noticed that. The time was going fast, especially when there were no deaths and almost impossible recoveries happened. I had seen dozens of them.

People who had fallen from great height, those who had got in car crashes or fires, victims of severe injuries, survivors of electric shock – sometimes the condition seemed so hopeless that doctors, if only they could, would have sent those patients straight to the morgue. Everyone who saw them thought that they didn't have much time left. Nevertheless, after a while they, as if nothing had happened, walked out of the hospital.

In the hospital I had also got an affirmation to one assumption. "Hopeless" patients often stuck to life and recovered if they had family or at least a close person. While awake, they didn't hesitate to shout that they won't give up and will recover to everyone they saw. Their determination was worthy of admiration. When seeing that somebody is listening to them, these patients lowered their voice and opened up, telling about their loved ones, their reason to live. They often had pictures of them.

The situation was completely different with seriously ill or injured patients who had no relatives or who had bad relationships with them. There was an aura of doom around them, they had no stimulus to follow the doctor's orders and quite often they didn't even want to communicate.

I remembered the words of a patient. "As long as one has somebody who's precious to them, they will survive even in the most hopeless situations."

"Sammy has fallen ill," Susan said to me one evening. I had just come home from work.

"What's the matter with him?"

"Temperature, pain in the muscles, loss of appetite."

"Sounds like the common cold or the flu."

The first symptoms really looked like the flu. However, when two weeks had passed but Sammy still hadn't got better, we started to worry. I examined him, but realised that my knowledge in medicine is not sufficient enough and called one of the doctors from the hospital, Doctor Berring.

He couldn't give an answer immediately and said he had to check something.

Meanwhile Sammy had got worse. The temperature jumped to 104 °F and a strong headache started to torment him.

A few days later, when I was doing my shift, Doctor Berring found me and told me the diagnosis.

"Trichinosis," he said.

"Trichinosis?"

I had never heard of such a disease before.

"It's an infectious disease, caused by intestinal parasite trichinella."

"Infectious disease?"

"Yes. It can be contracted by eating undercooked pork or game."

"How dangerous is this disease?"

"It depends. Normally it's not too dangerous. In Sammy's case I expect full recovery in a few weeks."

We felt relieved when the doctor said that Sammy should recover soon, although it was difficult for us to see him sick. New symptoms came on top of existing ones. Doctor Berring visited us periodically. One evening he came out of Sammy's room looking very worried.

"Sammy should have recovered by now, but instead of it his condition has worsened," he said.

At first vitamins were prescribed for Sammy, later the doctor prescribed antiparasitic medication. I, too, had noticed that none of them really worked.

"We'll have to change the method of treatment."

"What do you suggest?"

"There are several medical remedies that could help, but they're very expensive. And... it would be better if Sammy would be hospitalised."

"How much will it cost?"

Doctor Berring said the amount. Susan was plucking her handkerchief and didn't say a word. I knew what she was thinking about. Susan didn't have such money. I had.

"Is it possible to take him to hospital immediately?" I asked.

Susan gave me a surprised look.

"Of course," the Doctor said.

"Then please do it. Don't worry about the expenses, everything will be covered."

Now he, too, looked surprised, but didn't say anything. He left the apartment to find a phone and call the hospital.

"Vincent, what are you doing? We don't have such money!" Susan whispered as she grasped my hand.

"Don't worry about it. When Sammy recovers, I'll tell you everything. I promise."

The next day I went to the bank. I couldn't remember the last time I had withdrawn money from that account.

I was a wealthy man but had lost all interest in money a long time ago. There was a time when I had followed my cash flow and chosen investments, but that, just like many other things, belonged to the past.

I went straight to the hospital. My shift started in a couple of hours and I decided to use this time to visit Sammy.

"Hi, Sammy. How are you feeling?" I said as I entered the ward.

"Lousy."

The temperature hadn't fallen, Sammy was sweating a lot and severe muscle pain was torturing him. His face was pale and he had become so weak that it was difficult for him to move.

"Why was I taken to hospital? I don't like it at all."

"Doctor Berring said that it will be better for you. You'll have new medicine prescribed and soon you'll be able to return home. But before that you'll have to spend some time here."

"I wish that moment would come soon…"

"Shall I bring anything from home for you to make your stay here more pleasant?"

"Yes, some books, but please bring books with many pictures and short texts."

"I'll bring your encyclopaedia then. I'll see what else I can find."

"When will mom come?"

"In the evening, right after work. Both us will visit you as often as possible."

Sammy felt tired and soon fell asleep. I went to find Doctor Berring to ask him more about the new treatment.

The Doctor was kind enough not to question me about the money, but I saw that he felt both curious and concerned. I explained that the money was earned in a legal way and I have enough of it to cover all expenses of the treatment. It was enough for the Doctor.

Unfortunately, such an explanation didn't satisfy Susan.

"Vincent, where does the money come from?"

"Don't think about it."

"Not to think about it? Are you kidding? I can't sleep at night because of it! Please be honest to me. Where did you borrow the money?"

"Nowhere. It's my money."

"*Your* money?"

"Yes. It's from a life I left behind. The only thing that has remained is the money."

Concern in Susan's look was now replaced by puzzlement. She was looking at me as if she'd be doing that for the first time in her life.

"What else I don't know about you?"

This question was left unanswered.

I spent most of the time in the hospital. I checked up on Sammy as often as I could and spent my breaks with him. On my days off I went to the hospital and spent the whole day there. Sammy was currently the only inhabitant of the ward, there were almost no other children in the hospital and he didn't feel good enough to leave the ward and go to visit other patients. I brought some books and toys for him and helped to while-away his time by reading to him or telling stories. Susan came every evening after work.

Luckily, the treatment had shown good results and it looked like Sammy could return home already next week. Waiting for his return, Susan had tidied up Sammy's room. Usually she never did that saying that self-reliance must be taught to him since early days.

One evening, when Susan and I were at home, somebody knocked on the door. It was one of the nurses. She informed me that Doctor Berring had asked us to come to the hospital immediately.

The Doctor met us at the door of Sammy's ward. As we saw his face, we realised that we're going to hear bad news.

"Sammy's got heart problems," he said.

"Heart problems? How is that possible? He's only nine years old!" Susan exclaimed.

"It's one of the symptoms of trichinosis," he explained.

"Another symptom? Sammy had almost recovered," I said.

The Doctor sighed.

"That's why it was so unexpected."

"Can we see him?" Susan asked.

"Of course."

We entered the ward. Sammy's body was covered in sweat, breathing was heavy and he looked terrified. I knew that heart problems were one of the most unpleasant and panic-causing.

Susan rushed and embraced Sammy. Both burst into tears.

"What are you going to do?" I asked the Doctor.

"It looks like I'll have to prescribe medicine for the heart also. Poor child, he has already suffered so much and now this… I've never seen such a heavy case of trichinosis during my whole practice. And that's thirty years," Doctor Berring said.

It seemed unimaginable to me. Just a few days ago Sammy's condition was stable enough to think about his discharge, but then suddenly he got worse in the space of a few hours. Heart problems didn't go away, the temperature jumped to

104 °F and didn't go down for five days, treatment didn't have any effect anymore, but even that wasn't the worst. Sammy's livers were severely damaged and it meant that he'd never fully recover.

"I want to go home," Sammy said in a very weak voice.

After another conversation with Doctor Berring we had gone to see Sammy.

"Sammy, here in the hospital it's possible to take better care of you," Susan said.

He closed his eyes and took a deep breath. Talking was difficult for him now.

"Take me home. Please. I don't want to stay here anymore, between these white walls and foreign people. I want to go home."

I looked at Doctor Berring. He nodded in defeat. Sammy's condition was so bad that there was no difference whether or not he stays in the hospital. Sammy was dying.

I took unpaid leave to take care of Sammy. Susan continued to work. She said she had to keep herself busy otherwise she'd collapse.

Temperature, severe muscle pain, weakness, loss of appetite – every day was a torture for Sammy. I had to change his sheets several times a day because they were wet from his sweat. Luckily, at least he didn't have insomnia.

Sammy was afraid to talk about his death and what could come after it. Susan avoided talking about it because it was too hard for her, I didn't talk about it because I thought that I have no right to do that. Many years ago, I had fooled the fate to keep my body forever alive.

When looking at Sammy I felt that my strength has almost left me. The history was repeating itself again, I was forced to see a person close to me dying. I went to the bathroom and washed my face. The cold water flowed down my cheeks and made me feel better for a moment. I looked in the mirror. The next moment I was overtaken by self-hate again.

Damn body! It had immortality and eternal youth, but, at the same time, so much was forbidden to it. I felt terrible inside, but couldn't even cry. I was torn apart by pain, but I couldn't, at least partially, get rid of it.

Susan and I had started to talk less and less recently. We kept our suffering inside us.

One evening when Sammy was sleeping, I was standing by his bed thinking about our powerlessness. I even thought – why him and not me? If I could save Sammy by giving my own life away, I would do it with no hesitation. He had his whole life ahead, no matter what kind of life it would be – full of happiness or challenges and difficulties. What mattered is that it would be a real, full-bodied life. Me... I had nothing but misery ahead.

I didn't notice Susan entering the room. She looked at Sammy and her look was full of sadness.

"Maybe there is a hope," I said.

She shook her head.

"You know that there isn't any hope."

"If there would even be the faintest chance to save him..."

"Medicine can't help him anymore. But *you* can help him." As she said that, she gave me a look I had never seen before.

"What are you talking about?"

"Vincent… If that's your real name… I've come to know you quite well in the past two years. I knew that there's something strange about you. And recently I feel it more and more. You barely eat but are stronger than many other men. You can work without rest for hours, stay awake until the dawn and suddenly you turn out to be a wealthy man. You're in your early twenties, but have so much wisdom and experience."

"I've experienced a lot in my life."

"Whoever you are, you're not a human. I don't know how, but you can save him."

"No, I can't do *that*."

Susan grabbed my hands and said in an imperative voice:

"Save him. Turn him into what you are."

"I can't do that."

"Why?"

"Because it won't be a life."

"Won't be a life? You seem quite alive."

Susan was almost hissing at me. Although we hadn't raised our voices, it was an angry whisper.

"You can't imagine what it means! Yes, I'm alive, but I feel half-dead inside. Only when I'm with you I can feel anything else than dejection."

"Transform him," she insisted.

"I can't. Sammy will never grow up. He'll always remain as he is now – a little boy."

"So what? At least he'll be *alive*!"

"That wouldn't be a life. Years would pass, he would develop mentally, but his body would never change. You'd age and die and he'd stay alone in this world."

"In that case transform me too and I'll always be with him."

"You don't understand what you're asking. Look at Sammy. Can you imagine how it would be to remain a child forever? Me, I'll always be only eighteen years old!"

"What?!" Susan exclaimed. Her shout was so loud that I drew her out of the room in order not to wake up Sammy.

I'd never reveal this fact to her, but now I had to make her forget the idea about Sammy's transformation. I hoped that she wouldn't ask about my true age. I guess the same thought had come into Susan's mind.

When we met I told Susan I was in my late twenties. Initially she felt uneasy about dating a younger man but I had hoped that eventually she would forget about our age gap. Hard life during my human age had matured me early and I had always looked older than I actually was.

"Yes, biologically my age will always be eighteen years. I was so young when it happened. Too young. I made a huge mistake and I'm paying a high price for it."

"Vincent, you're such a hypocrite! You say you'd do anything for Sammy, but now you're allowing him to die!"

That night, for the first time Susan tried to sleep as far as possible from me. It didn't surprise me. I knew she would grow cold towards me. Sleeping next to her, I pondered over our conversation.

I had spent a long time among humans and hadn't caused any suspicion for years. I had moved from a city to a city, from a country to a country and always arrived at a new place as a foreigner with a made-up biography, simple and believable. I had a humble lifestyle and hid my wealth. Sunlight and pretending to be a human didn't cause difficulties for me. After all, once upon a time I was a human too. Of course, things were easier when I lived alone, living together with Susan made certain things more difficult, however, I coped with it. I didn't want to share my secret with her because I thought that thereby I'd saddle her with a heavy and unnecessary burden.

Now it turned out that Susan had had suspicions since the very beginning of our relationship. Why didn't she say anything earlier? Didn't she find it important or... was she afraid of me?

Susan had called me a hypocrite. I wasn't angry at her, although those words hurt me a lot. Susan was a mother who tried to do everything for her child. Me... I viewed

Sammy as a son, while he, because I was younger than his mother, viewed me rather as an elder brother or an uncle.

Susan was wrong. If money could save Sammy, I'd give all the money I had; if a particular doctor could save him, I'd bring him to Chicago from anywhere in the world. But there was nothing that could save Sammy. I had accepted it. Susan had not.

Susan continued to beg me to transform Sammy. At first, she was insistent, then pleading, then insistent again. When she realised that my "no" really means "no", she dramatically changed her attitude towards me. Susan couldn't sleep in one bed with me anymore and ordered me to move out of there. Now I slept in the living room.

"Where do you think you're going?" Susan asked me one evening when I was going to enter Sammy's room.

She put her arm on the door jamb, thus obstructing the entrance. Susan's voice sounded menacing.

"To see Sammy, of course."

"You want to feast your eyes upon his suffering?"

"What are you talking about?" I was upset. Once again, Susan had hurt me with her words.

"My son is dying and you're letting it happen."

"If only you'd listen to my story..."

Susan didn't want to listen to me. My tragic life story didn't interest her, she didn't want to know what a torture eternal life was. Every time I tried to explain it to her, she interrupted me.

"I absolutely don't care about your life. If you don't want to help Sammy, get the hell out of here!"

"I will not go anywhere," I said as I moved her arm away and went into Sammy's room.

Susan reacted by swearing at me.

Another door had closed for me. Once I already lost a child and a woman I loved and now it was happening again. Sammy would soon be gone and Susan was already lost.

I knew that there would be a day when I lose everyone who's close to me. I had a choice: to destine myself to eternal loneliness, but I couldn't do it, or to find people with whom to spend together at least a few happy years. I also knew that I'd have to pay dearly for each moment of happiness.

Was there a curse that followed me and destroyed the people I loved? My own son was still-born because I didn't listen to the warning that creatures like me can't have children. Elisa died because our child had died and because she realised that the man she had married wasn't a human. Sammy was dying of a disease that was lethal only in a minority of cases, while Susan would never recover from the death of her son.

Sammy died on an autumn night. The sky was cloudy and only a few stars were visible. It had been raining and rainwater hadn't soaked into the concrete yet. I was lying on the sofa with my eyes open, Susan was in Sammy's room. He was spending more and more time asleep recently, although his sleep was often discontinuous. The doors were open and I heard Susan's nervous voice. I rushed into the room. Sammy had woken up and was fighting with shortness of breath. Susan was hoping that it was just another attack, but I felt that it was the end.

Suddenly Sammy's breath became rhythmical. He took a deep breath a few times and laid back into the pillows.

Sammy glanced over the room, as if he'd be giving the last look to everything, and then turned to us.

"I wish I could stay here with you," he said. His voice sounded serious and calm at the same time.

Susan couldn't say anything. She, too, had realised that this was the end.

I went to Sammy and touched his forehead.

"Sammy…"

Suddenly I saw that his face had changed. His eyes lit up and he smiled. I looked into his eyes and understood that he doesn't see this room anymore. He was seeing something we couldn't. The next moment his eyes closed and he exhaled for the last time.

I could sense that Susan was looking at me.

"Vincent, how could you let this happen?" she asked.

This time her voice was neither accusing, nor reproachful, just full of sadness.

After Sammy's death Susan felt nothing but hate towards me. She reluctantly allowed me to pay for the funeral so Sammy could have a nice service and be buried in a sunny part of the local cemetery and then threw me out of the apartment. Also, she forbade me to come to the funeral. Of course, I ignored the ban and watched the funeral from a distance. When Susan left – she had spent several hours at the grave – I, too, went to Sammy's grave and stayed there for a while. Just a few months ago Sammy was a joyful boy, who laughed, played, and went to school. Now he was buried in the cold ground and Susan blamed me for that. I had done everything I could for Sammy, but Susan had different thoughts.

"I hope that someday your mom will understand why I refused to transform you. I didn't want you to die, but I couldn't destine you to the same life I have."

Susan's hate didn't hurt me anymore. I just hoped that one day she'd realise the meaning of my words. For her own sake.

This was the third time when I had lost my family. At first I lost my sister, parents and brothers, but back then I had no time for mourning because I had to fight for survival. Then I lost my child and Elisa and sought oblivion in partying, trying to spend as less time as possible alone. Now, once again, I was surrounded by the pain of loss and I had to seek oblivion. I decided to turn to medicine more seriously and become a doctor.

Sparks

"Lockwood! Make up your damn mind!" Yuri exclaimed.

Then he turned around and went out of the room, slamming the door behind him. I didn't shout. I didn't run after him. I wasn't even angry. I just closed my eyes and made a deep sigh. He was right. Yuri called me by my surname only if he had something serious to say or when he didn't like my behaviour and lately he was having plenty of reasons for such a reaction.

We were together for less than a year but cracks had already started to appear between us. I was the one who was responsible for them.

According to simple logic, everything should have been quite the reverse: after all, I had had several long-time relationships and a marriage in the past, while, if I could believe his words, the longest relationship Yuri had ever had lasted eight months but no. Yuri's behaviour was impeccable. He perceived my mood very well: he was always around when I needed it and let me spend time alone if I wanted. He even suppressed his egotism and narcissism, while I sometimes behaved as a bride against her will who was working on a runaway-plan. I could be cold, nasty and petulant, but even then Yuri was understanding. However, his patience had some boundaries. The worst was, I didn't want to behave like this – I liked being with him.

After I had said "yes" and didn't try to contain my feelings anymore, an explosion-like reaction happened in my head. I forgot all doubts, the fact that just yesterday I had been a proud bachelorette and flew into Yuri's arms. The year 2007 hadn't really started when it already seemed unimaginable that just a few weeks ago I had decided to reject him. We were a great match, both intellectually and physically. When our relationship started we didn't want to spend even a moment separate from each other.

Yuri was a master of surprises. One of the most beautiful ones took place on my birthday. Yuri took me to Finnish Lapland. We stayed at the Ice Hotel and on January 29th, my birthday, Yuri, as a real gentleman, took me by hand and invited me to go outside. What I saw there took my breath away: there were thousands of candles placed in the snow. Some of them were ornamental while others created a long path. Yuri took me to a place where my name was made out of the candles and told me 166 reasons why I'm wonderful – one for each year of my life. I was so touched that I couldn't express my feelings in words. But I knew that he could see them in my eyes.

Yuri's apartment only had one bedroom and I lived in a serviced apartment so we had to go house-hunting. We went to a few viewings until we spotted a house in Berkshire we both liked. Yuri dealt with everything that was related to the purchase and furnishing of the place. Moving in was a bit of comedy stuff sometimes – I gave instructions to Yuri telling him what has to be in the house... and also what I didn't want to see there, threatening not to move in if he wouldn't obey my orders.

"So, there has to be a good sound system in the house. And don't you dare to bring a gramophone instead!"

Or:

"Also there has to be a home cinema. And yes, it has to be good too. Remember, I'll check the brands you have chosen!"

Yuri got the place ready in a record time and we moved in at the end of March. The house was built in the 19th century and had five bedrooms, two reception rooms, two bathrooms, a large kitchen and a huge library. All four walls in the library were fully occupied by book-shelfs, floor to ceiling. When Yuri and I walked in there for the first time, Yuri glanced over the shelves and said that he had read more than half of the books there. I glanced over too and realised that the same could be said about me. We got the house part-furnished and created a nice mix of antiques and modern pieces. The attic was a true surprise. We de-dusted it and got rid of spider webs, and transformed it into a ballroom– in the evenings we often went there and waltzed around the room. Yuri had somehow managed to find a very good sound system. That could mean that either his knowledge about modern technical equipment was way better than I thought or that someone had helped him.

Sometimes I went to the attic alone and danced along to my favourite music, especially the song Wild Horses by The Rolling Stones. It was one of my favourite songs and, at the same time, a very personal song – once it had marked the end of an era in my life and the beginning of something new. It was released in 1971 and it was the time when Byron and I had become more and more estranged and I had alienated myself from my swinging London lifestyle.

The bedroom was one of my compromises. Most of the furniture was from the 19th century, except for the bed which was made to order. This king size wonder with a baldachin and silk and wool mattress had set us back a few thousand pounds. Another few hundred pounds were spent on the finest quality mattress topper, pillows and bed clothes. We didn't actually need any of it, we spent the money because we could. Yuri had also ordered blackout curtains. I thought they looked ugly but didn't say anything. I only objected when Yuri wanted to purchase a fur bedspread and a few rugs.

"No way!" I exclaimed. "I don't wear fur and I don't want to see any in our bedroom!"

For a moment, Yuri was speechless.

"I had no idea that you're such an animal lover."

"I'm a woman and women may sometimes have caprices."

"Luca, let me remind you that you feed on human blood. Don't you see anything absurd here?"

"No. Humans are humans but we're talking about animals," I said and gave him one of my irresistible smiles.

Yuri understood that there's no point to argue and gave up.

Another compromise was the home cinema. I wanted to watch DVDs, while Yuri didn't want the equipment to clash with the furnishing. In the end we hid the TV set and speakers behind a sliding door. The result satisfied us both – Yuri, just like me, enjoyed watching a good movie, mostly classic. I had nothing against it: I knew that Yuri prefers films made before the 1950s and I didn't force him to watch anything from other decades. Me, I liked films from any decade. My favourite was Citizen Kane, which was shot in 1941. Yuri, too, liked it a lot.

Our house wasn't large, but it came with acres of land and had a forest nearby. We didn't have any neighbours and both of us liked the place very much. With us, animals – horses and pigs – moved in. However, I wanted a real pet too and soon two adorable corgis, Max and Pax, joined us.

Sometimes we saw wild geese and ducks – it was a real countryside paradise.

Since there was plenty of space in the garden, I could turn to one of my hobbies – archery – again. I hadn't done it in years.

"Be careful when shooting. If you miss, you might have one hunt less this month," Yuri joked when I was setting up the target.

"It's been two months since we started living here. Have you seen any people during this time?"

"No, and that's another reason why I like this place so much."

And then there was the garage, of course. It wouldn't be a big exaggeration if I said that my favourite place in the house was the garage. I could spend hours cleaning and polishing my car. Yuri joked that he wouldn't be surprised if one day, after waking up, he'd see that the Pontiac, too, was in the bed.

"I'm curious... Are you going to move to the garage soon?" he asked as he walked in.

I had squatted down and was removing dust from the car's tyres with a toothbrush. Yuri found this sight amusing.

"No. I love my car, but I'm not obsessed. Besides, I prefer to lie next to you."

xxx

One of the vampire rules: boredom must never appear in your life. It meant that we always had to search for something new.

In order to expand my knowledge, I had mastered Spanish and now could read Jorge Luis Borges works in original.

There were many Spanish-speaking writers I liked but Borges was my favourite. I wanted to learn Italian next. Yuri decided to find something new to read and had mastered Russian. It surprised me – I had thought he already spoke the language.

"My ancestors came from several countries and represented various nationalities: English, German, Nordic, Russian, but my parents were English speaking. My name was supposed to be spelt with "J" but my mother changed it so that people wouldn't mispronounce it," he explained.

Yuri and I liked to spend time outdoors and could walk for miles, especially if we went to the forest. I liked to lie down on the moss and look at the sky. For humans such an activity could end with catching a cold or worse, but for me it meant only a wet spine and dirty clothes.

Once, when Yuri and I were in the forest, I started to banter him and, in addition, tried to trip him up but lost balance and both of us fell over. I was lying on the moss, feeling amused, when suddenly I heard a sincere laughter next to me. I had never heard him laughing like that before.

"It can't be! You're laughing!"

"I'm in the mood to laugh, what's so special about it?"

"Yes, but not like this. Indeed, I have a positive impact on you."

"Yes, you have. Luca, you make my life better."

Unfortunately, this idyll didn't last long. I had everything, including what I had feared the most: a serious relationship. I had opened up, I had trusted, didn't get burnt and I knew that this relationship could last for years, if not decades. I don't know why this short-circuit in my head happened, but already in June I started to behave like the "old" Lucretia. Yuri, too, couldn't understand the cause of such changes.

His suggestion about making my mind up was right in time. Unfortunately, I didn't know how to achieve it. I looked at the clock. It was two am and Yuri never went to sleep before dawn. I knew that it would be better if we stayed in separate rooms for a while. In the end, I went to the bedroom at seven am.

Although I had gone to sleep after him, I was the first one who woke up. I was watching Yuri sleep, trying to figure out how to apologise for my behaviour.

When he opened his eyes, I gave him a guilty smile and said:

"I'm difficult, I know. But it's not your fault. Really."

"Lucretia, what is going on in your mind?"

He gave me a very serious look that I hadn't seen for a while.

"Remember, when we met during hunting and I said that being with me won't be easy?"

"Of course. I assured you that I'm difficult too."

I caressed his cheek.

"How can you stand me?"

"Because it's worth being with you."

Yuri was trying to save our relationship, so he forgave me one more time.

xxx

It was the evening and we were in the library. The table was full of newspapers and magazines. I was sitting at the table with my feet up. I had a magazine in my hands and several newspapers on my lap. Yuri was sitting opposite me and was also going through the papers.

"Ashley Ann Rogan. Looks adorable in her new outfit. How else."

"Since when you're reading tabloids?"

"Every time when I need it."

"What a pity that we have to postpone her."

"Yes. At the moment she receives huge media attention. It's too risky to attack." I said.

Ashley, a good-looking and brainy socialite, was accused of pocketing tens of millions of pounds via various pretences. The case was never brought to court due to lack of witnesses. I do believe in coincidences and so does Yuri, but the sudden death of one and disappearance of two sounded too suspicious to us. Especially given that it happened within seven months. That's when we decided to pay her a visit. We were planning to go after Ashley together. Vampire style romance.

"Huh..." I said after a moment. "If we cannot get her, we need to check out what we can get. What do you suggest?"

"Scott Selfridge. Killed his wife during an argument. Has a criminal record because of aggressive behaviour. Released because of lack of evidence. Do you want him?"

"Why not? I'll teach him how to treat a woman," I grinned.

"Maurice Craig. Production and distribution of child pornography. Released because it turned out that some evidence was collected in an unlawful way. All right, this one is mine."

"Give him to me!"

"Why? You don't have children, so don't try to speak about maternal feelings."

"You didn't have children either."

"You know, unlike women, men can never be absolutely sure about that."

"Oh, dear... Again. If I wouldn't know you, I'd think that you're just a bragger."

"But, since you live with me, you know that I'm not only a talker, but also a doer."

I waved at him with a newspaper.

"How about if we do what we need to do? Otherwise we'll never finish..." Then I changed the tone and spoke in a very sweet and pleading voice. "Give him to me."

In addition, I made puppy eyes.

"All right. You know that it's very difficult to say "no" to you, don't you?"

"Thank you. If you want, you can take that bastard who beat his infant son to death."

"Hmm... I'd say that it's quite a fair exchange. All right, enough for this time."

Yuri threw the newspaper on the table and stood up.

"I'm leaving. Will you wish me luck?"

"Good luck."

He smirked and went out of the room.

He had just finished planning our "menu". We did it several times a month. Yuri and I attacked only criminals and other nasty people whom, in our opinion, the world wouldn't miss much. We followed the news and if we heard that someone had avoided punishment only because of a skillful lawyer or lack of evidence, we entered the game. We did have to do some research, though, to avoid going after someone who had been falsely accused.

For me, four "meals" a month were enough, Yuri usually needed six or seven hunts. Just in case, we usually added extra people to our list, because *force majeure* could always happen. For instance, a person could get arrested, killed or simply disappear.

A few days later I was in the library, going through some documents, when Yuri came in. He immediately noticed a ring with a huge violet amethyst on my right hand's index finger. He had never seen the ring before although I wore it from time to time – it was one of my favourite pieces of jewellery.

"Interesting ring. Where did you get it?" he asked as if by the way. From his tone it was clear that he supposed that the ring could have been given to me by a man.

"It's a gift from Byron," I said, continuing to check the documents.

"Who's Byron?"

"My husband."

Right after I had said these words, I realised that I shouldn't have done that. I bit my lip, but it was too late.

"Your *husband*? Are you married?"

"I was."

"You were *married*? To a *human*?"

Yuri didn't even ask if Byron was human, he already knew it – vampire couples didn't marry.

"Yes, I was."

"And who said that vampires and humans do not match? Interesting – years ago you gave up your relationship with Nigel, but later *married* a human!"

"Hey, you can't compare that!" I exclaimed. "When I met Nigel, I was twenty-three years old, I had been a vampire for only two years and I had havoc in my head. When I met Byron, I was one hundred and twenty and my mind was more or less made up."

"For how long were you married?"

If we had started to argue, there was no point to lie or hide something.

"Nine years."

"Nine years…" Yuri said in a strange voice.

This incident created another crack in our relationship.

Officially Byron and I divorced in 1973, although we separated already in 1970. I knew it would happen. I couldn't stay with him for more than ten, maybe twelve years because of my secret. Besides, we had started to drift apart. Byron had always been secluded and a man of few words, but over the years, particularly because of LSD, he became even more secluded and started to live in his own world where there was no space for me. By putting in some effort, we could probably have saved our marriage, but neither of us wanted it. I had to move forward, while Byron was satisfied with how things were going.

I decided to try something new and went to uni where I studied Art History. I left London's bohemian circles, but not the city, and from Luca Mortensen I transformed back into Lucretia Lockwood. The only thing that remained changeless was my visits to Brighton. I wanted to change the environment I was in completely and move to the States, but I knew I couldn't do it while Cedrick was alive. He was nearly 70 years old then and I didn't want to rely on the hope that we would still have a lot of time. I'd always be able to leave and return while his time was limited.

Cedrick died in May 1976. I attended his funeral, but stood aside because I didn't want anyone to notice me. I knew only a few of the funeral guests. However, Marie noticed me – apparently, she had the sixth sense. She had invited me and felt that I was somewhere near. Emil, too, noticed me although he tried not to show it. I didn't join them. After the funeral, I didn't return to my hometown until 2002 when I scattered Vincent's ashes in the sea.

After Cedrick's death nothing held me in London anymore. In 1977 I moved to New York and dived into a completely new and foreign world – Wall Street, where I quickly made lots of money and became a local legend. In 1992 I realised that I was sick and tired of stock market fluctuations and the omnipresent materialism and moved to Paris.

xxx

Yuri didn't like to leave things unsaid and he had a very annoying habit – he could appear anytime and suddenly ask a question.

Our conversation took place in a room that had only decorative meaning for us – in the kitchen. We went there only to feed the dogs or tidy up. In fact, only I cleaned the kitchen. Yuri didn't care about how it looked, while I couldn't stand litter and dust.

I was cleaning the work top when the door opened and Yuri came in. He stood facing me and leant against the dining table.

"How come you didn't tell me earlier about your marriage?" he asked and gave me a serious and piercing look.

"Why should I tell you everything?" I retorted. "I don't ask you to recount your life since childhood until today."

"Recount all my life to you? Never. There are a lot of memories I won't share with anyone."

"I can imagine what kind of memories they are," I smirked.

"Don't try to change the subject. Why did you stay silent about something so important?"

Yuri gave me another serious look and didn't say anything for a moment. I knew what he was thinking about – Yuri couldn't understand how, given that I had to hide my true identity, I could spend almost ten years with Byron, while with him, who was a vampire too, I couldn't normally spend even a year under one roof.

Since I didn't want to explain to him the uniqueness of mine and Byron's relationship, I had to get out of the situation somehow. Being unable to figure out something better, I went to Yuri and pressed my body against his, putting one arm around his neck. My lips were half an inch from his lips and, in my most charming voice, I said:

"Because it belongs to the past. How about if we leave it there?"

Then I pressed his lips against mine. He replied to my kiss. In the moment when I thought he should have forgotten all rebukes he tore himself away.

"Lucretia, you know very well that I succumb to passion only when I want it."

Then he untied himself from my embrace and left the room.

"You know, if you were a human, you'd make a great prosecutor!" I shouted.

Many times in my life, I had ascertained that work is the best remedy for silly thoughts, depressive thoughts, any other kind of thoughts or bad emotional experiences. Luckily, in our place there were always plenty of tasks to do. I cleaned the small stable where we kept our two horses with enthusiasm and heartily spent time in the barn feeding our pigs.

I had just thrown another portion of pig feed into the rack. One of the pigs came up to me and caressed my hand with her muzzle.

"Dinner is ready," I said and scratched the pig's ear. "What a lovely creature you are. Unfortunately, an underrated one. Otherwise humans wouldn't perceive you only as a piece of pork chop."

After I had finished the sentence, I realised what I had just said and it made me chuckle – a vampire criticised human food choices. Ha.

After I had finished, I walked out of the barn and took the amethyst ring out of my waistcoat's pocket. Since Yuri had found out its origin, he looked at the ring more than he looked at me. I put the ring back on my finger and sighed. How to explain to Yuri the magic that had existed between me and Byron? I was wearing this ring because, firstly, it was one of my favourite pieces of jewellery and, secondly, it was a gift from someone who used to be very dear to me. The ring reminded me of nine wonderful years of my life.

However, I had no nostalgia – I knew that the past is past and these times would never come back.

I needed a neutral topic to start the conversation with. I waited until Yuri went to the library and asked the question which, in fact, I should have asked already a year ago.

"Vincent has been dead for five years. Have you done anything with his money?"

"No," Yuri said. His voice sounded absolutely unconcerned.

"I had already thought so. May I know the reason? Please don't say that you had no time."

"I didn't view it as something urgent," he said.

Indeed, when you're immortal, why rush?

"I see. However, for Vincent it was very important. How about if we deal with it now?"

He gave me a look that said "as you wish", then opened one of the desk drawers and took a thick folder out of it.

"Here's everything he left me. Including his last diary. I suggest you read it."

I spent the following days in the company of numbers and documents. Vincent's total wealth – 6 million pounds – looked like nothing when compared to my £150 million or Yuri's £9 billion, but it was money too and Vincent had entrusted it to us.

"We have to come up with the best scenario for Vincent's death and make his last will," I said.

"That I'll leave up to you."

"Why me? He was your friend too!"

"Because I suspect it will involve a creative use of modern technology and this is the field you know way better than I do," he replied.

I couldn't not agree to that.

The work on Vincent's last will took me another week or so – I devised his money to dozens of charities around the world. Yuri forged Vincent's signature. According to my plan, Vincent had died in a plane crash five years ago when his small private jet, flown by him, crashed into the Pacific Ocean due to technical problems. The place where it "happened" was so remote that no proper investigation was possible. Therefore Vincent could be legally declared dead and our last promise to him was fulfilled.

As I finished dealing with Vincent's money matters, I turned to his diary. It was hard to read it and each new entry filled my heart with sorrow. In the last entry Vincent had listed all the most important things in his life. Most of them were sad: death of the relatives, brothers' betrayal, transformation into a vampire, death of Elisa and their child, Sammy's death... Loneliness, depression and sadness. Poor Vincent...

It was especially sad to read the entries about Sammy. I didn't know the story of him. Vincent had never mentioned Susan and Sammy, just like I had never mentioned Byron. There were memories we didn't want to share, even with each other.

Vincent knew that Sammy couldn't be saved, while Susan didn't understand it and persistently asked Vincent to transform Sammy into a vampire. She didn't understand that eternal life can be worse than death. Even for an adult it was sometimes difficult to accept immortality and eternal stillness of the body. How would a child feel, from year to year looking at the mirror and seeing that his body doesn't change, even for a bit? In one moment, he inevitably would start to hate himself and then... Vincent had made a very hard, but right decision. I would have done the same in his place.

Once again – poor Vincent. No wonder he lost the will to live.

I closed the diary and put it back into the drawer.

"Rest in peace, my friend," I whispered.

xxx

For the past few days, I had felt a strange elation: the grass seemed greener, the sky – bluer, the birdsong – nicer and so on. I was doing household chores and feeding animals with bigger enthusiasm and my mood was surprisingly good. Odd, but these changes had started right after Yuri had gone to London for a week to meet several of his financial advisors, look for new investment opportunities and attend a lot of other business meetings. He had decided to stay in his apartment instead of going back and forth.

Recently I had often caught myself listing the cons of being in a relationship and with nostalgia remembered the times when I had lived alone. I didn't have to consider anyone, I didn't have to care about anyone, I could do whatever I wanted. For instance, at the moment I was listening to music, mostly rock'n'roll and my favourite songs from the 60s, from dusk till dawn or from dawn till dusk (depending on what time I woke up at). There was only one thing that was spoiling my little paradise: the knowledge that Yuri would soon return.

Come to think of it, there was nothing strange in the fact that my enthusiasm about this relationship had diminished. The passion had decreased and a new period had started. It was natural.

However, something was wrong. Maybe it was because I had agreed to the relationship and cohabitation so easily? Otherwise I didn't know how to explain this change of heart.

The clock was showing eleven pm. I was sitting in the library reading when the door opened and Yuri came in. He sat next to me and caressed my face.

"I didn't notice your return," I said.

"I arrived a minute ago. I wanted to see you before I go to sleep."

Yuri looked exhausted. There were dark circles under his eyes and his voice sounded very silent.

"I almost haven't slept this week. Early morning meetings, afternoon meetings, evening meetings, trying to sleep at night... I'm glad it's over. "

I caressed his face.

"You better go to sleep now. You already look half asleep."

"I am."

Now his voice was even more silent. He stood up and slipped out of the library.

I continued to look at the door after he had closed it behind him. I was touched – Yuri was completely exhausted by the lack of sleep; however, he had come to see me instead of going straight upstairs.

I felt guilty now – Yuri had no idea that all this time I had almost celebrated his absence.

I returned to my awful mood. Once again, I had become shrewish, reticent and easily irritable. The reason for such changes was quite clear: they started soon after Yuri's return. Because of me the atmosphere had become tense again and it was obvious that soon there would be a new argument between me and him.

"Are you rejecting me because of Byron?" Yuri suddenly asked me one evening.

"What?!"

His words made me dumbstruck for a moment.

"Are you rejecting me because of Byron?"

"No! How could such a thought ever cross your mind? Byron belongs to the past. I think he's not among us anymore. Even if he's alive, he'd be nearly seventy now!"

"If Byron belongs to the past, why are you so attached to it?" While saying it, his gaze was fixed to my ring.

"Have you determined to infuriate me tonight? I'm wearing this ring because I like it. I can confess: at least half of my jewellery are gifts from my ex-lovers, so every time you see me wearing a piece of jewellery, you can ask who gave it to me!"

"Why have you changed so much?"

Although Yuri's question was reasonable, it only added fuel to the fire.

"I haven't changed. This is who I am. I once warned you about it, remember?"

"Really? As I've noticed, you're short-tempered only towards me. I have the impression that the better I treat you, the worse you behave."

"Oh, it looks like you've already found a solution. Treat me badly and maybe I'll start to behave better."

Now he was infuriated too.

"I always forgave you when you suddenly, without any explanation, rejected me; I didn't say anything when you once disappeared for several days without a warning and, upon return, didn't find it necessary to tell me where you'd been; I'm trying to understand why you treat me as if I had done something wrong to you. And you know, it's starting to sicken me. You know that I'm trying to start a new life and it's not easy for me. I had hoped that you being in my life would help, but instead of it..."

"What? Is that the reason why you're with me? I'm a tool that you're using to adapt to life in the twenty-first century?"

"That's not what I said. I've never perceived you like that. Your personality was what attracted me. That's why I want to be with you and learn from you."

It was too late. His words couldn't cool me down anymore.

"Really? You took me away from my usual life and brought me here. You tried to fulfil all my wishes, no matter what I wanted. You tolerate all variations of my mood. Why? To be sure that you won't lose your key to the new life?"

"If you were a human, I'd think that you have PMS, but since you are a vampire, I have no idea how to explain your sometimes incoherent behaviour!" Yuri's voice sounded venomous.

I thought that I couldn't become any angrier, but after these words...

"That's it! I'm sick and tired of this farce! I think it's time for us to part ways!"

Yuri's reaction was instant:

"Lockwood, you are insane!"

His patience had finally ended. If Yuri could flash lightning with his eyes, I would have been struck by a thunderbolt right in the forehead.

After this argument our relationship worsened so much that we couldn't stay in the same room anymore. I moved out of our bedroom. As I later found out, Yuri, not knowing that I had moved to another room, had done the same.

Yuri now occupied one of the spare bedrooms and barely came out of it. Sometimes he didn't leave his room for several days. If we met each other somewhere in the house, he ignored me or gave me a look that could cover a

Caribbean island with a thick layer of ice. I knew that I had hurt him a lot, but I felt no regret and wasn't going to apologise. I was mad at him because at the moment I had to take care of everything around the house.

"Cabron!"[3] I hissed while I was cleaning the stable.

When I wanted to buy animals, Yuri reminded me that they may live for twenty years and in case we decided to move somewhere else, we'd have to take responsibility for their future fate. "You become responsible, forever, for what you have tamed," I had replied to him with the words of Antoine de Saint-Exupéry. And now this solicitous and responsible man was spending days locked in his room, while I was spending a lot of time cleaning and feeding.

---

[3] Male goat (in Spanish), but it is also used as a slang word and can mean different things. In this context it means "bastard".

Unfortunately, or luckily, my mind couldn't work in only one direction and it started producing arguments in Yuri's defence. If you're a vampire who feeds only several times a month and who has spent many years in solitude, it's quite easy to forget that there are creatures who need food several times a day. Vincent once said that if Yuri calls someone a friend they can consider themselves very lucky. He was right. I remembered the many surprises Yuri had made during our relationship. Of course, he had some imperfections – I had nothing against it because a man who has no imperfections is a wrecker of a woman's self-confidence – however, he had so many qualities too.

Physical work and contemplation made me calm down and suddenly I felt shame for my behaviour. In anger I had said to Yuri that I didn't want to be with him anymore, although… I didn't want to lose him; I just couldn't continue to live as I did before the argument.

xxx

I went outside to the garden. It was a beautiful winter evening. It would have been more beautiful if the yard was covered with snow, however, the dark ground and moonlight looked nice too.

I noticed a silhouette – Yuri, too, had come out of his room. He was sitting on a bench and was immersed in thoughts. As soon as he sensed that he's not alone anymore, he turned his head and looked straight into my eyes.

"What will you allow me to call you tonight: Lockwood or Lucretia?"

"I would like to be Lucretia. Really." I sighed. "I have to apologise to you for all the nonsense I told you that night.

You know that something is wrong in our relationship, but still, I didn't want to be so sharp."

"I've already forgiven you."

"Even this time?"

"Well, until last night I had decided to cut you out of my life, but then I had a revelation. Remember what Vincent wrote about me in his diary? All my life was sealed by lack of love and care. I lost my parents when I was a child, I grew up alone and had no friends. I cared for no one but me and during my time as a human I met only a few people who deserved to be treated well. Vincent wrote that I became a vampire because my life was empty. I was empty. He was right. You... as a human, you were heavily betrayed and when you were reborn as a vampire, your heart was full of bitterness and you had to toughen up, killing all of Miss Westmoreland in you. Life has made us who we are. You are used to constant changes and uncertainty, while I like stability. I guess we rushed everything: this relationship, living together... It suited me, not you."

Unconsciously I had moved closer to him. He stood up and took my hands. Indeed. That's exactly how it was. The explanation of my behaviour turned out to be so simple.

"Amazing. Vincent is helping us from the grave. I wish we would have understood it earlier. It would have saved us the last few arguments..."

I cuddled up to him. Yuri, too, put his arms around me.

"What shall we do?" I asked.

"I'm offering you the following: one of us leaves for a while, the other stays here and takes care of the house and our animals. After a few months we'll meet again and have a fresh start."

"Excellent. I'm for it. I think I even know which of us will stay here."

Yuri was going to release himself from my embrace, but I didn't let that happen.

"Wait, are you going to leave tonight?"

He smiled and tousled my hair.

"You're unbelievable. At first you want to get rid of me, now you don't let me go."

"I know. But it's the reason why you like me so much, isn't it?" Now I was holding him even tighter.

On the one hand, I was pleased to have a break from this relationship, on the other hand – I was delighted by the thought that a few months would pass and we'd be together again. And this time I would not ruin anything.

Printed in Great Britain
by Amazon